CHIMERA

A Novel

S. M. Lynch

"If you want to change the world,
go home and love your family."
—Mother Teresa—

PART ONE

HIDING IN MONTREUX

Chapter One

The aircon hits me like a decadent waterfall as I walk into the store. My hand immediately snaps out for a shopping basket and I stride through, taking my usual eight steps around the baby food section, which leads to the cold drinks aisle. (I say aisle, but it's not huge in here, in fact it's tiny by American standards, but right now, this store is my world, my only lifeline.)

The bell over the door only stops ringing once I'm stood staring at the cold drinks beyond the glass doors of the refrigerators. Either the door's feeling as lethargic as I am, or someone came in right after me.

Something doesn't feel right as I stare at the neat row of strawberry smoothies, which are all I'm living on right now, owing to the whopping heat and everything in this town being meat-based—and I'm a vegetarian.

I see my own reflection in the glass fridges and there's nothing new there. My dirty-blonde hair, piled high on my head, looks like it needs a good wash. I need to stop recycling my mascara and realise that eyeliner is not a good idea in this weather. I stand back and see my thighs are looking thinner, sort of wobbly, lacking air or something. Deflated. I must be losing weight. It's not good. This place isn't good for me—but then I am on the run and beggars can't be choosers. My check shirt and my cut-off shorts give away the fact that I don't care about my personal ap-

3

pearance right now. I can't remember the last time I used an iron. I can't remember the last time I washed the white spaghetti-strap top beneath my check shirt. There's no full-length mirror in my crappy hotel room, so I just live day to day ignoring how I look.

So, no, nothing different about me.

So, what is different, then?

I know something is.

I come in this store every day—same time, same purchases—and today, there is something discernibly different.

I don't know what it is yet.

I open the fridge door and my sweaty hand basks in the cold as I reach out and start filling my basket with smoothies. I should get something more substantial. I could pick up a couple of crispy cremes, although I can't be sure if they're really vegetarian. Maybe some fries then?

I could visit the diner down the road and get some takeout, but then... that'd involve interaction, and round parts like these, people usually have your life story out of you before you've even been served your first drink.

The thing is, the only routine I feel safe enough keeping at the moment is this one involving purchasing smoothies—nothing else.

And now this small, insignificant daily routine feels threatened, too.

Midway through collecting my usual six smoothies, I look sideways and catch the eyes of the store assistant, Nate. I know he's called that because he wears a nametag. We don't ever really speak even though, for the past couple of weeks, we've made eyes at one another each time I've been in here. Trouble is, he's never looked like he does right now—afraid and wary. He usually wears a warm, inviting smile—but not today.

Right now, he's wearing concern.

The unsure look in his eyes has me turning back and collecting my remaining three smoothies in a hurry. I try to push the drinks into my basket without making it look as though I'm starting to worry, but I am—I'm starting to worry. I'm living on a knife's edge, day after day. It's been like this for three months and it's not getting any better. The bottles refuse to situate themselves in the basket and I nearly have them toppling to the floor. I'm struggling to push them in line, when usually they fill the basket perfectly. I only buy six because the most the basket can take is six.

I shut the fridge door and stand staring at my own reflection again. Shabby hair. Tall physique. Unlaced Caterpillar boots. Basket in hand. Usual haul from the drinks aisle. Nothing out of the ordinary.

I force myself to pull in bigger breaths of air and then I notice the rest of my surroundings. The usual hustle and bustle of the store is absent. This is unusual. This is, after all, the only store on this block and the only one servicing many other blocks, too. The rest of the inhabitants really must hate me for always stealing most of the strawberry smoothies, every day. Either that or Nate has a big stockpile out back, having noticed strawberry smoothies have become his biggest concern.

Anyway, it's not right that on a Sunday morning this store is empty. Not when there are fresh crispy cremes to be had, not to mention corn dogs (any time of the day), fresh coffee...

Ah, god. Fresh coffee. If only I felt safe enough to purchase fresh coffee. Asking for that would mean spending time making the coffee and I don't have time to waste. I only have time to shove six bottles of shit into my basket every day, have the handsome store assistant bag them up and send me on my merry way as if I don't have an issue—which clearly, I do.

My dad taught me that you seek your spot and always stick to it, and the drinks aisle has been my spot every time I've come in here. There's the baby food aisle near this one which is always stacked high with nappies (or diapers as people here call them), thus providing a protective wall between myself and any assailant. Then there's the fact that I can see the whole entire shop reflected in the glass whenever I'm at the fridges. So, I'll always know if I'm being followed.

Aside from the shop being empty, there's nothing to concern me apart from the fact that the bell rang for longer than normal after I entered the store. Either it's just me and Nate all to ourselves in here, or the bell is possessed... or my pursuer is hiding.

It occurs to me I don't have a gun... but I bet Nate does.

I turn and look at him, making my way slowly towards the sales counter. I watch his eyes and make the decision to continue on my usual path. He is fearful for me, I can tell. I'm reading it from him as I approach. Something's happening. Something I'm unsure of. But I know he's probably got a gun behind there to protect himself—and the store. If he has, he'll protect me, too. He likes me, I can tell. Always with the eyes. Always bagging up my shit without asking me if I need my shit bagging up. Always with those big hands of his, that tan, the strong build...

He could protect me, right?

I sort of lunge my basket towards him and he catches it, cradling it as if I just threw six rugby balls his way, and now he's trying to stop my bottles from flying to the floor by pressing one of his large palms to the tops of them.

I receive an exasperated sigh and he uses a moistened index finger to separate a plastic bag—and the routine exacts itself as it normally would.

"$17.94," he says, in a soft Texan accent. His voice almost persuades me he's an innocent, but his eyes are telling me things not-so-much innocent as deviant.

"Quiet in here today," I say.

He quirks a brow. "I don't question it when it's quiet, I question it when it's busy."

He's settling for ordinary shopkeeper banter, but still, I can tell he's nervous.

"Where is he?" I whisper, and Nate looks frozen for a second, before he passes me my change from a $50 note. "Don't be scared. Just answer me," I persuade him.

He discreetly points to the other side of the shop where there are more fridges, except those are filled with alcohol, not soft drinks like the section I always venture to.

"You got a gun?" I whisper.

He gives a nod.

Seconds pass, but they feel like aeons. Bloody hell, I've probably been inside this store for no more than two minutes and already it feels like a day.

I remind myself that this isn't my fault, that me running isn't down to me—but someone else. I must remember what my father taught me—that this could be coincidence. This could be a dude sticking up the joint. Maybe there's a gang in town that just arrived and that's why everyone's at home this sunny Sunday morning. Or maybe, for once, the inhabitants have all gone to church…

"Put 'em up, lady," I'm told, and I turn, thankful I don't have the huge bag of smoothie bottles in my hand yet.

I put my hands up.

Everything slows down.

Take control, Beatrice. That's what my father would say.

Focus and relax.

Take in your surroundings.

I breathe in and hear the whizzing of the fan above our heads, a bit of tape caught on one of the blades, flapping every now and again. The sound takes me out of the situation we're in and someplace else. I centre myself and reboot.

Use your mind.

Your mind is your most powerful weapon.

Don't be afraid.

From the look of him, he's nothing but a lowlife thief, not one of the hired killers my father's enemies might send to catch me.

He's not spent half his life in the gym. He's not clean shaven. He's not wearing the uniform of a trained killer. This guy has a ketchup stain on his Eagles t-shirt and all the signs of alcohol addiction—swollen, puffy lips, purple nose, shaking hand, dry tongue, inert eyes.

His gun looks like it's seen better days, too.

"You don't want to do this pal," Nate says from behind me, "let the girl leave the shop and I'll give you money, okay?"

Nate sounds calm. Level. Sure. He doesn't sound scared. Funny how you can be taught not to be scared, but when it comes down to it, you're still scared. Nate's not scared, though. He's definitely in control. I hear the subtle click behind me of him chambering a bullet. It's a handgun, but I'm hoping he has something else, too—something like a shotgun, just in case. In my peripheral vision, I notice Nate's forearm resting casually on the countertop, but beneath it he's most probably readying the gun. Or guns. Preferably plural.

"You must be fuckin' kiddin' me. She'll get out of the way and then you'll let go that piece you've got under there." The robber has a definite northern accent. Boston, maybe Chicago. I'm not an American so I can't tell. Anyway, what I know is that Texans are cool. Northerners—not so cool. Funny how it's the other way around back home.

Part of me is ready to fight at the thought of Nate having a piece under the counter, ready and aimed near enough in my direction—my body the only thing in the way of him putting a slug in this loser trash in front of me. I have to be cool to get out of here alive. I still have stuff to live for. I need to believe Nate's got a steady trigger finger and won't try to curve a bullet around me.

"What do you want?" Nate asks, sounding bored already.

"All the cash you got."

Nate gives a nod. "You'll let the girl go first?"

"Naw. She's insurance. Clearly you got a thing for her. Empty the register. Then I go, then we're done."

Nate rings open the till and bags up what's in there. I see the perplexed look in the thief's eyes.

"There's barely 200 bucks."

"You said empty it. Business is slow today, what can I say?"

"How much do you want?" I ask the degenerate man in front of me.

"Why? You gonna pay me in sweets, little girl."

I may be young, but I'm not little. The guy in front of me is 5'2 at most while I'm 5'9. I may look nothing much right now, but he's sorely mistaken if he thinks I'll let him take me for a mug.

"You've got one more chance before I kick the shit out of you," I warn him.

"Not so regal as she sounds, is she?" he laughs, looking at Nate.

You're stronger than they imagine, Beatrice.

While he's having his fun at my expense, I kick the gun out of his hand and quickly take it up myself.

"How much do you want, you old prick?" I check for bullets before chambering one.

He holds his hands up. "Okay, okay. I'm gone."

Thank goodness for that. Stupid idiot.

He backs out of the shop, but not before giving it one, last shot...

While my back's turned to address Nate once more, the man I'm now internally referring to as Thief-Loser-Dick-Fucker-Punk-Ass Scumbag grabs me and holds a knife at my throat. It pinches but doesn't slice. It feels like a love bite—except his weapon has the potential to deliver more disease than a kiss ever could.

Nate brings a shotgun up onto the counter, and warns, "You heard her, how much is your life worth, you fuck?"

I knew he would have a shotgun. The sound of its presence and potential to harm our assailant eases my anxiety, so does the sound of Nate's assured, dulcet tones.

I have my eyes closed, waiting to hear my fate. Nate's still confident of our survival—his breathing level and steady—calming me.

"Kids these days, you're all so fucked up. I'll be seeing ya, then."

My heart's pounding as I listen to his footsteps, counting them as he retreats. They seem endless. The robber man has even smaller strides than me. I don't know why that should perplex me—he *is* much shorter—but I just don't get how he thought he could stick up a store this morning and get away with it. Is he a complete idiot?

He finally exits the shop and that's it, he's gone. That feeling I had earlier disappears with him. My father taught me to smell trouble. No, I tell a lie. He taught me to predict it. I take a breath before heading for the liquor aisle. From the shelves I drag out a bottle of Jack Daniels and hand him another fifty off my roll of notes.

"Keep the change," I tell him, as I'm leaving the store.

"I should walk you home," he yells.

"No, I'll be fine."

I'm gone before he can say anything more.

I jog back to my hotel, seeing no sign of the robber, nor anyone else for that matter. I lock all my doors and windows.

What they're lacking in mirrors in this here hotel, they certainly make up for with security measures. Window bars. Windowless front door, reinforced. Chain. A safe bigger than the minibar. I guess the Texan businessmen passing through like to keep themselves to themselves because this place sure isn't as generous with the décor as it is with the safety measures.

I reassure myself I'm safe, so long as I'm tucked up in my hotel room. It's just that something about all that earlier did not feel right. I don't quite know what happened just then—but it's time to leave this place.

I'll stay one more night, then leave town before dawn.

Chapter Two

The view out of the window as the sun goes down isn't one that's any different to the other sunsets I've watched while I've been here in the US. It's beautiful. Even with the night approaching, it's still hot, and I'd rather watch the sky than Netflix, any day. As I'm looking through the window though, staring across the dead grass in front of the hotel, I see a familiar shape heading my way. I tell myself it can't be. Then there's a knock on the door.

"It's me, Nate, from the store," he explains, when I don't open up immediately.

"What's up?"

"I got you some dinner."

I look over my shoulder at the waste bin, full of empty smoothie bottles, and realise I probably gave myself away, didn't I? Or else why would he have taken pity on me and bought me dinner?

"I'm a vegetarian."

"Oh... well, there are options here. C'mon, let me in before I annoy Sam."

Sam's the owner of the hotel. I clocked his nametag as well as Nate's.

For some reason in America, loiterers are frowned upon. All over. Americans don't loiter. They drive from place to place, or they run. They <u>do not</u> loiter.

Gingerly, I open the door. I wouldn't want to cause trouble. Sam weighs at least twenty-five stones and he has several shotguns behind his counter.

"You've left me with no choice, *Nate*."

I take the door off the chain after peering through to check it really is him, and he watches me intently as I lock up again, like we're cellmates.

"Are you okay?" he asks, a tremor in his speech. "I mean, after earlier?"

"I'm fine." I replace myself at the window seat, checking nobody followed him. When Nate and I are in the same room, bad things seem to happen.

He places two bags of takeout food on the small, square table in the seating area and lets me know, "Well, I got fries. That's a good start, right?"

Thank goodness my nervous laughing drowns out my growling stomach as he walks towards me with a brown paper bag full of fries. I try not to look desperate for sustenance, but I can't help but start ramming the salted, hot potato sticks down my throat, as fast as I possibly can. In fact I'm glad he brought food as it's overpowering the other smells in this room—smells I've sort of become immune to now, but I know they're still there.

He returns to the table and rummages. "I guess I'll be having both these burgers, then. I also brought ribs and onion rings. Donuts, too."

"Pass them," I signal with my hand, a little more brusquely than is my usual style.

It doesn't even matter if the donuts aren't strictly vegetarian, not right now, not when I've had one hell of a day. When he brings out a bottle of coke, too—I point to where three quarters of a bottle of Jack Daniels remains and he gets the idea.

"So, what are you doing in town?" he asks, lounging back in one of the armchairs. I'm still at the window, shovelling fries and onion rings and donuts, in whatever order they'll fit inside me quickest.

"I'm a travel writer." It's not a lie, but it's not entirely true, either. I do write (occasionally), and I do travel (a lot).

"And you came here? To Longlake...?"

He's looking at me as though nobody would visit this place to write about it. He's not wrong. It's just a passing-through place between other places. It's where men come to fish or hide out from their wives for a few days—or do shady backroom business dealings. This dustbowl little strip is a nothing place between all the other beautiful places nearby, with their forests and their Hilton Hotels and their valets and their pristine sidewalks. Earlier today when I walked to the store, I saw a piece of trash on the sidewalk. You don't see that unless a town has really gone downhill.

"Longlake, so that's what it's called," I mumble, as I watch him take chunks out of his burger. It does look good, but then Dad once told me what really happens to meat and where it comes from—and it put me off for life.

"Who are you running from, girl?"

I pause midbite and blink fast, trying to control how his forwardness is unsettling me. I've not sat in a room like this with anyone, not in three whole months.

"Three months ago, my dad, my mum and my sister were killed. I don't know what else to do but float around."

I see all kinds of emotions cross his face. He's picking his next move. He's trying to decide how to treat me sensitively but also, how to get the rest of my story out of me.

"You were there, when it happened?" he asks.

I shake my head. "No. I was working in Florida when it happened."

"Oh, you were...?"

"Umm. I'm a model. Well, I was..."

"What do you model?"

"I model underwear and swimsuits designed for the bustier lady. I'm what you call a plus-size model."

His face scrunches up. "Either you lost a bunch of weight recently or those other models really are stick-thin."

I giggle a little. "I've lost a little weight, but if you're not a sample size, then you're a plus size in the industry. I'm a US size 6 or an 8 but that puts me as a plus-size. I can't get work at home, at all, hence why I model mostly in the US. I've got my work visas and everything. I'm not illegal."

"So, why in the hell are you running? Come on, you have got to admit..."

"Well, as I told you, I wasn't there. I found out on the news that our family home in Edinburgh had blown up and the problem is, how do I know the news was telling the truth when they said it was an accident?"

He nods like I'm filling in all the blanks. "Scotland, huh? You sound so English."

"I wasn't born there. I was born in Yorkshire. In fact, I was educated at an all-girls boarding school until we... moved."

His jaw is clenched as he thinks through what I've told him. "So, after they were killed, you decided to just... hide? I mean, after you saw on the news..."

He's asking a shitload of questions for someone who works in a store.

I cross my arms—and my legs. "You're awfully forward."

"You're awfully British."

He puts down his burger and drinks some of his JD and coke. He leans back in his chair and raises one leg across the other, tapping his fingers on the sofa arm.

"You clocked that guy pretty good earlier. Martial artist?"

I deliver as much ferocity in my stare as possible before giving in and revealing, "My father taught me some stuff."

"So, your dad was in a dangerous job?"

I should ask him to leave, I know; he's veering dangerously close to all the truths I've been running away from. The problem is he's very attractive and something about him makes me believe I can trust him.

When I don't reply and fix my eyes on the ragtag pile of food in my lap instead, he guesses, "So, they were killed... and you were scared. You didn't go home... and you've been floating ever since."

"You sum it up so eloquently."

"A woman like you must have a boyfriend. Why would you abandon everything? Even him?"

I look up and sharpen my gaze. "You ask too many questions."

"You betray too much with your eyes."

I throw back some JD and coke and answer, "He's Scottish. He and I... we're on and off. It's no big deal. He'll probably just think I've found someone else and ditched him. He won't be reading anything into it other than that."

"So, he hasn't tried to contact you?"

"I ditched my phone. Like I said, I don't know the truth. I don't know who to trust."

"Like you said, you don't know the truth, but you didn't answer me when I asked about your father, so all I can deduce is that he had a dangerous job, hung out with the wrong people, and that's why you're now running. Am I right?"

I refuse to answer him but the smug smile in his eyes lets me know that he thinks he's guessed right.

Cocky git.

"I'll tell you what I think, lady. If your family was killed altogether, you figure that maybe the perps thought you'd be included. Maybe the trip to Florida was a spur of the moment, last-minute gig. Maybe you weren't home when it happened, but you were meant to be. Maybe you're running 'cause you know they're coming for you next."

He doesn't say anything else. He takes up his burger, eats it, and starts on the next. I have to listen as his jaw works on that meat like he doesn't give a damn. What gives him the right to question me? I mean, really? Except maybe he saved my life earlier today... He protected me when I had that rusty old knife pressed to my throat.

"Maybe everything you say is true," I counter, "but maybe I wonder why a guy like you is holding the fort at some crummy shop in some godforsaken town in the middle of nowhere. Maybe I wonder a lot. Maybe I'm not stupid."

"Circumstance and stupidity don't always equate," he growls, almost. "Maybe I'm not dumb, maybe neither are you."

I ignore his comment and continue with the last of my carbohydrate feast. Meanwhile he gets to work on what remains of the meat feast he brought. When I'm done, I have to undo the top button on my shorts and I catch him smirking. The lowlife! (A lowlife with the most gorgeous blue eyes I've ever seen.)

I collect my trash and his, dumping it all in the waste paper basket, which I really should've lined with a plastic bag beforehand. His ribs were greasy, it appears.

"So, what now?" he asks.

"What do you mean?"

"Well, I'll need payment for bringing you dinner. Should I wait in bed naked while you go make yourself more comfortable in the bathroom?"

My jaw drops and I even almost dribble, because the absolute, sheer arrogance of him has me wondering how I could kill him and dispose of his body easiest.

"You're joking, right?"

"Maybe, maybe not," he says, amused.

He's joking, he's totally joking. I shrug off his attempt at 'getting me into bed'.

"Well, I'm gonna lie down in my carb coma for a while. Knock yourself out with the TV though." I throw myself onto the bed, hands over my eyes. Food is a shock to the system. My stomach is pumping that shit as fast as it can around my sorely deprived veins.

"Well, only because I don't have anywhere to be."

"Yeah, that's why," I reply, my accent deepening in line with my sarcasm.

He switches on the TV and discovers I have a Netflix login. I hear the familiar bleeps of him scrolling through the menus.

When he presses play on some old action film, I roll to my side and it feels like I just got off a rollercoaster.

Everything spins and I can't help it, I close my eyes.

WHEN I WAKE UP, IT'S pitch-black and I fly up in bed, my heart pounding. I must have been having a bad dream. Looking around the room, I find he's gone. There's a note by the TV: *See you at the store, N*

I hurry to put the chain on the door. How could I have been so stupid? Letting my guard down...

I rush towards my handbag and nothing seems to have been taken. I punch my password into the safe and it clicks open. Inside, my stash of money is intact.

There's only one thought in my mind as I consider what just happened. I told Nate all my secrets. Now he's out there, telling god knows who about what has happened to me. And I've been surviving all this time, too. Just fine. And now I've gone and cocked everything up. Now there will have been no point to any of this. None whatsoever. I may as well have been back home three months ago, being torched alive like the rest of my family. All this running has been for nothing. Besides, I won't ever get free, will I? I'll always be looking over my shoulder. It doesn't matter how many assumed names I adopt or how many times I dye my hair, I'm still me. And now Nate knows exactly who I am.

I start stuffing my few clothes in a bag. I need to get back to my car, which I parked on the edge of town, in an abandoned barn. I bought it in New Orleans and it's taken me this far.

I almost faint and then I remember, I can't handle my drink. I need water. This heat takes everything out of you.

I dash to the bathroom and start splashing my face and my neck, in between sucking water from out of my cupped palm.

"Beatrice, you are so fucked up," I tell myself, shaking my head because I look like my face got ran over by a bus and then stamped on. I need to sort this shit out.

"Beatrice, huh? Nice."

I do a slow turn, seeking him. When I realise he's not in sight, I know he can't be hiding in the other room because there's nothing but tables and chests of drawers in there, and no space beneath the bed. The only place he could be...

I slowly draw back the shower curtain and find him stretched out in the tub, a shotgun hugged to his chest.

"What are you doing?" I demand.

"Ssshhhhhh," he growls. "I'm not here."

"What do you mean, you're not here."

He puts his thumb over his shoulder and gestures towards the outside, where he allegedly believes there is a threat, lying in wait.

"Earlier," he barely whispers, "I left, but only after leaving the bathroom window open. I snuck back in. I figure they'll be back."

"Who'll be back?"

"Go back to bed and we'll see."

I narrow my eyes. "Who are you?"

"Just a guy," he says, with a shrug. "A guy who found out you're staying here. So, *they* could find out too, right?"

I don't believe he's 'just a guy', any more than he believes I believe him.

I roll my eyes. "Who's they?"

"How the hell do I know? You're the one with a target on your back."

There are too many questions for this time of night, and although I won't be able to sleep, I shake my head and leave the room, heading back to bed. Staring at the wall is better than staring at him.

Chapter Three

I've been in and out of sleep all night, so when day breaks, I feel dead but I know I have to get up. He's not moved from that bathroom all night and nobody has been by to kill me... so maybe we are both being paranoid. I mean, he's paranoid to the extent that he wrote that note, to make it look like he'd really gone... Maybe that was for my benefit (in case someone did come by to take a pop, then they would believe the ruse that the hotel room's only occupant was me). Nate could have snuck up on the assailant, and then...

Who knows?

Hell, maybe my mum and dad's house *did* explode because of a gas leak. Maybe tragedy is responsible for me being orphaned. Given my father's profession, it's not that easy for me to accept their demise was an accident... especially because the news reported that the whole area around the house for a half mile was cordoned off and evacuated. Surely a gas leak wouldn't require those sorts of measures?

"Are you awake?" I murmur.

"The more pressing question is, am I alive? I can't tell 'cause I've lost all feeling."

"I've got to leave town. Alone."

"Is that safe?"

"I don't believe I'll ever have the luxury of feeling safe, ever again."

"You got a car?"

"I've got one, yeah."

"Where?"

"Hidden."

"I'll come with you."

I run to the bathroom and draw back the shower curtain. He looks like shit. His tall frame has been bent double in the tub all night.

"You're an idiot so with all due respect, I have to say goodbye. Thanks for the smoothies, and for the carbs and all, but now I have to go. Alone."

"Sure, okay," he says, nodding his head.

He leans back in the bath and rests his eyes. Infuriated, I gather my toiletries from the bathroom and add them to the clothes I packed last night. I stuff some gum in my mouth, drag a brush through my hair and pull my boots on. Nobody will be on the road at this hour, will they? I can get down the road unnoticed, escape scot-free and be done. I'll move onto the next place, and then...

Well, in the next place, I'll not get myself involved with anyone or anything. I'm done living. It's time to hide for real. Either that or die, right?

But what about living? Don't I want to start living?

Well, at least not here, not in this dustbowl town.

My hand is on the door handle when I'm reminded my money's still in the safe. Shit. How could I leave without my money? Well, I have plenty more in my account, but still... hard cash comes in handy. I punch in the code and start filling my bag with the dough. As I'm shoving, I have a flashback to the day my father explained to me why we all needed secure, untraceable bank accounts...

The memory is cruelly ripped away as I'm dragged into the present, almost winded as the safe door flies at me, knocking me to the ground. My ribs scream for a moment, before I catch my breath. Once breathing again, I see the hole someone just blasted through the so-called reinforced hotel door. The bullet got through and hit the safe door, which I just had open, and which protected me.

"Beatrice!"

"The money..."

"Fuck the money."

There's still a wad in the safe, only about $10,000, but still.

My mind's a blur. More gunshots ring out. Nate encourages me to crawl towards him in the bathroom, where he is also on the floor. We hear someone drilling open the front door and Nate hurries me towards the bathroom window. I lower myself from the ledge as much as possible before dropping with a thud to the ground, my ankle crunching beneath me. Nate jumps straight out and lands inelegantly beside me, like he's used to all this.

My heart's clanging against my ribcage and I feel numb and sick as we take a few seconds to think, our backs pressed against the wall beneath the bathroom window.

My life flashes before my eyes. My mother's smile. My father's steady hands. The day my little sister was born. Why do these people think it's okay to keep taking?

It's not okay.

"I don't know what to do," he mumbles next to me, the shotgun held to his chest.

"Wait," I whisper.

There's nowhere to run without being spotted trying to make our escape; the hotel is surrounded by open land and there is nowhere to hide, no getaway car nearby I can see.

"Wait," I encourage him again, motioning he keep his back right against the wall.

I move into more of a squat position and place myself directly beneath the window, my eyes looking upwards.

The lock on my hotel room door is shown who is boss and we hear footsteps enter the room I formerly occupied for two weeks. It's a fifteen-foot drop from the bathroom window, so this attacker (whoever he or she is) could've got into my room through the window if they were capable of climbing, but instead they've chosen to assault my hotel room door instead. The gap at the top of the bathroom window is slim, which tells me our attacker is maybe big and wouldn't slide through as easily as Nate or I did. Maybe they're too overweight to climb. If they'd have climbed, they'd have had the element of surprise, except Nate would've been lying in wait in the bathtub and all bets would be off before the shootout ever began. How nobody has heard the gunshot and drilling and come out to help us, I don't know. Are my neighbours terrified of getting involved? Is this drama usual for these parts? Something tells me it is not.

Listening carefully, I only hear one set of footsteps dashing around the room above us. This is someone who works alone, probably someone masquerading as law enforcement or something.

Then something occurs to me. There are no drainpipes to climb, so how did Nate get back into the room earlier if the bathroom window is a storey up? Either he lied to me or he's good at climbing plain walls with no grips. Right now anyway, he's the least of my worries.

"He's alone," I tell Nate, "come on!"

We chase along the back of the building and parked in shadow, around the corner, is a clapped-out Winnebago that looks as if it's been sat there for yonks. It's probably Sam's.

"You thinking what I'm thinking?"

"YES!" I shout.

We jump into the vehicle and Nate finds keys in the sun visor above the driver's seat.

He guns the machine and sets off. I open the glovebox and find a handgun. Checking it, I find it's loaded. As we pass the front of the hotel, I see our assailant's vehicle is a blacked-out SUV with chrome wheels that are probably worth more than the entire hotel put together.

"Slow down," I urge him, and as we're passing, I blow out one of the tyres on the SUV. That ought to slow down our pursuer a little.

As we swerve onto the road, there is gunfire against the back of the Winnebago, but we're free before too much damage is done.

"Two miles down this road, you'll eventually come to an abandoned barn. Stop there. We need to ditch this thing."

"Good plan," he says.

"You should go back. You've done nothing wrong."

"Neither have you."

"How do you know that?"

"Yeah, well how do you know I'm innocent?"

"I guess I don't, do I?"

He's flooring the vehicle and it's still only doing 55. It would never take us very far.

"Maybe I have nothing better to do," he says.

"Maybe you fancy me."

"Don't flatter yourself, Beatrice." He snickers like he doesn't care how he comes across and it's strange how that pisses me off.

We come to the place and I point it out. "There!"

We swerve off the road and hide the Winnebago behind the other side of the old barn. While he's parking, I rush into the barn and throw my luggage into the boot of the Jeep Cherokee I bought in New Orleans at a steal. In cash. It's not as fresh now, not after being parked here for two weeks, so I wind down the window quickly and check the gas gauge. I've got about 200 miles in the tank. I've been so lucky. Anyone might have seen me hide the vehicle here and they could have syphoned off the petrol.

"Beatrice, wait!" he shouts as I begin reversing out and knock the barn doors open as I do.

I skid to a halt before heading back onto the road.

He comes to the driver's side window and gives me a foreboding look.

"Tell me the truth, *Nate*." If that's even his name...

He taps the rubber window seal and tells me, "I knew your father, William Fleming."

I stare into his eyes. He couldn't know that name unless he really knew my father. I don't keep anything about my person that could give away my true identity, neither did my father. Only his family knew the real him.

"Get in, and keep quiet," I instruct him, and he does so without complaint.

We eventually meet a proper highway and I don't know where we're going or how we got here, but I only have one question on my lips.

"What was the grocery store then?"

"I tracked you from New Orleans and noticed a tail right before Longlake. I bought the store off a guy, paid twice what it was worth. Everything was fine until that prick tried to stick up the store. Somebody must have been watching. They don't know who I am, but they know you. They saw you work over that dude. They could'a hacked into the CCTV. They'd have seen your moves. They now know you knew about your daddy. They know you've been trained. They've witnessed it. They know you know, so that's why you've been set up for the kill. You know too much."

I keep driving.

All this time I thought I was alone, that nobody was following me. I may as well have had a satellite signal beaming right out of my head.

I don't know if I can trust Nate. I don't know anything.

"Just answer me one thing, Nate?"

"Sure."

"Is that your real name?"

"It actually is."

It sinks in.

We don't use our real names.

I only spoke my real name out loud last night—because I thought I was alone in that room.

Which means Nate, or whoever he really is, isn't to be trusted.

I can't trust anyone, can I?

Nate may have figured out my father's real name, but Nate isn't one of us. He can't be.

The Collective doesn't use real names…

I drive on anyway.

Nate may prove useful yet.

He may help me discover what really happened to my family, and then after we're done, I'll ditch him somewhere and move on with my life.

"I was being sarcastic by the way," he says, "about my real name. My name's… not important."

"If your name's not important, then I assume you have a passport with a not-important name in it."

"I do."

"Good."

He looks puzzled, but then he settles in once it clicks.

I point the car in the direction of Houston.

Let's go back to where it all started.

Chapter Four

"I have no idea what the point of this is," he complains, as we stack our paltry luggage on the rack above our heads. All he has in his bag are the clothes he had on yesterday. He had to buy new stuff from Atlanta after we took a flight from Houston, and that was after spending seven hours in the car on the way to the airport. From Atlanta, our next stop was Heathrow, London. Our current mode of transport is a cabin on the Caledonian sleeper from London to Edinburgh. It is tiny, true, but it will also give us time to rest before we get to Edinburgh, my home turf. At least there aren't as many guns in the UK.

"We've been awake for hours and hours. We've crossed time zones and been oxygen deprived. I'm not getting into another aircraft just to have my energy zapped even more."

"Jeez, show me how this thing works then..."

I pull down the top bunk and he launches himself up.

"Okay, I take your point," he says, and within moments, I hear his breathing change and his leg flops over the edge of the top bunk. It's not even that late, but then all we've had are little snatched windows of sleep on aircrafts.

The train's not even set off yet. We're still at Euston.

I could totally ditch him. Maybe he's on my side. Maybe he's not.

Maybe he's gorgeous, but that still doesn't mean he can be trusted.

I could leave him right now. He may not wake until morning. He is tired, after all.

I could be halfway across Europe before he even realises I've gone, and he could land in Edinburgh alone, and with nobody to back him up or show him the lay of the land.

I don't even know why I'm here.

Why didn't I come back home months ago?

I missed the memorial. I missed everything. I haven't even buried my family. I couldn't. They weren't given the privilege of having their remains buried. They were incinerated in a blast that forced the authorities to create a half-mile cordon.

Three million pounds dropped into my account just days after they died and that's all I know. Dad planned for his death, and maybe a trusted friend of his knew I was still alive, so they sent me that money. Unless... Dad had some sort of provision where if he didn't log into an account within 48 hours, it would automatically deposit all that money in my account for me, I don't know. But what about Phoebe's account? Did she get money, too? Or did he know she was going to die alongside him and Mum? And that's the problem. I don't know enough. And even if this Nate guy is rotten to the core, right now he's my only lead—and we've got this far. Maybe I shouldn't have been running all this time. Maybe I should have been seeking answers from the start. Maybe then, I would have them already. Or perhaps, in the words of my father, "Everything in good time, and everything as it should be." He was a great believer in things working themselves out.

I stand staring at Nate as he sleeps. He's got golden highlights running through his dark-brown hair. He has a classic American tan and big hands. He's tall, has a strong nose and his jaw wears the most gorgeous designer stubble. He's the most stunning man I've ever come across. I just have no idea who he is or what we're doing. This could end up a train wreck.

Too bad it's too late, I realise, as the sleeper judders into action, taking us onwards in the direction of Scotland, the land of whisky, haggis, landscapes seemingly out of this world—and a place in which I've spent time knowing that one day, things could go wrong for our family.

So how in the hell does this cute American factor into all of this? I guess eventually, I'll find out. Until then, I just have to pray I stay alive. After all, so far he hasn't been a bad travelling companion. He doesn't try to fill silences with stupid talk. He even picked up some books to read in the airport, and appeared to read them on the flight from Atlanta to London. Maybe that was part of the act, or maybe he really is a reader. I read Classics at St. Andrew's, but at this point, sharing information like this seems too much of a risk.

I think about sliding my hand into his jacket pocket to check what he has in there, but what's the point? If I'm dead, I'm dead, right?

The Collective would have had me killed by now for sure, if they'd wanted me gone. Nate found me, didn't he? Even him. He's a little immature for sure, so if even he could find me...

It seems to me like they just want to know what I know. Or else they think I have the key to something my father might have left behind.

Whatever is going on here, all I know right now is that I need the oblivion of a whisky-induced sleep.

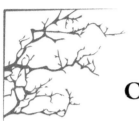

Chapter Five

P AST
     I was fifteen and our whole life had just been turned up-side down. It was like we were in a witness protection pro-gramme, except I had a suspicion that what my father had done was completely illegal—and I wanted to know why this was our life now. I needed to satisfy my curiosity. Sure, our new house in Edinburgh was bigger than the old stone cottage we used to oc-cupy in rural North Yorkshire. Not only was it bigger—and only a couple of miles up the road from one of the greatest cities in the world—it was also more stately. My new school had an entirely different curriculum and still, I didn't worry about that; I was clever, I'd catch up, and Phoebe was young, so this wouldn't get her down, either. It was just that my raging curiosity about why we'd had to ship out of Yorkshire so suddenly wouldn't be quelled. Dad would only tell me so much, so I resorted to sneak-ing around corners.

One night, it was blowing a gale outside, and even so I could still hear my parents arguing downstairs. I snuck across the creaky landing upstairs, only moving every time the gale blew, so they wouldn't hear my footsteps.

When I got to the stairs, I slid down the bannister rail and managed not to make a sound. Even above the gale, footsteps on the stairs would be heard—ours was a Victorian mansion, the stairs creakier than the ones in Shakespeare's birthplace, which my dad took me to one time.

I slid along the waxed flooring and edged my way to the ajar living-room door.

Then, I heard voices.

"Who are these people?" my mother demanded.

"It's too dangerous for you to know anything."

"*What* are these people?" she asked, her Yorkshire accent so broad, meaning she was angry—and upset. She could speak well but it took effort. Her West Yorkshire accent was thick and rough if she was tired and couldn't concentrate.

"The Collective. That's all I can tell you. They're called the Collective."

She scoffed. "That means fuck all to me."

"Marie, you better pack this in."

I'd never heard my mother swear before then. It was a shock.

"I knew the dangers, oh I knew," she growled. "Changing our identities? I could handle. Changing our location? I could handle. But this? You, working for this Collective... whoever they are... and going away... weeks... months at a time... *this... this* I cannot handle. I won't."

"What do you expect me to do, Marie? What?"

I could tell their argument was becoming physical. There was a shove. I couldn't see what was going on, but from the sounds of it, Dad had Mum pushed up against the sideboard.

"I got us out. I told you I'd walk, let you and the girls go free. I'd walk away and you'd be fine, but you wouldn't let me go. Instead, I got us all out, together. Safe. We're safe here. Nobody knows us. We've never kept friends. We'll be fine here. I told you, I warned you it would be this way—"

"You didn't warn me about the true cost though, did you? Did you?"

I sensed my mother was getting ready to vacate the room and not give my father anymore of her time. I stepped back into the hallway a little, ready to hide myself in the downstairs toilet if need be. I had my hand ready on the doorknob and everything.

"I swear, Bill... I swear—"

"Swear, what?"

"I'll make sure you never see your girls again."

"That's an empty threat and you know it. Beatrice will never go for that."

"It's Annalise, remember? Annalise. You renamed her Annalise," my mother spat, venom flying from her lips (and I could tell that even from the corridor, while unable to see her).

"You can take them, but I'll still find you. You don't mean it anyway. You know you don't."

My mother swung the living-room door open, so I twisted the bathroom doorknob and sank bank against the door, letting the room swallow me before she caught me. She had her back to the hallway as she left the living room anyway, her argument with Dad still ongoing.

Once I was shut in the bathroom, I heard my mother race upstairs. My father followed soon after. I allowed myself a couple of minutes grace before I re-entered the corridor and smelt whisky on the air.

My mother always became argumentative when she'd had whisky, even Phoebe and I knew that. I started climbing the stairs, one at a time. Whenever my mother whined softly under my father's caress, I took the next step, and the next, or if the wind battered the house hard, I'd take two steps. Eventually I was back in my room and listening to the wind flying up and down the chimney behind my headboard. From where I lay in bed, the wind drowned out all the other noises.

IN THE MONTHS THAT followed, I realised what my mother had been complaining about that night. Dad started going away for work, sometimes for weeks on end. He'd always worked away, but now it was for much lengthier stints. Whenever he got home from those long periods apart, they'd argue, drink and have sex. Rinse and repeat.

My mum had been a landscape gardener in Yorkshire, but she didn't seek work in Edinburgh. She tried to convince us it was because she didn't need to work anymore, but I instinctively knew it was because she was depressed. So, instead she dedicated herself to us, our lives and our education.

I'd be lying if I said I didn't enjoy it when he wasn't there. Without Dad around, we were lighter, freer. The weapons he used to hide around the house in Yorkshire were now gone. We'd had to leave behind the grandfather clock we used to have in Yorkshire, and I missed that—because the way it used to chime was familiar, elementary even. I also missed being able to walk over the top of the heather in the warmer months. I missed the snow tractor and the old settle Mum had had in the ancient kitchen. Our Edinburgh mansion was clearly more expensive, had a more modern kitchen and huge rooms, plus we were neighbours with famous authors and retired brain surgeons, but it was never quite home. It was where the Williamsons hid out, pretending they weren't actually the Flemings.

When he was away, sometimes I'd hear her crying in the downstairs toilet, thinking we couldn't hear because we were upstairs with the telly on. We could tell it was because she was missing him and couldn't bear it.

I vowed never to love a man because of the pain I heard in her cries.

I vowed never to allow a man to hurt me in the same way he was hurting her.

I vowed never to fall for an assassin, too. Even though it was never said, I knew from the way my dad had lightning-fast reflexes and weapons stashed all around the old Yorkshire house, that whatever it was he did was dangerous, and he was in a profession where he could get guns—and guns weren't easy to get hold of in England.

For some reason there were no guns stashed around the Edinburgh house, but Dad was paying the price for our freedom—and in a way I was grateful. He'd been piling the weight of the world on my shoulders since I was small and now I was free because he was away all the time. I skipped Krav Maga classes, I concentrated on my Duke of Edinburgh award instead and got involved with a rambler's society Mum was into, walking out and about, all over the Scottish countryside. When he wasn't around, I wasn't thinking about which people walking down the street were carrying guns, knives, or suicide vests. I wasn't thinking about which dickheads wanted to rape me. I wasn't thinking about anything other than living my life. I wasn't living in fear anymore. I wasn't thinking about constantly having to potentially defend myself. I wasn't thinking about my little sister being kidnapped and used as bait. He was gone and as far as I was concerned, the threat had disappeared along with him.

I'd always been clever and Dad had put pressure on me to learn about the world 'in order to protect myself', and in a way, my academic education would never falter, mainly because I shared my father's thirst for knowledge. However, with him gone, I looked at everything in terms of enjoyment and fun—rather than as a method to prepare myself for the dark and dangerous world he was involved in. It was as though he'd one day expect me to follow in his footsteps, and that was never going to be for me, not at all.

I thought I was being mean, but looking back, my overall instinct about it all was right: our lives were better off without my dad, it was just that Mum loved him too much to fully let go.

I wasn't sorry he was gone from home all the time, but I was sorry that my mother lived in constant agony.

If only she'd escaped him while she still had the chance.

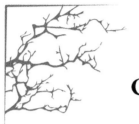

Chapter Six

It's stupid o'clock in the morning as we begin the approach into Edinburgh, but we're both alert. As we wait in our sleeper, we go over the plan again...

We've already booked our hotel rooms online and all we need to do once we make it to our budget hotel is check in at a computer screen—no human interaction required—and through the power of the internet we've also swung early check-in.

After checking in, I'll give it 30 minutes and then I'll leave the hotel and head out towards the area of town where my family used to live. Nate will follow behind me to see if I'm being pursued. If they already know I'm home, then they know the first place I'll go will be my burnt-down old house. Nate will quickly be able to determine if we're in danger. I'll need to wear something to cover my head and mask my face in case I bump into someone I know, but... it's said that assassins know their mark just from their walk. They don't mess about.

"If we make it," he says, "then I'll do as you suggested and wait in the gated park across the road. If you can tell if any of your old neighbours are still around, we'll come back another day and pick a way of finding out what they know. We can't just roll up and ask them. We don't know if they're being watched, too."

I nod my head.

"Are you sure you can do this?" he asks me, because once we exit the sleeper train, we're to make our own way. He'll pretend he's not looked up the hotel on a map, and that he's a dawdling tourist, while I'll get to the hotel in quick time and make a stop at a café along the way, stocking up on much-needed food. He'll grab something from a bakery en route, too.

"I can do it."

"It must feel weird to be back."

I look down at my lap. "It's weird to be back in jeans."

"You've lost a lot of weight, huh?"

My old pair of 501s are just a little bit baggy, he's right. "I've starved myself, I guess. Punished myself for running. I don't actually know why I was running, really. Not now. Maybe it was the shock. Maybe I ran because I didn't know what else to do."

"Running might have saved your life, who knows? Let's just hope we find out."

"Well," I chuckle, nervously, "I just need a few good drinks inside me, a few egg sandwiches and some cake. I'll be swelling these jeans again, no problem."

I see in his eyes he's wrestling with a response—some cheesy comeback or something cliché, like he likes me just the way I am. His eyes dart from side to side as the train bumps to a halt.

"Okay?" he asks.

I pull a woollen skull cap over my head, even though it's August. I can probably get away with it because even in August it's freezing—in comparison to Texas, anyway.

He leaves the train before me, rushing ahead to avoid the crush.

I dawdle a bit before exiting. Out on the platform, engine fumes and perfume and body odour surrounds me and I feel the world spin on its axis, the people crushing me. It's just that I haven't been somewhere so populated in months.

I push on through Waverley Station and remember to breathe.

I know this place well. Know it like the back of my hand. I just have to put one foot in front of the other. The trouble is, I'm subconsciously looking around, trying to spot Nate.

He could be going to find a place in the rafters, somewhere to shoot me down from.

Just who is he and what does he want from me?

I was in Texas just the other day and now I'm back here, in the city where *it* happened—that event that took away my entire family. My Phoebe. My beautiful mother, and my father. Part of me hates Dad for bringing this down on his family, but I hate the perpetrators even more.

I have to remind myself to pick up a burner phone along the way. Nate's going to get one, too—and we'll exchange numbers much later tonight, when he deems it safe enough to creep into my hotel room and devise the next stage of the plan with me.

I smell food as I make my way out of the packed station, which is bustling with tourists and students starting a new term, plus people on their way back to England after spending the summer here. The smells bring back memories of warmer, happier times; shopping days with Mum and Phoebe; rare days when Dad and I would jump on the train up to Inverness and do a bit of sightseeing, feeding the historian inside me. Phoebe never liked history or books or anything I was interested in. She wanted to be an actress. She was six years younger than me and only eighteen when she died. She was going to drama school in Oxford. She'd be there already if she was still alive. She'd be looking forward to freshers' week and maybe meeting a cute boy or two, making friends with some of the girls in her Halls of Residence. She'd have been the centre of attention, with her stark red hair, sexy accent and big, green eyes. She would have lit up the world.

As I'm passing through the station, I ditch the woollen hat once I realise it's warmer today than I thought it would be. I rummage in my handbag and find my sunglasses, the thick black ones. Donning them as I exit Waverley, tears slide unseen down the sides of my face, my fake dirty-blonde hair catching and soaking up how I really feel.

I'm broken and devastated and I've been running because I could be next.

Maybe I ought to be next.

That way I get to be with them again, don't I?

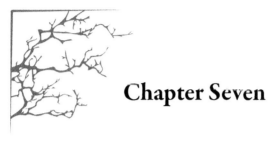

Chapter Seven

Hotel check-in and procurement of a burner phone has so far been easy. (I even got a second burner phone, just in case—because Nate has yet to prove himself as far as I'm concerned.) Now I'm working my way towards my former home.

On foot I reach the tram stop near Edinburgh Castle and suddenly I realise I haven't donned a hat, or even my sunglasses. By returning home, I've allowed myself to be lulled into a false sense of security. Or maybe it's just that for almost ten years of my life, I was safe here. Maybe that's it.

I don the glasses anyway.

After five minutes on the tram, I catch sight of Nate stood near the front, glaring at me. He looks furious in fact. I would smile or glare back, but I don't have the energy. So what if I've gone off script? Earlier today I told him I'd walk all the way to Morningside, giving an enemy plenty of time to capture me, or at least attempt capture, and here I am going the naughty way home—the way that doesn't involve a long walk or me having to see every little memory on every street corner as I walk by.

After 20 minutes on the tram, I jump off and look Nate in the eye when he follows me off. He looks exasperated because I keep looking at him. Everyone exiting the tram alongside him can tell we know one another. There's no hiding the ruse. I'm too tired and facing too much. I can't be bothered with charades right now.

"So the fuck what, Nate?"

"So the fuck what, so the fuck what!" he repeats. "You know the drill. I cover your back."

"I value my liberty more than my back and I should've told you that earlier. Besides I am sick and tired of pretending." Maybe that's why I'm back in Scotland: I can't be bothered to lie anymore, not to myself and not to anyone else either.

He huffs and puffs alongside me, but we walk on anyway. As the tall buildings around us swallow all the daylight, it feels suddenly colder and drearier and he mumbles, "I've never been so cold in my whole damn life."

"Get used to it."

"I've never been this far north before."

"I can tell."

"How?"

"You're exceptionally bronzed."

We walk on in silence and turn a corner. I feel it before I see it.

Something like a wall of ice descends from the sky and lands right in front of me, like a shield, or a barrier to me walking onwards. If I didn't feel cold in the shadows before, I do right now.

"You can do this," he says, and placing his hand on my forearm, he urges me on.

I walk right through the sheet of ice and begin shivering as we draw closer.

The charred remains of our six-bedroom, three-storey, detached property in affluent Morningside is nothing but a pile of ash, and even a satellite view could tell me that. We don't need to be right here to determine it's been burnt to the ground.

We reach the middle of the street and stand on the opposite side of the road.

Mum's rose bushes are all dead, front and back I assume. The apple and pear trees look skeletal, even now, in summer.

It's a shell, still standing, but a shell nonetheless. I can see the outline of where life once existed, just there. The first-floor master suite was at the front of the house, but Mum liked her privacy, so she and Dad had the whole top floor as their own while I had the master and Phoebe had the junior suite. We had a couple of spare rooms which schoolfriends of Phoebe's would stay in. I've never kept close friends.

"What was his cover?" Nate asks, standing beside me still. I'd almost forgotten he was even here.

"He told people he was a travelling salesman."

"What about your mother?"

"She was a landscaper. It was her real job, too."

"I can see the gardens were once nice."

His words bring down that wall of ice around me again. A part of me, which I've buried so deep down inside, feels as dead as they are.

It's scary how unemotional I feel right now. Maybe this just isn't the time or the place. Maybe I still need those answers.

"The curtains on both the neighbours' houses either side are still the same. They can't have moved. The same ornaments in the windows..."

"We should keep walking, then," he says, steering me away. "Maybe catch a drink at that bar we passed on the way up the hill."

"It's okay, we should go back into town. There's more choice."
I stare at my feet, watching as they move, even as I feel like it's not
me moving them.

Once we're around the corner, I can't walk anymore and my
legs buckle, like they're jelly. He catches me and holds me up. I'm
bundled against him.

"Oh my god," I whisper, because that's all I have left. Just a
whisper.

"I've got you."

A whole chunk of my young adulthood is now just a pile of
charred remains and I can't even bury my family properly. Bits
and pieces of them are still in that house and even despite the police cordons, and the tape surrounding what was once my home,
anyone could just go in and start picking through what was once
our life together.

My whole world is shattered, but it was lucky it was only the
three of them who died, because whoever intended to murder my
parents wanted to make sure the job was done. In fact, I'm surprised the whole entire street didn't go up in flames. It's clear the
incident was no ordinary gas leak. For sure, people usually smell
gas and report it before it does that much damage.

Which means someone has to know something.

Someone must.

Chapter Eight

On the tram going back into the city centre, we sit together this time. There's no pretending we don't know one another. I mean there's no interaction either, but I'm not pretending. I'm barely even breathing, really. I want to put my head between my legs but instead I'm just trying to focus on the path ahead, mentally counting down the familiar streets that mark our way ahead. I keep counting and counting. We're getting there slowly, up and down hills, over crossings and round corners. A short journey ends up feeling very long but every new point along the journey that I anticipate comes to pass and we end up making it back in one piece. That's not to say Nate isn't still wary. I can tell from the way he's continually scoping our surroundings that he is.

Once off the tram, he steers me via the elbow towards a Starbucks. We wait in the queue and I realise how I've missed good coffee. How I've missed life in general. It's late morning, not lunch yet, and thankfully the queue goes down steadily.

"I've got friends," I mumble.

"We don't have friends."

"I've got places, people would put me up."

"We don't have places."

"I've got money."

"Money means nothing, and you know it."

We make it to the front of the queue and the server gives Nate a huge grin. She looks enamoured.

"What can I get you?" she asks.

"A cappuccino, a hot chocolate and two blueberry muffins. All grande... please," he adds, as if manners are an afterthought for him. She doesn't even blink. Or breathe. It must be the accent.

"Okay then," she mumbles, when she notices me glaring. I don't want to be in this queue any longer than I have to be.

I'm about to argue that I can make my own choices when he shoots me a look I can only interpret as, "Shut the hell up while I think."

He clicks his heeled cowboy boots on the floor as we wait for our order. Nate pays in cash. He must have exchanged some dollars for pounds at some point—unless people like him always have a variety of currencies about their person?

People like him...? The thing is, I don't want to believe Nate is what I think he is. I think he's the same as my father. But I don't want him to be the same. The same means death, doesn't it? It means constantly living with the threat of it. Always there. Everywhere. Death. Preparing for it. Also living it. Not living. Death.

We reach a corner of the seating area and I watch the muscles and bones work in his wrist as he carries the tray in one thick, steady hand. Is that hand going to protect me? Or will I never be able to trust anyone? Is there only me now? Is this my life? Because of my father's job, will I always be looking over my shoulder?

"You trust nobody outside the family, Beatrice," Dad always used to say, and with those stern eyes of his staring at me as he said it, I never disbelieved him. Never. Just because Nate knows my father's real name, that doesn't necessarily mean he's one of

the family, does it? Sure, Nate likely worked with my father, but
how do I know I can trust him? All I know is that I want to trust
him. I want to trust him, because well... because he's freaking gorgeous. Wanting doesn't make something right though, does it?
Just because I want him doesn't mean he's good. He could be
very, very bad.

Nate pushes the blueberry muffin and the hot chocolate my
way.

I don't like either.

He shakes his head at me. "Sugar. You need sugar. You're
amped up, you need sugar to calm down."

Everything is tasteless on my tongue as it goes on its merry
way down towards my stomach.

After I've started to get the feeling back in my legs and I'm
breathing normally again, Nate asks, "You said you're a model,
right?"

"Yeah."

"Is that a cover?" He stares at me, challenging me to lie.

He has my hackles raised and he knows it. He can't help it.
And I can't help it that he pisses me off so easily.

"My father wanted me to be just like him, but I fucking told
him no. I said *no*. So, it's not a cover. I'm a fucking model and I
don't actually give a fuck if you believe that or not."

When my fist lands on the table as I assert my honest response, the drinks spill everywhere and for the first time since we
met, he looks sorry.

"So, why do you know *stuff*?"

I shrug. "He knew something like this would happen... eventually. He prepared us. Well, he prepared me. Phoebe wasn't in-

terested in protecting herself. She never took it all seriously... the danger, I mean."

"So, why did you?"

"Because..." I huff. "Phoebe and I were very different. She wasn't an airhead, she just preferred to see the good in everything. She thought all for the best. She and I were very different personalities."

There is liquid trickling down my face and I haven't even got the energy to hide my emotion right now. I'm detached, even from my own tears. I stare out of the window to our side and avert my gaze from his.

"You're a model... but you graduated with a first-class degree?"

Fucker's done his research. I almost want to laugh out loud at the absurdity of all this.

What is it about being back in Scotland that makes my thoughts more colourful? I guess the mild manners of the Deep South are out of the window now.

He holds out some Starbucks paper napkins towards me and I dab my cheeks absentmindedly. Maybe he's embarrassed to be sat here with a crying woman.

"It's a way of earning money, so what? I was going to travel the world after I got enough money together, or what I thought was enough anyway."

"Your dad couldn't have given you the money?"

I turn and stare right at him. "I wanted to make my own way in the world, but I also did modelling to piss him off. Satisfied?"

"You loved your father, then? You're angry, so you must have loved him, otherwise—" He's there in his chair, his arm draped over the one next to him, like he doesn't give a damn. And yet here he is, having travelled all this way with me.

"It was complicated between us. He was distant... absent... but yeah, you could say I loved him."

"You just hated his job?"

"He never spelled it out what it was he did, but I knew. I just knew." I lean forward and snarl, "I hated, and I still hate anyone in his line of work, just so you know, just so we're clear."

His jaw ticks and he looks away, so I can't see his fear. He can't hide it forever though, can he? The fact that he is just as scared as the rest of us is becoming ever more evident.

I wring my hands under the table after finishing my sugary drink and food.

"Did you have your own apartment?" he asks.

I shake my head. "No, but I spent a lot of time at my boyfriend's place."

"What's his name?"

"Doctor Arthur Doherty. He's a professor at St. Andrew's."

His eyes narrow and he leans in closer. "You fucked your professor?"

"After I wasn't a student anymore, yeah."

"He fucked one of his students?"

The look in Nate's eyes right now is one I'd love to punch my way through, just to get rid of it. I've never felt this aggressive towards a man in all my life. I don't know what's come over me.

"We got together after I graduated, so I wasn't a student then."

"Was it the elbow patches? Maybe a monocle? What was it?"

I scrape back my chair abruptly and tower above him as I sneer, "Get out of my life."

I turn on my heel and walk out of Starbucks.

I start walking back towards the hotel. I'll get my stuff, go back to the train station and book a ticket to St. Andrew's. Arthur will take some convincing, but he loved me, maybe he still does. Maybe he could forgive me? But then, what if the bad guys come after me while we're together? Arthur will get caught in the crossfire. Maybe I could send him a note and ask him to meet me somewhere. We could run away together. I'll use my money to get a fake passport for Arthur. Arthur and I can live happily ever after, somewhere else.

If only I really loved Arthur, but I don't, do I? If I did love him, I would have done whatever it took to get word to him that I was okay, not cut him off altogether. Mum and Dad did whatever it took to stay together. They couldn't be without one another. Arthur was just my university crush. I wanted him because everyone else wanted him. I think I also got together with him because I knew it would piss Dad off. I knew modelling would piss him off, too. I did love my father, but we had beef.

His job and what it did to my mum was that beef.

Soon enough I'm standing outside the budget hotel once more, and that's when I realise I really have no fucking clue what I'm doing. None at all.

I walk a few paces and take one of the benches, sitting in the middle of the garden in front of the hotel.

Nate drops onto the bench beside me after catching up with me ten seconds later.

Doesn't he get bored of following me around?

"I never even called Arthur after I saw it on the telly. I just... I heard the news... and that was it, you know? The warnings my dad had given me started to ring in my head and they came into effect. I put Arthur out of my mind. I mean, he might even think I'm dead. That I went and jumped into the sea off Florida or something. I know I should let him know I'm alive, at least. The thing is, I really just don't care about him. I used him to hurt my dad. I used him because I was lost. I know I owe him an explanation, but I... I mean, should I tell him I'm okay?" I look to Nate for help on this matter.

"You should, but you can't," Nate reminds me. "Arthur and your old friends and anyone you used to be associated with will be being watched. They won't know their iPads, their phones, laptops and TVs are hacked. Everything they do on Facebook is probably being printed out daily. They won't know their every move is being watched. The Collective is just waiting for you to show up."

"Why, though? WHY?" I demand, pulling my hair.

He shakes his head. "I don't know. Aside from being afraid of what you may or may not know, I don't know why they would still be chasing you. I don't know. As for your parents' neighbours, well, you saw that pile of ash. Everyone in the borough has probably been bought off. Nobody is going to cave."

"There's one person," I assure him, "and I know how I can speak to her. You have to trust me."

He turns my face and holds my cheeks in his hands, declaring, "I do trust you."

"Tonight, then. Tonight. Before that, I'm going to rest for a bit if you don't mind."

"Okay," he agrees, and I walk into the hotel and leave him where he is.

IT'S 4.30 IN THE EVENING by the time I feel ready to do this thing. Figuring that Nate will already have a trace on my phone (the one with the number I gave him), I ditch that one and tuck the second burner in my back pocket. I stuff all the necessary get-away items in a small backpack, which is more of a handbag on string really, but anyway...

I pack my cash, my passports (all of them), and the only thing I have left of my family—a photo of us all that I've kept in my wallet for years. We were in Florida at Disney World and it was one of the rare times we were all relaxed. I was 15 and Phoebe, nine. We had those dumb Mickey ears and it was one of the rare occasions Phoebe and I got along. With me being much older than her, and much cleverer, she despised me until she reached 17, then she finally seemed to warm to me. I never hated her. Like all other teenagers, I just tossed her off as my immature little sis and made like I was indifferent. Mum always said Phoebe would eventually grow out of it—and she did, thankfully. Just in time for us to put things right before her death.

It was a long shot—this being a budget hotel and all—but earlier I asked reception if they could perhaps perform me a service. I'd researched which shade I wanted, using the internet of course. Anyway, the hotel went out and bought me hair dye and now I'm no longer dirty blonde. I'm back to my natural copper. It took me ages to find the correct shade online. Nate probably knows about that, too. He can probably find out anything about me. Anyway, me dyeing my hair back to its natural colour isn't me flipping two fingers at the people after me—or Nate—it's just me trying to get back to normal, if there is such a thing anyway.

What I'm hoping is that Nate thinks I'm paranoid about venturing out alone—hence asking the hotel to get me the dye—and he won't be expecting my next move.

Earlier today I noticed a linen store next to my hotel room and as one of the chambermaids was collecting stuff from inside the room, I noticed the window inside. All hotel rooms have locks on the windows, but the linen store doesn't. I stole the chambermaid's universal key card in case I'd be needing it. Now I'm needing it.

Now I've got my baseball cap on and my backpack and a plan of attack in mind, it's time.

I open my hotel room door as quietly as possible and look out into the corridor. There's nobody about.

Quickly, I step into the corridor and let my hotel room door close behind me quietly. I swing my arm out and the key card in my hand slides into the slot on the linen store. Maybe they need windows in linen stores to keep the room aerated, who knows?

As quietly as I vacated my hotel room, I enter the linen store and breathe a sigh of relief once I'm inside and the door's shut. I rush to the window and look out. There are people passing by on the street below but if I'm quick, they might not even notice what I'm about to do. One of the other reasons my sister hated me while we were growing up, was that I was six inches taller, and a hell of a lot more athletic. I used to go rock climbing in the country and tackle the wall down at the gym. I'm only on the second floor here and this is an old building. The room below me has a little patio I can drop down onto.

Soon enough I'm prising open the window, swinging it out-wards.

I climb up onto the windowsill and judge the drop down. It's nothing. Just the same as the drop from the hotel in Longlake, if not a couple of feet more.

I slide out and slowly lower myself, my leather-gloved hand clinging to the edge of the wooden sill. Before I let myself drop, I touch the window shut to make it look like it was never opened at all, as I deftly lower at the same time—letting go.

Thankfully, as I crouch on the patio, I don't spot anyone in the hotel room beneath the one I just vacated. I jump over the wall and I'm free. I'm on the street.

I start walking quickly towards the National Gallery, which is half a mile away. My mum and dad's old neighbour Rosie works there. Or at least, I hope she still does.

I make quick work of the route. I'd run but I'm grossly out of shape and I don't want to draw attention to myself. Glancing over my shoulder, I don't see Nate following me. I've outsmarted him all right.

At the door I stuff a few American notes into the donation box. I won't be needing them anytime soon. I do a little lap around the gallery, pretending I haven't seen it all before. Some things never change, thank God.

After I've pretended like I'm here to see the stuff on the walls, I walk into the gift shop and keep my head bowed. It's quiet, being that it's nearly closing time. I pick up a couple of Rab-bie Burns-themed postcards, still wearing my gloves as I handle them. I'll send one to Arthur and another to my best friend, Gwen. I'll simply tell them I'm alive.

Rosie's at the cash desk and takes the cards from me without looking up.

"Don't look up," I whisper.

She shudders in response to my voice.

"You're alive," she says. "They said it was a gas explosion. I wondered if you'd been caught in it too. Nobody would tell us anything, nobody knew."

"Well, I'm alive."

She looks up and tries not to look shocked when she sees me. "I'm glad."

"Did someone come and pay you off? Say as little as possible, by the way."

She nods. As long as she doesn't say anything to incriminate herself, this is all on me. There are far too many CCTV cameras around here.

"Did you see anyone?"

"Yes. No. I mean..."

I hand her my cash and she rings it through the till, handing me my postcards in their paper bag.

"Before it happened... during... or after...?"

She looks more animated when I say after.

"Male or female?"

"A guy," she mumbles.

"He had an accent?"

"American," she says.

"Southern?"

"Yes."

"Six-four, dark, blue eyes..."

She nods fast.

"He asked questions? Was he the one who paid you off?"

"Yes, and yes."

I want to thump the counter, but I refrain.

"He was polite, but he had that edge," she says. "He said it was money not to talk to the papers or the police about your mum and dad's comings and goings, but it was said with a warning look. Please be careful, Annalise."

She calls me by my fake name. I remember the day we had to tell Phoebe that her name outside was Heather. She was confused. She was nine. Mum used to say it was an imaginary friend when friends of the family asked questions about 'Phoebe'. That was before Phoebe grew up to realise why Dad and Mum weren't really Greg and Mary Williamson, but William and Marie Fleming.

"I guess this is goodbye, Rosie," I say.

"Take care, wee 'un," she says with a wink.

I make my way out of the gallery, heading towards the exit. I need to get as far away from Scotland as possible. I need to leave and just not exist. That's what I need to do.

As I'm rushing away from the gallery, I get the distinct feeling I'm being followed.

I swirl around and there he is.

"Beatrice."

"Don't you dare use my name," I growl.

"Let me explain." His hands are in his pockets and he looks defeated.

"I don't trust you, not as far as I can throw you."

"Then let me earn your trust," he says.

"What are you? Some sort of cleaner? What?"

He toes the floor. "You could say that."

"And what? WHAT?" I demand, raising my voice, even as commuters push around us on their way home from work.

He walks towards me. "You were the last job on my cleaning list."

I can hardly breathe. "What?"

"Now I'm running, too. I couldn't..."

I don't like the look in his eye, but I hate the alternative too—that he hates me, or that he hated my family enough to kill them.

"Who lit the torch?" I demand.

He shakes his head. "I don't know. I don't. I knew your father. He was a good guy. I liked him. I was shocked when I heard their plan."

"This was internal for sure?"

"He must have done something... pissed someone off, right?"

"He had a family, why would he...?" Even as I'm asking the question, I'm remembering the time he uprooted his entire family, moving us from Yorkshire to Edinburgh—and it was down to his own ineptitude, for sure. Perhaps he was a sloppy assassin?

"Well, they took him out, and I was the cleaner. All I know is that they'd tossed a few grenades through an open bathroom window, after already breaking a couple of gas pipes. I had to clean up the evidence before the authorities discovered the truth."

I shake my head. "Did you see their bodies?"

His jaw ticks, before he lowers his voice, trying to be sensitive to my emotions. "There was nothing left but indistinguishable, charred remains. It was assumed you'd have been with them, and we thought you were. Then your bank card flared in Florida. When I told them this, they made you a part of my clean-up job even though that's not what I do. Somebody made a big fuck-up, obviously. The intelligence was that you'd all be together. It was your younger sister's birthday."

I rub my forehead. "So I'm alive because I'm a shit sister?"

"You forgot her birthday." It's a statement he makes with no opinion on the matter; it's just the reason I'm still alive. Well, that and the fact that Nate allegedly doesn't have it in him to kill me.

Chapter Nine

I didn't think I'd be coming back to my hotel room tonight. I mean, I haven't even slept in it yet, but I still didn't think I'd be coming back to it. I can't believe this is my life right now—this rollercoaster ride of uncertainties—but evidently it is. This day feels so long. This past few months have dragged on for an eternity. I just went next door and shut the linen room's window properly. Nobody must have noticed as it hadn't moved at all since I left the hotel through it earlier on.

I'm pacing the floor, trying to think like Dad. What would he do?

Not only do I have a target on my back, but Nate does too.

"Is there anyone my father might have trusted? Someone we can trust now."

"You know how it goes, Beatrice. We trust no one."

I'm shaking my head. What else is there to do?

"How long do we have?" I ask, turning to face him.

"I don't know. A day or so. Eventually facial recognition will lead them right to us. We've been careful but all they need is one small sighting and they've got us. We've been through airports, railway stations... and now you've been inside one of the country's major galleries."

I don't know what's worse—that I'm running or that I'm now responsible for him, too. He saved me, so I don't have a choice. I have to stick with him.

I stop pacing and stare down at him, trying to read something from his expression. Maybe, answers. I don't know. He's just sitting on the edge of the bed, as though he's already come to terms with this. It's only me who's struggling with the reality.

"When did you first learn he was an assassin?" Nate asks me.

The question takes me aback. I take a seat alongside him, not too close though.

"I knew his job was dangerous from about the age of ten. It was little things. He kept weapons around the house, in odd places. A crowbar in the airing cupboard. Mace in his robe pocket. A Glock in the cloak cupboard, always on a high shelf, so we couldn't reach it, but it was there. He also had this look. In certain situations, I mean. He would look different. It was when we were in Orlando and I was fifteen that there was a situation. There was a hostage crisis and it turned out to be just some kid off his meds, but my father diffused the chaos within minutes. After we got home from Disney, I asked him if he was secretly in the police. He said he wasn't. I begged him to tell me. I tried to wear him down, accusing him of not trusting me. He said he couldn't say a lot, but he said..." My voice sounds cracklier than I want it to, but I continue, "...he told me his job involved life or death situations, and that was all he could tell me. He'd always been distant, but he became more of a stranger than ever after Florida. It dawned on me how much danger he was putting us all in. He never came out and said the words, 'I'm a killer', but I knew. He used to say that there was the world we saw on the surface, and the one beneath, and the surface world only exists because of the work people do behind the scenes. I thought assassins didn't have loved ones, you know? Lone wolfs. Working alone. Living alone. I'd read a lot of Lee Child novels, you see."

Nate nods his head, understanding.

"Anyway, after a while, resentment set in. It had always seemed normal up to then, you know? He encouraged us to know self-defence, and there were weapons around the house, et cetera, but then to actually find out why we were doing all that... I started to see things I didn't see before. I realised I didn't want the life he'd chosen. It was his life, not ours. To make things worse, our whole entire existence changed dramatically after we left Yorkshire for Edinburgh and had to start again, with new identities and everything.

"I presumed with all the coverage of the Florida thing, maybe he'd caught too much attention. It was a constant guessing game, wondering what was really going on in his head. All I knew was that soon after Florida, he said we had to go, and we went. After that, after we came here I mean, I slowly began to rail against his overriding warning to prepare myself for battle. I rebelled, and by rebelling, I mean I actually started living my fucking life instead of fearing every sodding threat that might never cross my path. You could say Arthur was just one of my rebellious acts, some guy 15 years older than me, but really he was just a guy I enjoyed the mind of. He was really smart, as you Americans say, and it was easy because deep down, we both knew it was never gonna go anywhere."

"I see," Nate says, chewing his thumb.

"And then, there was my modelling. Dad had always wanted me to follow him, I could tell. It went unsaid but it was the way he entrusted certain ways of thinking to me, like he was preparing me for something, to be like him. Anyway, he would always have this face on him whenever I said I was going on a modelling job, like I was off out to sell sex or something. I could tell he hated what I was doing.

"Before Edinburgh, he'd go away for like a night or two, and be back as if it was nothing. He had this demeanour of having done his job, and that was it. After Edinburgh though, he'd be gone for months at a time, and we never knew where, not even my mother knew where he was. She'd speak with him on the phone and he'd tell her he couldn't say anything... then she'd get mad. As a consequence of her grief, Mum wrapped Phoebe and me up in this sort of domestic cocoon and nothing major was ever expected of us after that, except when he'd come home and he'd suddenly be all up in my face, demanding a progress report sort of thing. It was one extreme to the other with my parents. You can imagine that after witnessing that toxic dynamic of polar opposites, I decided I didn't want it for myself. Marriage, I mean. Domesticity, you know? Washing the same knives and forks, plates and spoons, day in, day out. Having roots, but being trapped. Being stuck. I didn't want that. I think the only reason my father had that at all was my mother. Otherwise he would have been that lone wolf he was born to be. I could never imagine wanting to be tied down, no way, not if it meant being as stranded as my mother was. She was basically in love with a guy never there."

I stop speed talking and a wave of pain washes over me, making me rub my chest.

My upbringing wasn't normal and the way my family were taken from me was even more bizarre.

"It's okay, you can cry if you want," he whispers, but when he reaches out his hand, I pull away.

"Ha, you'd love that, wouldn't you? Me, all weak and needy, vulnerable, so you can do with me as you please." I feel wretched as soon as the words have come out. All Nate has been trying to do is help me.

"That's not what I'm saying."

"So, what are you—"

"You need to let it all out."

He's right, I do. The little cry I had in Starbucks earlier was just a result of shock, really. It wasn't a proper, emotional outpouring, more physical.

The problem is, I've never cried in front of anyone else, not in as long as I can remember. Not while I've been an adult anyway. Not proper crying. Not grief-crying.

I stand up and walk to the window. "I can't cry properly until I know the truth."

"I came here with you to see if it might give you closure, or I thought, maybe it'd trigger something in your mind, some explanation as to why this happened... but it appears we're both clueless, together. Whatever reason they had for killing your father, the Collective is unlikely to tell us. We might never know the whole truth, and we certainly can't afford to risk being out there, showing our faces. Most certainly, we can't be seen to be actively investigating all of this. What we need to do is hide. Until we figure out a way to survive..."

"So, what do you suggest?"

"I've got a safe house in Switzerland. We just need a vehicle."

"It's safe? I mean, not to sound stupid, but it's for real safe?"

"Nobody but me knows it's there. Your dad would have had a safe house too, you know?"

"Where?"

"I doubt there will be any record of it. Its location probably died with him."

"But..."

He walks towards me and takes my hand. "You have to let go. He's gone. It's just you and me now, for how ever long it takes us to figure things out."

I look down at our joined hands, thankful for him suddenly. "Okay."

"We'll take the linen closet window at midnight. I dusted my room for prints already. I'll dust yours and then we'll leave. Take everything, leave nothing. Until then I'll go out and acquire a car or something. I'll bring pizza back. Any preference?"

"Just vegetarian," I whisper.

"Okay. Don't go anywhere."

"I won't."

The door clicks shut and I feel that pang again, the one telling me to leave this place and never return—escape Nate and never come back.

Even if I still don't trust him, he's the closest thing I've got to a way of finding out what really happened to my father, mother and sister.

So, I sit my arse down and stay put. It's a new thing for me, but I'm determined.

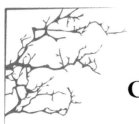

Chapter Ten

It's taken us two days to drive from Scotland to Switzerland—Montreux to be exact. We've taken it in turns to drive and I've slept on nothing more than the backseat of the Audi A8 he picked up in Edinburgh. I haven't asked him how he got it, and I don't want to know.

It's dark and I'm tired and I can't process our surroundings right now, even though the last hour or two of the drive has promised our destination will be most likely out of this world.

We reach a house up in the mountains, a log cabin set in complete darkness. As I look across Lake Geneva, all I can see are distant shapes, blurry outlines. My eyesight is hazy. I'm exhausted. He takes my arm and carries the meagre luggage we've brought with us.

"You can sleep in here," he says, directing me to a bedroom. On the way, I notice there is more than one, but that's about all I notice. The house is laid out on one level but apart from being able to distinguish these few traits of the house, all I can tell is that it's dark, and blobby, and all the same. He tugs my shoes off and envelops me in the sheets and blankets. A bed has never felt so good.

"I've gotta go get rid of the car, but I'll be back. You'll be safe here, I promise."

"You promise?" I mumble, already with my eyes closed.

"I promise."

I hear him leave and lock me inside the house. I stretch out in the bed and the mattress seems to catch me as I fall.

WAKING UP BY A SWISS lake is something everyone should try once. My bedroom has French doors which open out onto a balcony. I've not been awake more than a minute, but I have to see more, so I wriggle out of the sheets and walk across the room, unlocking the doors and stepping outside. The fresh air hits me first, then the postcard view. White-topped mountains frame the sheer-blue lake and all the alpine scenery leaves me breathless.

"Good morning," he says, scaring the bejesus out of me.

I turn and catch him on the next balcony, sat with his feet propped up, bare-chested and content. He's drinking coffee with his laptop resting on his knees.

He looks amused. "I didn't want to wake you, but..."

"What time is it?"

"Near noon," he reveals.

"Shit."

"Coffee in the pot."

"I'd better shower first. And burn these clothes."

"I did some online shopping last night. Should be here soon. Until then, there's a robe in the bathroom and some dried food-stuffs in the cupboard."

"You ordered me clothes?"

"The weather can change here as quickly as... well, the weather."

"Okay." I take a moment. "You shopped? After forty-eight hours on the road?"

"I'm used to this lifestyle, Beatrice. I grabbed six hours and I was awake again."

"So, you've been up since..."

"Six a.m., yeah. You snore a little, by the way. It's cute though."

"Shut up..."

As I turn around and try to locate my stuff, I notice I have a shower cubicle in my room. It's behind a frosted door, but it's just frosted, and... it doesn't seem to have a lock. My morning shower is usually where I do all my crying—get it out of the way first thing—have done with it. Curl up into a ball and let rip. I normally do that in completely privacy.

I return to the balcony, hands on hips.

"Where's the family bathroom?"

He peers at me, annoyed. "Pardon me?"

"You know, the thing that normally has... I don't know... a tub." I just need somewhere he won't hear or see me crying. Ugly crying. With only a frosted door and no lock, he could try to intercede and stop the crying, when I don't need that. Sometimes I just need to cry—in private.

"There's a hot tub out back. Would that be preferable?"

"I'd imagine the hot tub needs booting up, all the levels checking, and then filling, et cetera?"

"Yep."

"Go on then. I'll take the tub."

He sighs and salutes me before going out back. "Yes, ma'am."

I take in the view a little more while I listen out. When I hear the tub start to fill up, I head for the kitchen and grab some coffee, pouring in some of the dried milk substitute he has. While he's busy doing his thing, I take a moment to walk around. I find his bedroom and discover it's the same layout as mine, only his shower is on the opposite side. The house has these two matching bedrooms and I notice there's an adjoining door between them, but it seems to be locked. It looks that way anyway. His bed is made and yet I can tell he slept in it. There's a dent where his head lay. The room smells like him, too. It smells of Hugo Boss and Argan oil. If that's all he has to put in his hair, he's lucky. It looks effortless every day. There's no t-shirt stuffed under the pillow so I assume he sleeps naked, or in just his underwear. I better leave his bedroom before he starts getting ideas.

His 'safe house', if that's what he wants to keep calling it, is a beautiful place. It's sprawling but it's not intimidating and it's cosy enough to feel like a home from home. There are rugs and throws, cushions and big, open fires.

On the patio out back, I place my coffee mug on the side of the hot tub and begin undressing.

He looks embarrassed when he sees what I'm doing. "Let me get out of the way. I'll show you how to work the controls."

"Nate, I'm a model for Christ's sakes. I get my tits and arse out every day of the week. Calm down."

"Well, I'm a good American boy who believes in modesty, not your European flash-your-particulars-everywhere philosophy."

I throw my head back laughing. "I admit, I didn't bring a bathing suit. I mean, in the rush of trying to stay alive, it didn't cross my mind. However, I'm going to keep my undies on and we'll pretend I'm wearing a bikini, okay? So, chill out."

"Oh... okay."

I dip myself into the hot tub and sigh as I relax back. "Oh god, this is good. Fill it up."

"Can I ask you a question?"

I point to my coffee mug and he passes me it. "Sure."

"If you're a model and your boyfriend was a leather-patch wearing fuck, I mean, how did that work?"

I press my lips together. "What do you mean, precisely? And think very carefully before you speak."

"If your tits and ass are out every day of the week, didn't you get hit on in your line of work?"

"Everyone male in modelling is gay. It's the rule. You're gay. If a straight man steps into the dressing room, the whole place comes to a fucking halt."

He chews his fingernail. "You're fucking with me."

I raise my eyebrows. "I am. And you're a little naïve, aren't you?"

"I'm traditional. And flesh, like yours, shouldn't be for everyone."

I sniff. I can't help it. "Well, my flesh isn't for everyone. Ever heard the saying, you can look, but don't touch? Saying that, even Arthur rarely touched me. He was a horrible drinker and could barely get it up some nights. It was sometimes nice to have someone who didn't want anything from me."

"You didn't love him?"

"No."

"What about him? Did he love you?"

"Yes. In the way that sad, stunted alcoholics love beautiful women, because they think shagging someone with youth and beauty will in exchange, save them."

"So... that's it then...?" He looks disturbed.

"God, how old are you?"

"Thirty-two."

My eyebrows have never raised so high. "Wow, you look... you look..." He looks way younger than thirty-two.

"I'm joking, I'm twenty-five." He tilts his head and I see him regarding me in that way of his, trying to trip me up.

"Well you act like a teenager around me. It's seriously irksome."

"Hey, I'm just trying to figure out why a gal like you wasted time with a drunken, stick-up-his-ass fuck and works a job where her particulars are on show all the time. That's all."

"I told you already," I exclaim. "I didn't want anything permanent. Plus, I just wanted to piss off my father."

He turns the taps off once the tub is full and starts the bubbles. "You dated a guy much older? Solely to piss off your dad?"

"Well, I've recently found myself with a lot of spare time to think, and yes, just a few days ago I reached that conclusion, so yeah, I guess I may have dated him to piss off my dad. But anyway, Arthur had great taste in clothes, not a patch in sight. He was—hopefully still is—handsome. Charismatic. But yeah, a drinker. It's probably why he's not married yet. It was all good when I was a student, and for those nights where I wanted to get off my tits too, but otherwise he wasn't any kind of life partner. Just a dude to bunk up with for a few nights a week. A little bit of a baby."

"So, you did screw him before you left college." Nate stands and shakes his head. "You should have had more respect for yourself, lady."

I now see how he works: Nate goes over old ground, again and again, extracting even more info from people than he did before. He's either very jealous or trying to wear me down, so he can prise more and more info out of me.

He leaves the patio and I look out across the mountainous landscape out back, wondering whether he's actually got a point—continually bringing up Arthur all the time. A chill comes over me and I fiddle with the hot tub settings to crank up the heat. If he thinks a model doesn't know how to operate a hot tub all by herself, he's got another thing coming. Hell, I could operate this thing fine, even while stoned and drunk on a litre of champagne.

I turn up the bubbles so they're loud, but I keep my tears silent. I don't even have to prompt them today—no forced shuddering in the shower required.

Chapter Eleven

I hear him get up to open the door for the internet delivery at around two o'clock in the afternoon, but I'm sulking in my room, annoyed with him. I guess it's also that I still haven't come to terms with my family's demise. I keep thinking that any minute now, I'll get a call telling me the whole thing was a big mistake, or that these past few months have been a nightmare and that I just have to wake up, like in *Vanilla Sky*. Maybe I'm really in cryogenic hibernation and I was frozen because I was in the fire, too. What I'm living right now is just a dream, or an alternative future, something to keep my mind occupied while time stretches on... until the doctors get that new technology they need to save my broken, fire-ravaged body.

If only...

Nate appears at the doorway. "Do you want your new clothes?"

"I have clothes."

"Yeah, but when were they last washed? And have you seen yourself lately?"

So, maybe for the past three months I have been living in my limited Florida wardrobe and nothing else, and my only way of washing my garments has been to use soap and water in hotel room tubs or sinks.

"Fine."

He tosses a sack of stuff towards the bed and it lands with a thud. "You're welcome."

Nate should have left me by the side of the road yonks ago, but that's the thing about him—he seems eerily determined to stick by me, even when I'm being a bitch all the time. More than anything, I know if he'd wanted to kill me, he would have done so already. For some reason he sees something to like about me.

I groan when I realise all this stuff has been bought off Amazon. He does know I'm used to good stuff, right? Right?

The first items I come to are a couple of lingerie sets. I'm often mistaken for having normal-sized boobs but that's because I dress them demurely. He's got me the right size. How did he know? I can sometimes be between cup sizes too, but he's gone for the upper end, which pleases me in a way I didn't imagine I could be pleased. He takes note. I mean... I don't know why I'm surprised. If he's anything like my father, Nate must be off-the-charts clever. Yeah, it's just that he's clever that he knows my cup size...

I try to put all those romantic notions I might have once held out for a guy like Nate right out of my head. He cannot be trusted. Nothing about this situation rings true and there are secrets I need explaining.

I pull on the first black lace set I put my hands on and, in the wardrobe mirror, I'm astonished to see myself looking human again—in underwear that fits and hasn't been wrung out so many times by hand, that it has become misshapen. It's not cheap stuff, either. He maybe just used Amazon because they deliver stupidly quick.

I unpack all the stuff he's bought me and lay it all out, staring at it. Pretty summer dresses and ballet shoes and skirts and tshirts. Plus, a denim jacket I really like, with bright floral embroidery on the shoulders I adore. Soon enough, all my new items are stowed away in drawers and the wardrobe. I'd wash them before wearing but over the past few months, I've learnt not to be so darn privileged.

I enter the living room wearing my old shorts, a new white tee and the denim jacket.

"Are you coming, then?" I stare at him, sat there still bare-chested, as if he's on holiday. If he's trying to drive me to distraction with the sight of his ripped muscles, it's not going to work. No... way... (I mentally count eight. Yeah. He has an eight pack. Feck.)

He looks at me like I've suggested we visit Mars. "I just filled the fridge and cupboards. We have no need to go out. Why else did I put matchsticks between my eyelids last night to make sure this shit got here okay?"

"Let's get one thing straight, matey boy. I will not be told what to do, not by you, not by anyone. Do you understand?" I bark, hands on hips. Maybe I feel like I need to test him a little in return.

He rolls his eyes. "We should be careful, you know that."

"Should shmud. If I stay indoors any longer, cabin fever will become permanent and I'll transmogrify into a couch or something. So I'm going, and you won't stop me."

"Fine." He leaps over the back of the sofa and dashes into his room. He emerges wearing a white Henley to complement the jeans he never seems to take off.

As we're leaving through the front door, he gives me a proper once over.

"What?" I demand.

"You look beautiful."

The honesty and sincerity of his words make a lump form in my throat.

"Oh," is all I can say right now.

Outside on the driveway there's a different vehicle, with a French plate. It's a car that won't draw attention anyway—a Ford Focus.

I don't make a fuss about the change of vehicle. I'm not exactly in a position to complain.

He drives us down the mountainside and we park near the lake, where all the action seems to be.

Walking along the promenade, he takes my hand and asks, "How long are we going to keep pretending?"

"What are you talking about?"

He spins me into his arms and kisses me, just a quick press of his lips against mine.

"Take your hands off me." I push him away, even though he's gorgeously lovely.

"Okay, so a little longer, then." He doesn't even have the decency to look bruised. He looks amused. How is it possible for one man to be this annoying?

"I don't trust you," I warn.

He holds his hands up. "I wouldn't trust me either."

As people walk past us, they notice the atmosphere. Women also notice the gorgeous man, while men notice my pasty legs. I will have to change that latter problem very soon. The other problem may not have a solution...

Nate's not just gorgeous. He's absolutely, soul-churningly beautiful and his kiss has left me weak at the knees. I want to throw my arms around his neck, squeeze myself into him and never let go. I want the oblivion of him and that's what scares me. I'm frightened I'll dive in too deep and I'll never surface.

"At least let me hold your hand, we may as well maintain our cover as a couple on vacation."

"Okay," I reply, willing my hand not to shake as I place it back inside of his. Luckily, he squeezes my palm so tight, there's no room for me to falter.

"That jacket looks good on you, Beatrice. I saw it and thought of you."

"Can you please stop calling me Beatrice?" I sigh, tired of hearing that name.

"What, then?"

"I don't know," I reply, as we pass one of the many sculptures along the promenade, this one depicting Freddie Mercury in concert. "Everyone called me Lis. I know that's not my real name, but that's what people called me. It's just, Beatrice sounds so formal."

"It's a good name. I like it. And I'm not calling you Lis. Beatrice is more regal, it suits you. I like it very much." He breaks all the rules when he kisses my temple as we pretend we're a couple strolling down the promenade. A part of me hopes that his act isn't an act at all, but how can I be sure?

The truth is, I'm not even sure there was ever any threat at all. Look at us now, walking around in public.

So why is this guy in my life? That's what I have to find out.

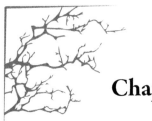

Chapter Twelve

We're just finishing up dinner on the patio out back, next to the hot tub. He made paella. He can cook! He's also still wearing the Henley (now complete with a few splashes of tomato juice). Still, he looks fucking ridiculous in a Henley, splashed or not. There should be laws about Nate wearing a Henley only in private. It hugs his pecs and biceps perfectly. This beast of a man knew exactly what he was doing today—pulling on a white fucking Henley. Lord almighty, preserve me.

"That was... nice." I don't want to sound too enthusiastic.

"I thought so, too." He stands up and clears the plates away. I watch him load the dishwasher.

It's been a nice day. Not too hot, maybe 25 degrees. We walked around for a bit, then stopped off for a sandwich at a deli-type place, then had a cool glass of wine at a bar. We haven't talked much all day, not since the kiss. He's been infuriatingly quiet and I'd rather him be obnoxious or cheeky. Anything. Instead, he's cooked me dinner...

When he returns with bowls of cookie dough ice cream for pudding, it's time for me to bite the bullet and ask him why we're here.

"Why Montreux?"

He looks up from his bowl. "It was my father's. This place, I mean."

I read something in his eyes. Grief.

"Is he...?" I chicken out of using the d word.

"...dead?" he asks for me.

I nod.

"He's dead," he tells me, gazing furtively out into the distance.

"Was he..."

"...one of the Collective?"

I nod.

"He was."

"That's how you got into this?"

He nods. He focuses on his ice cream.

"Did he bring you here?"

"No," he says, shaking his head, as if to reinforce his words.

"You inherited it."

He puts his spoon down, clenching and unclenching his fists. Eventually he looks up, out at the view in front of us, and with a vacant look, he reveals, "I was raised by my mom. I didn't ask why. I didn't know any different. When I was eleven though, this guy just turned up with a gift. A games console. He and my mom went and talked while I played with my new toy. After he was gone, mom sat me down and said the man who just visited was my father. She said that if I wanted to, I could spend every other Saturday with him. I said yes. I didn't really think it would mean anything more than getting gifts."

I can see he's struggling to hide his feelings. It hurts and I can tell.

"When did he tell you?" I ask Nate

His lip wrinkles a little, but he manages to divulge, "He never told me about his job. I only found out after he was killed in the line of duty, so to speak. I never knew what he did for a living.

Mom didn't know either." Nate holds his hand out, like he can see his father's image right in front of his face. He pulls himself out of the memory and takes a deep breath. "I think he kept his distance to protect us. Anyway, here we are now."

I frown. "Did your dad talk about this place at all? Was it special to him?"

"I don't know." Nate throws his hands up. "When we'd spend time together, he would talk about stuff in a generalised way. He would tell me there were some beautiful places in the world. Places he'd been. Places I could go one day. When he left me this in his will, I wondered if this was one of those places. Or if he chose to leave me a house in Switzerland for some sort of... political reason, you know."

"I see. So, how old were you...?"

"I was eighteen. When he died."

"I'm sorry."

"So am I."

He carries on eating his ice cream, but I only manage a spoonful or two more.

The sky has turned a phosphorescent burnt orange, having been cobalt blue for most of the day. The temperature dips in the evening and I start to notice it, so after he takes the bowls away I leave the patio and go inside, pulling one of the fur throws over my bare legs on the couch. After flicking through a few channels on the TV and finding nothing I want to watch, I throw the remote across the room and it hits one of the other sofas.

After tidying away the last of the dishes he sits on the sofa I just threw the remote to, digging it out from beneath his arse before getting comfy. He rests his laptop on his knees and sits back.

I give it ten minutes before asking, "What are you doing?"

He turns the screen towards me and shows me he's reading a book on his cloud reader. I feel a major pang of jealousy.

"If I make a list, can you get me some books?"

"You can read on my tablet if you wish."

I shake my head. "I have to read proper books. I had a beautiful collection, but obviously..."

"The tablet's on my bedside. Just order whatever you want. I'm all logged in."

"Oh... I can pay you back."

"It's fine."

In his bedroom I find the tablet and linger longer than I should. His room smells like him and in here, I don't have his eyes examining me. I can just enjoy his scent without him knowing.

Back in the living room, I find he's logged in as Nathan Buchanan. Maybe that's his real name, maybe's it's his working name? I'm past worrying now. Whatever happens, happens.

I get to work stacking up all my book purchases, until I see the amount I've spent. Then I remember I can cover it if he gets annoyed, so I choose one-day delivery at the same time.

After I've ordered all my books, I notice his tablet has the Kindle app, so I press the icon and I can see all the books he's bought and read. He seems to be a fan of fantasy, with all the *Game of Thrones* books archived as 'read'. He has a lot of China Mieville, Tolkien and even *Harry Potter*. Terry Pratchett. Neil Gaiman. Philip Pullman, Stephen King, and a lot of others I haven't read—plus a lot of American classics. I click out of his app when he asks, "So, you got what you wanted?"

"Yep." I put the tablet down, pretending I haven't been spying on his reading habits.

I could have a good dig into his order history too, but I doubt there will be anything in there different to clothes, books and other standard items.

"If you're bored and want an e-book just to tide you over, be my guest, there's an app on the tablet you're holding."

"I'm good, but thanks."

"Suit yourself."

I watch him as he furtively studies his laptop, which is probably synced to his tablet. He's probably studying what I just bought. His nose wrinkles.

"Nate," I interrupt him.

"Yes, Beatrice."

"Is this all we're meant to do now? Read and eat and stroll around town. It's pretty and everything, but I mean, how long are we going to stay here?"

There's that sigh of his again. Like he knows he can't control me, but he doesn't want to either.

"We could do the whole tourist thing, if you want? I don't know, eat around town. Visit the casino. Traipse up and down hidden cobbled streets. Take the railway up into the mountains and see the panoramic view, stay in a nomadic tent. Pay Chillon Castle a visit. Wait until next July for the famous jazz festival... or just enjoy this beautiful house and the beautiful view and be at ease."

I roll my eyes. "That's not what I meant, and you know it."

"So, please. Elaborate." He shuts the lid of his laptop and stares right at me, putting me on the spot.

I almost lose my nerve, but I take a hold of myself. "You and I, we're strangers. I get that we were in danger, but now... it doesn't feel that way."

"Well, I told you. We're in Switzerland now, Beatrice."

I hate it when he calls me that. It's the way he says it, as if to remind me I'm a lot posher than him. Or something...

"I need to know if there's a plan, if there's an end date, or something. I don't know. Like a day when you think it might be safe for me to finally go back home—"

He leans forward in his seat. "Home? Where is home...?"

"...and your job," I continue, "your profession. I mean, you said you're on the run, you said you didn't kill me because you couldn't and that now makes you their enemy, too. How do we know people aren't going to kill us in the night? How do we know anything?"

"We don't."

"Dad used to say—" I take a gulp. "He used to say that there's the world people think they know, and then there's the real one. And the real one is the world they can't handle. The one they can't handle is the one where there's a terrorist attack being planned in the mansion next door. The real one is where your neighbour's planning to break into your garage for the third time in a row, steal all your gardening equipment, flog it on ebay and push up your insurance premium yet again, all while using your misfortune to pay for his annual holiday to Tenerife. You never hear your neighbour break in because he copied the key you lent him that one time and he sneaks in quietly, then makes it look like a break-in after he's gone."

"If it makes you feel any better, I have friends and they would get in touch if they heard anything on the grapevine. Plus, I have a feeling that we're not interesting as long as we're holed up here, not bothering anyone. So that's what we're going to do: not bother anyone."

"So, you're telling me... we're trapped... in this... together. And there's no getting out? Is that what you're telling me? There's no shelf life to this? We could be doing this forever?"

"You've been here a day."

I stand up and flail my arms around. "You just said a moment ago that we could end up staying here until next year!"

"It's one of the world's most famous jazz festivals, just chill out. I just said that as..." —he throws his hands around, too— "...as a, stupid something. I didn't literally mean we'd stay here until next July. Like for the next ten months or something. I just said, we could. I didn't say we will. But we could. I own this property. Between us we both have cash. It'll get cold in winter but there's plenty of firewood in storage and the house has solar panels. There's a lot of credit saved up."

I pout. "I've been running for so long, that this doesn't feel right. Standing still feels abnormal."

"I understand that it must." He comes and sits on the coffee table between us, not touching me. It feels weird when he touches me, but even weirder when he doesn't. "Where do you have to be? Back in Edinburgh? On a shoot? Meeting friends? All those people wouldn't understand."

I implore his bright blue eyes. "Why am I here? Why? There has to be a reason."

"Maybe waiting patiently is the only way you'll find out. Perhaps the answers will come to you. You just have to trust me."

I have no idea if I can trust him. Will he murder me in my sleep? Who is he? Has he been telling me the truth?

I just don't know.

What I do know is that my family is dead.

Arthur probably thinks I topped myself and that's why I haven't been found.

It's not safe to visit old friends. It's not safe to trust anyone.

But maybe I have to trust Nate?

I have all my faculties and money, but I don't have a plan. I don't have trust—not in anything, or anyone.

I don't have a future, not until I know what really happened. Not until I can put all this to bed.

"I have to wait it out, then? But what am I waiting out, exactly?"

"We'll only know that once we've waited it out."

I blink rapidly. "I know I implied I'm a lady of leisure, being a model and all, but I actually worked very hard. I had a busy life, too. This has been bad for me. I've lost so much weight and I feel so weak."

He reaches for my hand. "So, we'll build you back up."

And just like that, he gives me renewed hope.

I need time so I tell him, "I'm going to go and read in bed. Do you mind?"

"No, shout if you need anything."

"Okay."

I lie in bed with his tablet, deciding to give *Harry Potter* another read. *The Half-Blood Prince* is my favourite.

As I lie in bed reading, tears begin to fall down my face.

Nate comes in a while later, carrying a glass of wine.

"I though you might—"

I try to hide my face. "I'm fine. Just leave it."

"What's wrong?"

"I don't want to talk about it."

"Okay."

He leaves the room.

I have the most awful ache in my chest. I want to have him hold me, kiss me, tell me it's going to be all right—but I don't trust it. I don't trust this growing feeling I have for him. I trusted the sordid illicit affair I had with my lecturer because there were no layers there, nothing else to know. It was what it was. Whatever's growing between Nate and I, it's undefined, and it's scary.

I cry into my pillow. I cry and cry.

His father protected him; mine didn't.

Even now my father's dead, I can still hear his voice inside my head: "Trust only yourself, Beatrice. Nobody sees things the way we do."

But were his words poison, or a warning of things to come?

Chapter Thirteen

The next morning, as I shower in my cubicle, I refuse to cry. It has occurred to me: what am I really crying for? The loss of a family I never really had? A mother who played along; a father who put all our lives in danger; a sister who concerned herself with so many other things, and never the fate we faced as the children of a dangerous man. I refuse to cry because in all honesty, I'm not sure what I'm crying for anymore. I can't bring them back. They're gone, and it's certainly not my fault that they are. I had nothing to do with it. So instead of crying, I should be laughing, and living, because even though they're gone, I'm free. I'm alive. Why should I cry every morning? Why shouldn't I smile? Why shouldn't I scream from the rooftops that I'm alive and I have days yet to live? Wherever they are, they're not in pain anymore, and I don't have to be either.

Maybe my father should never have had children, but it's too late to think like that now. If he hadn't, I wouldn't be alive. I wouldn't be me. Maybe if my dad had been strong enough to walk away before they fell in love, my mother might have married someone else, and he'd have been my father instead—but then, I wouldn't be me, would I? It's true that in a lot of ways, I am my father's daughter and I've tried to distance myself from our similarities because they scare me. Perhaps I veered from the path because of the dangers I knew he was up against. Maybe now is the time to face facts: this world is tough, and to survive you have to toughen up.

Then there's that man out there in his room next door to mine. Strong. Clever. Fearless. Is Nate my protector? Or is he my enemy?

I finish conditioning my hair and step out of the shower, determined to regain that girl I used to be—the one before Edinburgh—the house captain and the sports mad redhead waving a lethal hockey stick around. She was so much stronger and more determined than me. Maybe here, in beautiful Montreux, I can reincarnate her. I can become her again.

Or am I too jaded now? Am I too experienced?

Is what's left of me the person my dad created?

Am I what the world has made me? Am I mistrusting because of their deaths?

Will I never be the same again?

Perhaps not.

NATE FINDS ME ON THE patio at lunchtime. He's spent all morning on his laptop in his bedroom, doing whatever it is that he does.

"What are you doing? You'll singe out here."

He strips the shirt off his back and throws it over my bare legs.

"What the hell are you doing?" I demand, lifting my sunglasses to inspect him.

I shift on my sunbed and he squats down beside me, shaking his head.

"You're fair-skinned, you'll burn," he chastises, checking the bottle of sunblock I'm using. "What good is factor 20? You need 50 with this delicate tone of yours. Anyway, I thought the fashion industry loved alabaster?"

"Are you honestly giving me a lecture on my sunbathing habits? Are you?" I pick up his shirt and throw it at him.

He falls on his backside. Maybe I shoved him a little hard?

He rights himself and stands up, one eyebrow raised, jaw clenched.

"I'm too pale for the Swiss Riviera. It won't do," I tell him. "Especially not next to Captain Bronze."

"Really? Captain Bronze? Is that the best you could come up with?"

"Well, you think you're so indestructible, don't you? And you're far too tanned for a— Whatever you are."

"You're fair-skinned, Beatrice. Don't be an idiot. Take better care of yourself. I grew up in Texas, not the Arctic like you."

"You're a fool," I retaliate.

"You look better with red hair, by the way. It suits you. You should embrace who you really are. You know you don't have to hide anymore, not with me."

He swans back indoors and I almost chase after him—wanting to extend the argument—but then the doorbell rings and he goes to answer it. It's probably my delivery of books!

Something comes over me while he's gone. *"You don't have to hide anymore."* His words ring in my ears. Am I naked in his eyes? Am I so readable?

I check myself, because it could so easily be that his words are designed to lure me into a false sense of security.

Dad never said I had to dye my hair, but after we came to Edinburgh, I started dyeing it dirty blonde instead of red. Maybe because my whole identity was lost.

Maybe I'll never get it back.

BY EVENING, I'M REALLY into one of the books I ordered. Nate's scowling from across the other side of the room. He just brought over my dinner of gnocchi, which I am eating on my lap, my book in one hand, a fork in the other. I'm too ensconced in my book to care about looking at or acknowledging him.

"Thank you for making me dinner, Nate," he says sarcastically, putting on my voice, "oh, and I noticed you didn't include meat in the dish, even though you really like meat. I notice you've sprinkled cold pepperoni on top of yours because you're so thoughtful."

"You don't exist," I tell him. "If you'd wanted me to participate in life, you shouldn't have facilitated the purchase of all these books. You won't be getting me back for weeks now."

I point at the stack of books on the coffee table. I've already arranged them in order of how I'll read them.

"I'll know for next time," he grumbles, like he really believes there will be a next time.

He keeps talking as though we'll be here forever, and it is starting to get on my nerves. If I have my way, I'll stay another couple of weeks and then head to Paris, maybe. I have a friend there, Emily. She could put me up and help me find work. She's a model, too.

I'm so into my book, but that doesn't mean to say I'm not enjoying his food, too. Nate's style of cooking is sort of rustic, but I like it. He chops vegetables so they're chunky and I can taste more garlic than I think I've ever had in my entire life. My blood will be healthy and humming tonight.

After we've eaten, he asks, "Do you want dessert?"

"Maybe later."

I shoo him away and he takes a few puddings out of the fridge, eating them all to himself. He makes satisfied noises, as if trying to distract me, but I mumble, "Go away... but before you do, light the fire."

"It's not cold."

"It's not warm either, and I love the fire. Please."

He starts building the fire, complaining under his breath, even though I know he secretly loves building the fire. I know because eventually he starts humming as he works.

The only thing that could possibly deter me from my reading right now is the sight I see as I turn my head sideways. Nate is kneeling in front of the fire and his shirt has ridden up, revealing the muscles around his waist and lower back. I've seen him shirtless, of course. I know he doesn't have chest hair. He's smooth. It's just that seeing his skin like this, exposed just a little, and how his jeans are tight around his butt as he kneels... it's making me hot and bothered. When he stands up, I quickly avert my eyes and get back to reading. He brushes the dust off his hands and grabs his jacket, heading for the door.

"Where are you going?"

"You said to get lost."

"I didn't mean it, I mean, only metaphorically."

"Well, I'll go grab a couple beers. Back soon."

"You shouldn't drink and drive."

"Won't be long," he says, slamming the door shut.

I hear the car leave and I rush across the room, bolting the door. I didn't mean for him to go... I didn't mean...

I sit waiting for him to come back, but fifteen minutes pass, and he doesn't. Maybe he really has just gone for a couple of beers.

I take my book into my bedroom and change into my nightdress, the one Nate bought me. It's long, cotton, white, embroidered. Spaghetti straps. It's nice. I pull on socks, too. The heat really drops here at night and the house feels cold. All the glass that makes it feel like a greenhouse during the day makes it seem like a cool box at night.

I tug on my towelling robe and head back to the living room, pulling the sofa closer to the fire, but not too close. I grab a glass of wine from the kitchen and lie back, the fur throw pulled over me.

"Perfect," I whisper.

Chapter Fourteen

When Nate arrives back, I'm almost done with my book, but I have to get up to unbolt the door and let him in. I welcome him back without pleasantries: "Thirty pages to go. Thirty pages!" I hold up the book to him without looking at him. I can't be distracted.

I seat myself back where I was and quickly get back to it. I'm reading *Me Before You* and I'm praying, I'm hoping... I'm wishing...

They've finally admitted their love and it was in a beautiful, tropical setting, too. She's going to save him, I know she is.

Then page by page, I have my hopes and dreams ripped away from me. Louisa realises Will isn't going to change his mind; he's a quadriplegic and he's still going to go to Switzerland and end his life. He wants to finish it.

The world doesn't exist as I read the final pages—as she accepts his decision, but is all the more heartbroken for knowing that their six months together wasn't going to change them or anything like that, it was just that she never knew she should have been cherishing every minute she had him—because it was all going to come to this, in the end. Tears are falling down my face as she's kissing him goodbye, as she's pouring her love into his soul, still hoping he'll stay, but knowing ultimately, he won't. Poor Louisa and her simple hopes and dreams, and this complex, fiery man having come in and shown her that small isn't good enough—not for her.

After I finish the final page, I can't believe what I've just read.

I open the book at the death chapter again and re-read it, but I'm told yet again, he's made the same choice.

I go back and relive the euphoria of the night she kisses him and discovers he loves her, too. I put myself through the same pain, over and over, my masochistic tendency to force-feed myself emotional pain, again and again—to feel anything but nothingness.

The truth I've buried is that nothingness has been my life for so long now, I'm not sure who I am. I haven't been able to plan the life I always wanted because my dad told me at fifteen that we could all be dead any moment. He never said the specific words, but that's what I interpreted, and what's the point in trying when it could all be ripped away, just like that? Just like it has been for Phoebe, who will never get to do the things she always wanted to do.

In a fit of rage, I throw the book across the room in anger, and through sheer bad luck it ends up in the fire. I rush to try and rescue it, hating myself, but it goes up in flames.

I can't believe what I'm witnessing as I watch the most beautiful thing I've ever read whoosh up the chimney.

How could I do this? I must be a monster.

"What the hell is going on?" he asks, entering the room in his long underwear, shirtless. It looks like he's been trying to sleep. I notice on the huge clock which covers half a wall that it's almost two in the morning.

I notice the shock on his face and it suddenly registers with me, too—that I'm hysterical.

I rush from the room and dash to my bedroom, slamming the door shut. I throw myself at my bed and cry and cry and cry.

After around what I guess has been half an hour, he knocks on the door, asking, "Can I come in?"

"No!"

"Well, I'm coming in anyway."

I'm facing the window, my back to him, but I pull the covers tighter around me anyway. I feel the bed shift when he sits on the other side, behind me.

"What's going on, Beatrice?"

"I read the book and it made me sad... and I accidentally tossed it in the fire."

"Oh."

"I'm not crazy. It was an accident."

"No, I believe you."

"You don't sound like you do."

"Oh, I do."

"So why do you sound dickish about it all?"

"Dickish?" he snorts.

"Yeah, dickish. Like I'm a madwoman who needs checking up on."

"That's not it, at all."

I sigh, gathering myself. "Where did you go anyway?"

"I went for a think. Drove around a bit."

"Are you drunk?"

"No, and I've never been drunk in my whole life. That's not who I am."

"Did you go and find a woman? Is that why you got back so late?"

"I'm not that kind of guy, Beatrice."

"What's wrong with you, then? There has to be something wrong with you."

"If there is, I'm sure you'll find out, in time."

"Oh, I will."

"Nice to know where I stand." He abruptly leaves the room and I realise I've hurt him.

Worst of all, I've hurt me too, because I've started to care about him.

THE BEDROOM'S HOT AND unbearably sticky when I wake, so I know I've slept in and it's already late in the day. My eyes are encrusted with sleep and tears, my heart feels wrung out and I'm lethargic in the extreme. I don't want to leave the bed, but my stomach's gurgling.

I roll over in bed and find a few things on my nightstand. There's a travel mug with coffee inside it and when I open it, it's still hot. After sipping some, I find a brown paper package too and rip it open. Inside there's a brand-new copy of the book I tossed in the fire yesterday, this time in hardback. I open it and find it's signed!

"Oh my god!"

I find a note on the nightstand, tucked under a bottle of factor 50. It reads: *Wear sunscreen. I've gone for a run. N*

On the back of the book, I find a sales sticker which tells me he bought this book for me this morning from a store down in Montreux—and it wasn't cheap. More than that, it's the thought that counts.

I finish my coffee and dive into the shower.

It's a new day and I feel like taking it by the horns, so after I shower, I discover it's not too late, it's only eleven in the morning. It felt like I was waking mid-afternoon earlier, I was so exhausted. Now I've had coffee, I'm all better. I pull on my bikini and my cut-offs on top.

In the kitchen I get to work and brew more coffee, set the orange squeezing machine to work and make two glasses of juice. I pour ingredients for scrambled egg into a pan and start heating it up. I grab English muffins from the breadbin and smoked salmon from the fridge. Luckily, he has hollandaise sauce, too. Within no time, breakfast is served.

I leave his on the side, covered in the hood from the microwave plate, but he returns home in time to get it fresh.

"What's this?" he asks, panting and dripping with sweat.

"Breakfast, or maybe brunch, at least for you."

"Back in a sec." He waltzes into his room and produces a towel, which he uses to wipe away his sweat.

He seats himself opposite me and uncovers his food. "Wow, it looks good."

"It's my favourite breakfast. You had all the stuff I needed, too. Amazing."

"Right on."

He stabs his food and eats quickly. While he focuses on his food, I focus on him, hoping he likes what I made him. He has no complaints. After he's done, he lets me know, "Just grabbing a shower, thank you for breakfast Beatrice."

"Thank you for the book, it's amazing. You didn't have to."

"I know, but for the sake of your sanity and mine, I thought it necessary."

His bedroom door shuts and I hear him turn on the shower.

When he emerges, I'm on the patio, lounging. The factor 50 is by my side and has already been applied. He wrestles with the spare sunbed and sets it up next to mine. He brings out two bottles of water and starts drinking from his. He doesn't use the sunbed to lie down, he sits facing me, his shirt buttons undone, his legs spread, shorts on. He holds his hands together in front of him, his shades on, but I can tell he's got something on his mind.

"So, why did the book make you so sad?" he asks, his voice gentle.

"You'd find out if you read it."

"I don't read chicklit."

"It's more than chicklit."

"Well, you could just tell me, that would save me the heartache. Plus, I don't read as fast as you." I see his nose wrinkle, because he's trying not to smile. It makes him slightly more adorable, if anything. I bet behind his shades, his eyes are smiling. He's trying to hide it.

"Okay..."

"Please, tell me. I'm dying to know," he says, using dramatic hand gestures. "It must have been good to have provoked such a strong reaction in you."

I chuckle and fiddle with my sunbed, making it so that I'm less reclining, more sitting up.

"Okay, so, there's this girl, Louisa and she's a runner's widow, working in a café—"

"Okay, what the hell's a runner's widow?"

"Oh, it's like where the woman is a widow because her husband or boyfriend is never there. It's a British expression. The author never uses the term in the book, but I've heard it a lot.

Some friends of mine were runners' widows. It's because the guy becomes addicted to running and exercise in general, and everything in his life is geared towards running and exercise, even holidays and weekend breaks, all his spare time in fact. It's because he's basically addicted to exercise and because of that, you're left a widow, because you suddenly find yourself right down the pecking order in his life, which is now dominated by metabolic rates, run times and the latest in sportswear..." Maybe I'm not explaining it well, because he has a look on his face.

"I'm sensing this isn't the point of the book, otherwise last night, you were crying about running."

I throw my head back laughing. He laughs alongside me and touches his fingers lightly to my arm.

"Tell me more, then," he asks. "I'm on the edge of my seat, can't you tell?"

I laugh it off and wipe my eyes, replacing my sunglasses. "Okay, so she's with this loser runner guy and working in a café, even though she can't even make a cup of tea. She's really sweet, though. She knows the regulars and takes care of them."

"Chicklit much," he mumbles, and I shake my head.

"I haven't told you everything, yet!"

"Go on, then," he sighs, holding his head up in his hands, waiting for the big twist he's been banking on.

"So anyway, she loses the job in the café, because her boss has to let her go. When she gets home, you find out she's 27 and still living at home. Her sister is brainy but has a small kid, also still living at home. Her dad works but his work is so-so and her mum looks after their ailing grandfather. So when they learn Louisa's lost her job, it's like a big blow, because she contributes to the household income."

"Uh-huh," Nate says, still not convinced.

"So, in typical chicklit, English romantic comedy fashion, she goes to the job centre and it's a complete disaster. It's atrocious what people go through to find work in the UK, you know? I bet you don't have the same issues in the US."

"I don't know..."

"Anyway, she lands this job, working for a rich family. There's the son, who's grown-up, but he's quadriplegic..." —Nate sits up, listening— "...and Louisa finds him difficult at the start. He's had this life, where it was busy and big and he would go on holidays where he'd be throwing himself into dangerous situations, but then it was something as stupid as walking out into the road on a rainy day that got him into a chair, with all these recurring health problems and stuff."

"Oh, so there's more, then..."

"Yeah, much more. And then Louisa, over the course of time, realises Will—that's the guy's name by the way—has this desire to end his own life at Dignitas, and she starts doing things, like arranging trips, days out. She even arranges this hilarious day at the races. He gets stuck in the mud and it's undignified, but it's... I don't know... Anyway, they fall in love and she thinks she's saved him, she really believes she's shown him that life, even in a chair, can be good. She takes him to a tropical resort where everything's beautiful and she does things she never thought she would, and she learns things about herself, but she never thought it would be the end—she never thought he would still make the same choice he was always going to make. She always thought, deep down, she could save him. And there she is, more in love with him than ever, and he's in love with her—though he doesn't say that, I mean, he's too strong to admit it, he doesn't admit it because he's the hero and he can't be weak, even in his chair he's so strong—and anyway, he still makes the choice. Because it's his choice. And he dies. And she's left completely heartbroken. And he leaves her some money and tells her to live big. And it's just so completely devastating because it was like one minute he was there, living life, so strong and vital and vibrant, and the next he was reduced to this wreck, suffering constant infections, always needing medication, and it just makes you realise how quickly it can all be taken away, you know? And the worst of it is, they only met after he was in a chair. They only met because he was in a chair. Otherwise the café worker and the big London business dude would never have met, would never have known that despite all their social differences they would have always been perfect for one another. Oh, and don't get me started on the bumble bee tights..." I have a little chuckle to myself.

"Bumble bee tights?"

"It's so cute."

"I'm missing important info here," he says, removing his sunglasses and looking amused. "What about the runner guy? Did she felate this quad guy while she was still with the runner dude? Did she cheat on the poor running man?"

I can see the deviant sense of humour in him and I respond, "What are you talking about? Really? I mean..."

"I'm just saying, they could have done stuff. He still had his tongue, right?"

I'm shaking my head. "Oh my god, why did I tell you? Why? You're a guy. You don't understand."

"She could've positioned him places. Fingers. I don't know. If he was a big guy, it might not have mattered if he was flaccid. She could have still got what she wanted. Naked cuddles are nice, even without sex. It could've been nice. Don't say she couldn't have done stuff with him. And the things they can do with IVF nowadays, too..."

I sit up in my chair, absolutely flabbergasted. "Do you want to know what happened to running man, or not?"

He chuckles. "Okay."

"She did not cheat on him with the quad guy. She dumped him, and he went and got himself a running woman."

"Ah, well that's put my mind at rest. Running woman and running man, sailing off into the sunset together..." He uses grand hand gestures, which piss me off. He's mocking everything about my precious book.

"You're making a joke out of my heartbreak," I retaliate, "and it's not cute. This book has changed my life."

"I'm only making light of what's just a story. I've known quads, you know?"

I sit up and take note. "Yeah?"

"I'm from Texas, horse country. More people fall off horses there than have car accidents."

"Oh, really?"

"Some still make a real life afterwards, you know? I guess it entirely depends on your state of mind."

"I guess it does." I sit scratching my lip, contemplating his words.

"I mean, it's the power of the mind, Beatrice. If the mind's alive, somehow it survives, even if the body isn't working any longer. That book is just a story. It's one author's version; one decision made one afternoon to kill her hero off instead of letting him live. It's fiction. It's the author's prerogative to remind us that life can be taken away, any moment. The hero died, but it's life affirming for everyone else. It's just that something always has to be sacrificed, doesn't it?"

I peer at him. "So, why do you read, then?"

"I read because fantasy has a lot of sex and a lot of different species and worlds and ideas I often find myself wondering about. Fantasy takes me out there, to someplace else, a different corner of my own brain. A safe place to explore my deepest, darkest thoughts, thoughts a man can't really say out loud."

"You mean thoughts of quads getting sucked off by a woman in a pinny?"

"See, why are you even bothering reading Beatrice? You've got all the imagination you need to start writing that shit yourself. Kinky shit, too. Hell, I'd read it."

"You planted the idea there, Captain Bronze!"

He goes back inside, but I can hear him chuckling to himself as he sets some music going and starts cooking up lunch for us. I realise he'd never widow me to become a running man—he loves his food too much.

Chapter Fifteen

A nother evening rolls round, but this time I can't be bothered to read. I'm still letting what I read last night sink in. We're having pizza delivered and after Nate collects it from the delivery man at the door, I clear the coffee table so we can spread everything out.

We get to work on chomping through doughy, gooey, sumptuous pizzas, all lathered in garlic and various other spices. Nate turns on the TV and we start watching *Fellowship of the Ring*. It's in English, but with French subtitles. I'm not sure how they deal with all the different languages in this country, but they do. Nate and I settle back and after we polish off the pizza, he breaks open two bottles of beer and a big bag of Doritos.

We sit in absolute harmony, watching TV and eating, drinking. When it gets dark in the room and there's a commercial break, he sets the fire going and I light the candles on the fireplace.

When the film resumes, our heroes have reached Rivendell and are contemplating the fate of the ring.

"I could watch all three back to back, wouldn't bother me," I suggest.

"Yeah? You up for it?"

"Yeah."

He checks the TV and discovers the other two films are available on demand.

"You're on," he says.

"We'll need supplies at the ready, then."

I dash into the kitchen and raid everything we've got. Beef jerky. More chips, and dip. Chocolate. Popcorn. I carry it all to the coffee table and set it out.

"You've gotta admit, it's not a bad life here, Beatrice."

"No, it isn't," I admit, chomping through a handful of popcorn.

Nate's big hand rummages around the bag on my lap and he lifts out an enormous amount of popcorn, clutched in his big fist.

"Maybe we could do a few touristy things, then?" he asks.

"Yeah?"

"Why not?"

"I suppose we could."

"Can you ski?"

"I can, but I'm not a skier, not really. I'm a swimmer. A floater. A skater, but not a skier."

"I have no idea what to read into that."

"Me neither."

He laughs. "So, what about... maybe a bit of hiking."

"Oh, I love hiking. I could hike all day."

I turn and catch the smile on his face. He has to stop himself laughing.

"You know I didn't mean it like that."

"Okay... so, you like hiking," he says, insinuating something.

I throw a bunch of popcorn at his head. He sits picking it off his t-shirt, eating it.

"I actually like hiking. I've climbed the Five Sisters in Scotland, it's one of the bonniest walks imaginable. You'll have to do it someday, maybe we could—" I stop myself before I say anymore.

"I'd like that," he says, sounding oh so endearing, and yet I'm still not sure he's earnest.

"I've done a lot of mountaineering," I boast.

"Oh yeah, what have you climbed?"

I try to think of something dramatic, something that'll make me look good.

"Oh... I climbed walls at the gym... and a couple of vertical rock faces in the country." I can't help but laugh. "It's a lot more climbing than the average person, I suppose."

"I climbed Mount Hood, in Oregon," he says.

"Really?"

"Uh-huh, it was tricky but worth it. We had a team. It was safe enough."

"Cold, though?"

"Wondered-where-my-balls-had-gone cold, yeah!" We both laugh.

"Was it like the landscape on this film?" I ask. "Sort of like another world? I've always loved dominating landscapes, reminds me how small we are, how insignificant. Reminds you to be humble."

Nate turns and takes the popcorn from my lap, pulling me towards him. He holds my face and leans in, kissing me. I'm in shock for a moment, before I hold his shoulder and his side. He's warm and smells beautiful and he's very gentle to begin with, nudging and teasing my lips with his, his groan of approval guttural. I want to fall into complete and utter oblivion with this man. I want to jump, and I don't care the cost. He's utterly beautiful and the finest kisser I've ever known.

When our tongues meet, I open my mouth wider. We settle into a pattern of kissing and licking and gentle lip biting. He takes his soft, full lips away and I become more aware of the heat in my belly once he's not kissing me anymore.

He looks passionate as he stares into my eyes, stroking his fingers over my cheeks. "I just had to kiss you, you're so goddamned beautiful."

I'm stunned into silence as he hands me back the popcorn and continues watching the film. I want to ask for more kisses. I want to ask for lots more, in fact!

"You didn't tell me what it was like," I remind him, as the film reaches the point where the Fellowship is taking the pass of Caradhras, over the snowy mountains. "Mount Hood, I mean."

"I can't think right now," he says, "I'll tell you another time."

I turn and see he's crimson, from the neck up.

"Nate," I whisper.

"You deserve so much better than me. Let's just watch the film."

"Okay," I whisper, impressed by his restraint.

Chapter Sixteen

I t's been a couple of weeks since the kiss and things have been awkward ever since. I've never cared what a guy thinks before, but now I do. I would usually go for what I want without even thinking twice, but Nate is more than what I want—he's something different to what I've ever encountered before, and he's carrying around a guilty conscience, I can tell. (Unless he's very traditional and doesn't believe in sex outside of marriage, but I doubt it...) My reasoning is that if he didn't have a guilty conscience, he would have slid into my bed already.

So, to disperse the awkwardness, yesterday I suggested we finally leave the house, not just to buy groceries or have a quick drink out, but to embark on a full-day excursion.

Therefore, today we're on the rickety train, travelling to Rochers-de-Naye, which lies up in the mountains, 2000m above sea level. It's a clear day as we travel which will hopefully allow for some amazing views. The train is chugging along at a leisurely pace and we can watch out of the window as villages and other scenery passes us by.

Nate is sitting in the aisle seat, allowing me to watch out of the window. He has his arm resting on the back of my chair, looking over my shoulder at the scenery. We're both wearing shades because it is so bright. He went out and bought hiking boots for us both yesterday and North Face jackets, so we're wearing these too.

"It's beautiful," I whisper, "have you ever been up here before?"

"Nah, it's a touristy thing to do."

I turn and flash him a smile. "Well, I'm excited."

"Good, it's a clear day, we should be able to see for miles around."

The journey is slow and after spending a while watching out of the window, I turn to look ahead and when I do, I find myself slotting under his arm and he shifts his hand so it rests on my shoulder. The train keeps stopping and starting. It's electrical, so maybe it's temperamental? I don't know.

"What's it like where you come from?" I ask him. "In Texas."

"You really wanna know?"

"Of course. I want to know all about it. I'm guessing you don't originate from Longlake, that's for sure?"

"No," he says, with a wry smile. "I have a ranch just outside Del Rio. It's in the south. It's subtropical there and the humidity will be peaking right about now."

I keep looking ahead, just enjoying the fact that he has his arm around me. It's been two weeks since the kiss and all we've done in two weeks is brush shoulders in passing. The rest of the time we've been reading in our own corners or using the hot tub at separate times. He pulls up this wall sometimes and you can't get past it. He will answer you and be polite, but the wall doesn't allow for any intimacy, so I'm glad he's finally talking about the place he comes from. I want to know everything about him—good and bad.

"So, you have a ranch? You mean, you own it, or your...?"

He pauses to consider his answer. "I own it."

"Oh, so...?"

He takes a deep breath. I dare not turn to look at him. I might scare him off and he will shut down again.

"My mother grew up on a ranch, but tragedy befell her family when she was a teenager and she was lost, for a long time. I have people who run it for me, but she lives there."

I pick up on what he's not saying. "You bought her a ranch?"

"Why not? I have the money."

I won't call him out on the slight defensiveness of his tone...

"So, your job pays a lot?" I don't say it, but Dad never splashed out on anything. We had the house and everything in it, but otherwise he wasn't showy.

"It pays enough," he says, as explanation. "My dad left me some, too."

"I remember. So..." I chew my nail. "Home is a lot different to here, I bet? No snow in Texas."

"I never saw snow until I came here," he admits. "It happens though, once in a while, so I'm told. I mean the climate of Texas is a great deal changeable, there are storms and all kinds. The wind dictates what we get, whatever jet stream blows in."

"What happens on the ranch, then? I mean, what's the business?"

"We have horses and cattle and land. We drive the cattle from pasture to pasture and sell them when they get big and fat. It's pretty simple. I have people I trust to run the show, they don't need me."

"And your mum, she lives there...?"

"She has people," he reveals, but his bluntness tells me that his mother is not up for discussion.

"What's it like when you wake up there? Is it as beautiful as here?"

"It's different," he explains. "The heat is different. It's sometimes so foggy in the morning, it's like dragon's breath. The plains stretch as far as the eye can see; it's just so flat and arid and endless. In summer, Lake Amistad fills with people trying to keep cool, on jet skis or in boats, or swimming. Sometimes, it can get too hot, but I'm used to it. I guess when I think about it, no, it's not as pretty there as it is here, but it's home, and it has its charms."

"Scotland is said to be the most beautiful country in the whole world. Did you know that?"

"I didn't."

"Can you imagine just putting your hands in a stream and being able to drink straight from it?"

"I can imagine..."

"Some of the whisky is so good because they draw in notes from the sea air during the distilling process."

"Pretty good whisky. I'm not a big drinker, though."

"I noticed." He barely has more than a glass at a time. "And the forests, Nate? Do you have forests in Texas?"

"You mean, tropical rainforests."

"Oh, really?"

"Yeah. I wouldn't risk it."

"One time, I'd like to camp in the countryside, maybe the Cairngorms. Watch the sun rise and set every day, feel the fresh air seep into my skin and bones. The purity of it all, you know?"

"You mean the freezing coldness of it all," he chuckles. "The rock in your lower back that almost paralyses you at night. The threat of deer trampling your tent, maybe even rain washing it away!"

I laugh along with him, before getting serious again. "Dad was Scottish. I thought we'd gone to Scotland because he'd wanted to return home, but Scotland wasn't for him. He'd always take us on holiday to hot countries. He didn't have Scotland in his heart."

"Like you do, you mean?"

"I just think..." I take a few moments to pick the right words, because I want to get my meaning across. "He never had the propensity to stop and admire anything... raw."

"And your mother?"

"Oh, she would admire anything. A broken and chipped old doll. A dead tree. A homeless chick. She admired everything about life."

"So, you take after her, then?"

"I suppose I must." I've never thought of it like that.

"We're here," he says, and somehow, we've made it, our conversation having distracted us from the journey up.

We leave the tiny rail station, which is quiet because it's still early in the day, and we make our way to stand amid open land, where we're alone and can just admire everything.

It really feels like we're up in the clouds here. I can even see the odd fluffy cloud hanging above nearby mountains, and they're not as high as this.

You can hardly tell the difference between the sky and the lake, they're both so blue, accented starkly by the white-topped mountains nearby. There are lots of sheer cliffs all around and they stand as a reminder that we're tiny and this world is vast and perilous and unwieldy. Beautiful blue, yellow and white flora decorates the rocky mountainside and as I breathe in the scent of snow and wind and fresh grass, it feels like a dream. It feels like we're in a Peter Jackson movie without the camera crew, who've just popped to the canteen for their lunch, but will be back any minute now to film here, because it's so beautiful.

I can see all the houses dotted along the shoreline below; they look so tiny from up here, so insignificant. It's difficult to see where the lake ends, in fact; from up here it looks as if it's never-ending—as if it goes on forever. The coniferous trees stay standing in all weathers and people who visit at Christmas probably come because it's a real festive paradise. If we were here in winter, this would be covered in snow right now. The yurts on the other side, where some people stay during their holiday, would be buried in white stuff, no doubt.

"Here, take a seat," Nate suggests, laying out his coat for me to sit on. It's not so cold, but it's not warm either, so I keep my coat on and park my bum.

"Nudge forward," he says, sitting down behind me.

I'm thrilled when he wraps his arms around my shoulders.

"Is this real?" I ask Nate.

"It's real."

I turn and stare at his face. He's looking out at all the landscape and his eyes are so blue, they almost look translucent up here, the sky and the lake reflected in his eyes. He's a man truly happy right now, mirroring me, his awe and wonder the same as mine. He blinks and his long lashes flutter. He finally sees that I'm watching him watching the world. He turns his face and glances at me, then looks at the world again. He doesn't have a smile on his lips per se, but there's a smile in there somewhere, it's just that his lips haven't even moved a millimetre. It's hard to explain but it's a look of happiness I read from him, of complete and utter peace. He looks like he was born to lord it over a mountainside retreat like this. He was born for the country and to live in the fresh air—just like this—free and unencumbered and pure. To live simply and without all the influences of the modern world, like our laptops and tablets, phones and TVs, gadgets and gizmos, always distracting us from what's right here—all the time—just pure, uninterrupted beauty, all around us.

"Nate?"

"Yeah?" He turns and looks at me.

"I'm really happy."

I lean my head back against his shoulder as I crane my neck and look up into his eyes.

"So am I."

He doesn't do anything but smile, then he takes his focus back to the landscape.

I sink back into his arms and try to be patient, but what I'd give for a kiss right now, or what I wouldn't give—virtually nothing.

We sit staring at the world for a good hour, his arms wrapped tight around my shoulders.

When he kisses my hair, I feel him shudder, I feel him linger—I also sense his continued restraint.

"Shall we get some lunch?" he asks.

"Yes."

He helps me to stand and we stagger back to the buildings nearby, where a hot lunch should be waiting for us, to warm us through again.

He's transfixed on the world outside as we sit by large glass windows in the restaurant, and as I continue watching him—and not the fantastical world outside—I realise there's only one place I want to call home and one life I want to lead:

Anywhere his arms are, I want to live inside them, as his woman.

"Nate?" I ask.

"Yeah," he answers, as we await our lunch, the smells of the canteen driving me mad.

"Do you want to go out? Maybe tomorrow night."

He gives me a barely-there nod, glancing at me. "I know a place."

"Gives us both a night off, right? From cooking I mean."

"Why not?"

"Okay. Cool."

"Cool."

Our food is delivered, and I sit wondering if he realises I just asked him out. I'm not sure he does!

Chapter Seventeen

I'm in the changing rooms of H&M, trying on numerous outfits, and I'm being picky. Normally, I wouldn't even use a changing room. I can usually look at a garment and know whether it will fit or whether it will suit. I know this from years of being on the circuit and people telling me what suits me. Basically, anything suits me. I'm a model for Christ's sake.

We're going to dinner tonight, to some fancy place, and I can't decide what to wear. It's not about picking what will suit me, but about picking something that will tell him what I want, without me seeming slutty.

I decide to go with the old faithful: the saying that, 'If in doubt, wear black', because black never lets you down. It's not innocent, but it's not cheap either.

From the pile of clothes I've just shoved into the tub chair in the corner of my cubicle, I drag out a black silk shirt and throw it on. It floats down to my knees but has a thigh-high cut. I throw on a belt and fasten it tight at the waist. I just need some accessories and I'm done. Oh, and a pair of ankle boots. Then I'm done. And maybe a trip to the nail bar down the road. And the perfume shop. And the salon. And wherever else I can seek help.

I throw my hands up, looking down on the mess I've made in the changing room. There's no way I'm going to be able to carry it all out, so I'll leave it for the staff to clear up. Whoops.

I swear Nate should've come with me today. Trouble is, I think he wants to prove he trusts me, as much as I want to trust him, too. Everything's got serious—and so suddenly—it's making me crazy.

After scrambling around for accessories, I don my sunglasses at the cash desk and try to avoid the cashier's stare. Either she's staring at me because I look familiar, or because I just wrecked their changing room. Either way, once I've paid up I'm rushing down the street towards the nearest salon, as fast as my legs will take me.

WHEN WE ENTER DAVINDA, Nate's hand is resting on my lower back as we're shown to our table. Everyone in the restaurant has their eyes fixed on us. There's a big group of ladies on one table, perhaps seasonal workers having a night out before they all leave Montreux until next year, and every one of them seems to be fanning themselves.

We're taken to a hidden nook and I'm thankful of the moody atmosphere, low lighting, dark wood and exotic, instrumental music invading our ears. I get comfy with a few cushions propping me up in our booth and he sits close, so we're tucked right in a corner, together.

Ever since our trip yesterday, I've felt a crackle in the air between us. Something happened and I don't know what. Obviously, I've climbed mountains in Scotland and they were beautiful, but I didn't have an out-of-body experience in Scotland like I did yesterday. Of course, the greenery surrounding Montreux and Lake Geneva is lush beyond imagination when seen in the flesh. The snow-capped, ethereal mountains and the lake are truly awe-inspiring and breath-taking. The little towns and villages dotted along its edges...

However, it was as Nate held his arms around me, that I looked up into his non-smiley smile and knew that I loved him. In that moment, I knew it, and I've known it ever since. As we were taking the long and rickety train journey back down the mountain afterwards, he cuddled me all the way down in our seats on the freezing cold train. All the way down. Arthur would never have sat cuddling me for that length of time. He would have been busy reading tourist guidebooks or checking his email or reading someone's draft thesis on his iPad, telling me, "Sorry, but you know how it is."

I sure knew how it was—Arthur always wanted to work or drink. Anything to pass the time without having to emotionally unveil himself in front of me. The thing is, I know Nate's different. I need only find the right place to unplug Nate and all his passion will be unleashed. I want that passion more than anything. I've never wanted anything more than I want him—even despite our beginning.

After he orders drinks for us, he turns and smiles, taking my hand which is lying on the table between us. "Did you have fun today?"

I can't help but smile. He's so tactful. "You mean, did I spend a lot of money pampering myself?"

He smiles. "Well, it never crossed my mind. You just look radiant is all."

"Well, radiance came at a cost." I stroke my hand through my salon-styled hair. I just had a trim and some of the weight taken out of it, plus I had it straightened so it's lost its waves. Straight, it reaches past my breasts.

"You look beautiful, Beatrice. You always do, but tonight especially." He looks bashful and it looks so bloody gorgeous on him.

I blush furiously, I can't help it. Arthur never used to make me blush. I never used to make a mess of changing rooms either, not for him. Not for anyone. Only for Nate.

He leans in and brushes a kiss against my cheek. His breath on my skin makes my entire body break out in goosepimples.

"You bought perfume, too? Let me guess..." He continues inhaling me, making all the hairs on the back of my neck stand even taller. "Dior?"

I turn my head and our noses brush, our eyes focused on one another's.

Does he know how much I want him? I want to feel the safety of his body wrapped around mine. It's all I want. It's all I'll ever want. I want to see that smile every day for the rest of my life.

A little smile curves his lips before he whispers, "I've eaten here before. I think you would like the eggplant starter and then the veggie burger."

"Oh, you're so certain?"

"As certain as I'll ever be," he says, smirking.

He keeps his hand over mine when the waiter comes back with some wine for me and a beer for Nate.

"Ready to order?" we're asked.

Nate looks at me and I nod. He orders for me and then picks the shrimp and a blue cheese burger for himself.

Under the table our feet and ankles are touching and yet I still want to be closer. He smells gorgeous and looks even more handsome than usual, with a white shirt rolled to his elbows, revealing strong forearms. I've noticed he leaves the house early every morning to go for a long, energetic run. Whenever he comes back I can smell his sweat. It circulates the house and drives me wild.

After he's poured me some wine from the bottle, I take a sip and nod. It's delightful. What it is, I don't care, I'm just glad it tastes good.

"Have you ever been on a date before?" I ask, now I have Dutch courage.

He gives me one of those all-American smiles. "You got me."

"I guessed not."

"Most girls think I'm weird," he confesses.

"How so?" I drink a little more. The tang of the wine is offsetting my nerves.

"Well, I read a lot and I work with computers, a lot. I was always into computers, even before I knew about my father. I'm a high-level hacker, but don't tell anyone."

I smile, catching my bottom lip between my teeth. "If this is a date, and by the way you didn't deny it just then, perhaps you should have given me a proper kiss already?"

He almost spits out his beer and quickly places his bottle back down.

"Do you trust me yet, Beatrice?"

He has to spoil the moment, doesn't he? ...by asking the question I also want to know the answer to: do I trust him? The truth is, I don't know if I do.

I put my wine glass down and stare into space. "My father brought me up not to trust anyone, or anything. It's why I lost my virginity to a boy I didn't give a shit about. It's why I slept with guys I didn't care about. It's why I was with Arthur, because it didn't have a future. Maybe my problem isn't this situation we're in, maybe it's the mistrust that's been instilled in me. I didn't get the freedom you did, Nate. I didn't get protected."

He reaches over and tucks a few strands of static hair behind my ear. We're having a moment, it feels like.

Then our starters are delivered at the most inopportune juncture. He shoots the waiter a look and the guy promptly leaves us to it. I tuck into my starter, the moment having passed.

WHILE NATE VISITS THE bathroom, the bill arrives and before the waiter leaves the table, I open my wallet and pay in cash. I just want to get out of here.

Tonight didn't go the way I wanted it to. It started off well, but Nate seems to have this incessant desire for me to trust him. While I'm starting to, I don't know what it is, but as I told him earlier, it's not as simple as making the decision and choosing yes or no. I've been taught to trust nothing and nobody. It's going to be a hard habit to break.

When I see him heading back towards the table, I stand and walk towards him, letting him know, "I paid. Let's go."

I like that in my heels I'm almost as tall as him and he can't defy me because I paid. I don't need a man to pay for me. I don't need a man for anything really, I just want him. That's all. I want Nate.

I want him with me, naked, writhing. I want his kiss and his hands on me. It's that simple. I want him—and it has nothing to do with trust.

We head down the dark side street where he parked the car. There's no physical contact this time; no hand on my lower back; no hand-holding.

The car automatically unlocks as Nate gets closer with his key. I feel something's not right and when I catch his eye, it's like he can see something I can't.

Something behind me.

"Don't move," I hear—but it's not Nate's voice.

Someone else has crept up behind me.

Chapter Eighteen

"What do you want?" Nate asks the man, who has something digging into my back. I can't tell what it is. It could be a gun or the handle of a knife or just a pebble he picked up off the beach earlier, who knows? Anyway, Nate can see the discomfort in my eyes as I'm threatened. It's the unknown that scares both me and Nate. It's the unknown we fear, because it's everywhere. We've both been warned about it—and we both know we will do things to survive if we have to. It's the things we're capable of that scare us most. The acts we've yet to commit.

"Nobody needs to get hurt. Just give up your purse, mademoiselle," the guy says, in a truncated French accent, like he wasn't born here.

"Her purse? Listen, I've got money. Come and get it." Nate digs out his wallet and holds out a few thousand euros in cash.

The dirtbag holding me hostage produces a gun which he holds out towards Nate.

"No more fast moves, man."

The gun is being presented to Nate but there's still that thing at my back. A knife, perhaps? I don't know. A knife would be easier. He could slice me and there wouldn't be a sound. Not like gunfire.

"Okay, okay, look, I'm gonna toss my wallet over. You can take it all. There's more money there than there is in her purse. C'mon."

Nate starts to lower towards the ground to slide the wallet over, but I can see his other hand moving behind his back, like he's going to make a grab for something from his back pocket or the back of his jeans.

I judge the scene in the space of a couple of seconds:

If Nate pulls out a gun, the guy with the knife at my back might be frightened and desperate enough to either knife me or shoot Nate for no reason except he has nothing to lose.

I don't have to let chaos reign. I can overcome chaos.

Being that I can hear the rough breathing of the scum standing behind me, I gather power in my fist and clench it, and when I'm ready, I lift my arms as if I'm surrendering.

"You don't have to do this," I warn them both, and when they're each seemingly readying their weapons, I slam my fist right into my assailant's face and send him flying back, the pressure of whatever was at my back disappearing instantly.

I swirl round and clock him around the head with my boot.

He goes flying to the ground, knocked out.

Nate races towards us and steals the mugger's gun and what I now see was a knife, not yet unsheathed. I recognise my assailant. Barely, but a fleeting memory...

"He was walking by the restaurant, I remember," I say, out of breath. "I remember looking out the window because this guy was staring at me. I was paying the bill and he was staring at me. I had my purse open towards the window, so the waiter couldn't see my rolls of cash, but anyone passing by would have been able to. I'm sorry, but you didn't offer me the use of the safe and I didn't want to leave it there, and today I was spending, and I didn't know how much I'd need, and I'm sorry."

I can feel the anxiety rolling off Nate. He's scared, I can tell.

Nate empties the guy's gun and tosses it down a drain, along with the knife. He gives him a good kick in the kidneys and rolls him off the street and into the gutter. The dirtbag squirms and moans in pain, then Nate grabs my arm roughly and ushers me towards the car. I'm barely buckled in when he screeches away, flying around corners and bends as we drive back up into the wild countryside above Montreux, back towards our cabin.

Once we're there, he doesn't wait for me to get out of the car with him, he steams on ahead and flies through the front door. When I catch up with him, he's got the whisky open on the coffee table and he can't look at me.

I leave the room and head for my own space, slamming the door on my bedroom once I'm inside.

Two can play this game.

Chapter Nineteen

I'm struggling. It doesn't matter what I do, I can't sleep. The house is eerily quiet and I feel so wired, still. It's impossible to fall asleep when all I can think about is going to Nate to hold him, but then fearing what it might mean if I do. I shake off the duvet and wriggle out of bed, lifting my dressing gown off the chair next to the bed. I tie it at the waist; satin, with lace trim, matching my nightdress beneath. Both are floor length. I bought them earlier today and if things went well, I was going to wear them for him and ask him to come to bed with me tonight. Instead, things went tits up and now my heart feels heavy and it hurts.

Leaving the bedroom, I head for the kitchen and find him gone, his bedroom door closed on the corridor. So, he's got no intention of comforting me. Fine.

I hope he's sleeping peacefully, because at first light, I'm leaving. This time I'll make sure he won't find me. I have other spare passports, ones he doesn't know about, stitched into the lining of my rucksack. Alongside those passports are my other bank cards and he doesn't know about those, either. Dad prepared me well, including encouraging me to do self-defence.

Just because I defended myself tonight, he had to go and get huffy, didn't he? God, I could drive myself mad trying to get inside that man's head. Who knows what he's thinking...

I pour milk into a pan and turn on the gas. Probably won't work, but hey... What the hell. Anything to try and get me to sleep tonight.

While the milk warms through, I walk to the sitting area and watch the stars outside. You can't see as many here as you could in that dustbowl town in Texas, where I first met Nate what seems like months ago now, but there are still plenty to gaze at. My mother once told me there are fire gazers and then there are star gazers. She said I was the latter, not content to live the same as everyone else, always looking at the stars instead of inside my own hearth... or heart. She was very fond of a metaphor, my mother. She knew how to tell a story.

On the coffee table the whisky is still open. Perhaps I'll pour a little into my warm milk. That should help me fall asleep.

Given that he's left the top off the bottle, I think he may have gone to sleep drunk, or else he was so upset he forgot. Taking a closer look, he hasn't drunk a lot of it. It was half full yesterday and he's only drunk maybe three more fingers out of the bottle. Nate isn't a big drinker. Unless he's very good at acting and pretending, what I've learnt about him so far is that he doesn't drink a lot. He does like food, and reading. He likes keeping himself in shape. He enjoys the outdoors—but.he.does.not.drink.

So he must be upset to have been drinking tonight.

On the sofa beneath the fur throw, I curl up and watch the stars. Before I know it, I'm floating.

The next thing I know, there's this hideous beeping sound, raping my ears. I cover my ears and look around. The room is beginning to fill with smoke.

"Oh shit, the pan!"

"What the hell, Beatrice?" he shouts, sounding groggy.

"I left the milk pan on, I must've drifted off! Sorry!" I can't see him for all the smoke. It's ridiculous. I run for the patio doors and swing them wide open. I vaguely see him grab the pan and toss it into the stainless-steel sink, throwing the tap on and extinguishing the flames.

After the small fire's died down and he's switched off the gas, I'm standing in the middle of the room, and he looks at me, exasperated.

"You could've just lit the logs if you were cold!"

I laugh behind my sleeve and tears leak from my eyes. "I was making hot milk. I didn't mean to doze off, I swear!"

"I can't leave you to your own devices for thirty seconds, can I?" He doesn't sound drunk or angry or annoyed anymore.

"I'm sorry. And... for earlier. I'm sorry, Nathan."

The tightness in my chest grows as he stands there, panting. He's wearing his long johns thingamabobs and he looks magnificent. I just want him to hold me tight and envelop me.

"I was finally dozing off, too," he says, intimating he's had trouble sleeping as well.

I could've burnt us both alive tonight (difficult seeing as though we have a working fire alarm), but anyway, my reasoning for what I'm going to do next is that we nearly died tonight—twice—and there's one thing I don't want to miss out on before I die. Whether I die tomorrow, or next year, or in fifty years' time, I don't want to regret never having had his arms around me.

Once the smoke's all gone, and the fire alarm clicks back on green, I shut the patio doors.

"Are you coming to bed, Nathan?"

He stands, still staring. "Beatrice."

"Nathan."

I turn and walk down the corridor which leads to the bedrooms. I don't walk down to my bedroom. I take the door into his room. The sheets are uncharacteristically tangled, revealing he's been wrestling with them tonight, as much as I've been wrestling with mine.

I remove my dressing gown and leave it on his chair. He doesn't have piles of clothes all over his room, not like I do. He's disciplined.

When I see him standing in the doorway, not sure of himself, I ask, "Why were you so angry?"

His lip wobbles and he turns his face to the side. "Because I was so close to killing a man for you tonight."

"You've never killed before?"

"No."

"Okay, I understand. And I'm sorry, it was stupid of me to open my purse with so much money inside it. I won't do that again. Although in my defence, I didn't know some trigger-happy punk would be walking down the street the exact same moment I had my bag open."

"It's done, but I'd rather move on after what happened. We don't need the trouble."

"You want to go, already? Leave Montreux?" The thought of leaving this beautiful place has me breathless, when a few weeks ago, there was nothing I wanted more than to keep running. How quickly things can change!

He shrugs. "Maybe."

"That guy was in the wrong."

"Trouble begets trouble, Beatrice. People still might knock on our door, wanting to know why we didn't report it. I don't know..."

There's still that element of doubt. Does he think that guy tonight was an attacker of a different sort? Someone sent from the Collective to warn us this isn't over?

The problem is, we don't know anything for sure, and we can't hide forever. Hiding in Texas nearly killed me. Living could kill me too, but I'd rather live and die than never live at all.

"Nate, it doesn't matter what happened or what's going to happen. What matters is that we want one another, and we could be dead any moment. I'm tired of this now. I want to feel your arms around me. Come to bed."

He remains in the doorway, conflicted. I see it in his face, the contortions, the uncertainty in his heart.

I walk straight up to him and take his hand. "Are you coming to bed?"

He looks me right in the eye, and from these close quarters, I feel myself tremble and something in my stomach clenches, just from the look in his eye. He was genuinely scared tonight and he's trying so hard not to be afraid. "You don't know what it means if we do this, but I do, Beatrice. I know what this life is like. Eventually, they *will* come for us."

"Then let them come."

I wrap my arms around his neck and our bodies come together, flush. I press my lips to his throat and he groans. His hands land on my waist and I run my hands over his shoulders and down his back. His skin smells so fucking good.

"I want you, Nate. I want you," I say, gasping, imploring.

"Goddammit," he complains, leaning in and smelling my hair.

The moment his arms wrap tight around my body—his submission final—I relax, and the tension falls away, all of it.

"I want you too, beautiful girl," he groans, inhaling and kissing my throat at the same time, "I want you too."

His kisses mark me, claiming me for his own. His touch stains me, drawing heat out of my skin wherever he touches. I almost fly off my feet with his wondrous kisses.

God, when his lips touch mine... I feel faint as the biggest wallop of heat hits me, right between my thighs.

He plunders my mouth more savagely than the last time we held one another, his tongue rampant this time, all his passion unleashed finally. He lifts me and carries me to bed, covering my body with his, his urgent, wet kisses making me throb for him as he lies, long and hard between my open thighs.

He's kissing my face and trembling in my arms as I hold him around his back. His skin is smooth and warm and slightly damp to the touch. I melt into his body and tears leak from my eyes as he ravishes me.

My cheeks are on fire as he kisses my throat, in a way nobody has ever kissed me before. He lingers, he tastes, he teases. I have his soft hair between my fingers, directing him, begging him not to stop, my head thrown back in ecstasy.

He slides down the strap of my nightdress and digs his teeth into my bare shoulder. I grind against his body and pull on his hair, groaning as he tugs down my nightdress and takes my nipple in his mouth, his fierce suction making me cry out loudly. It occurs to me that what I thought were orgasms before now, weren't orgasms at all. He's nearly making me come from nipple stimulation, and it's a feeling I have never felt before, not in my whole entire life.

Nate grabs a hold of my arse in his hand and squeezes my flesh, moving back to kiss my mouth, even more viciously. I brush my groin against his thigh and fight back against his kiss, letting him know he can be a little rough if he likes. He bites into my bottom lip and I can't breathe for the heat in my stomach. My upper wall is screaming out to be touched and fucked.

"So goddamned beautiful," he groans, kissing my belly over the satin nightdress as he makes his way down to between my thighs. He pushes my nightdress up my legs and exposes me to him, grunting as he stares at the silken entrance to my body. I haven't a clue what is happening until he strokes his tongue over my clitoris.

I arch off the bed, "Nate..."

Fire explodes at my centre and I squeeze my eyes shut, sure I'll never feel this way, ever again. I'm in love for the first time—the only time. Nothing has ever felt this good.

"Say you're mine," he demands.

"I'm yours," I gasp.

He grunts and I scream as he replaces his lips on my throbbing clit.

I rest my feet on his shoulders to spread my legs wider and he reaches for my hands, holding my fingers tight as he licks my sex, then kisses my clit, indulging himself.

I arch off the bed and into his mouth, begging him, "Please, go slower, please, I'm going to die..."

He laughs against my flesh and the vibrations only make me pant harder. He squeezes my fingers and warns, "I'm going to make you come, Beatrice. Then I'm going to make love to you."

"PLEASE!" I yell, as my cheeks feel like they might combust. My clit is engorged and I can feel every little touch of his lips and his tongue, magnified by need and all my sensitive nerve endings, which are currently on fire.

When I come, it obliterates me. Kills me. He's cruelly destroying my ability to see past him and he's already smashed down the wall I built around my heart, so long ago. I have no chance of escaping this, not now. I need him so much. He has no idea. And now he's just proven that I didn't have a clue before. I didn't know anything.

I feel detached from what happens next as he kisses the insides of my thighs and down to my calves, his kisses against the arch of my foot making my skin tingle. It feels like it's not happening to me, but I want more, so much more.

I reach for my nightie and tug it away, lifting my hips to get it off.

"Fuck, you're mine," he groans, his eyes darkened by lust.

He lingers over my navel, taking a deep inhale, and he sucks on both of my breasts until I'm near manic with longing for him to come and lie on my body and take me in his arms.

He nips at my collarbone and licks the suprasternal notch at my throat—until I'm a quivering wreck all over again.

My hands are pushed above my head and I can barely see, even with my eyes open. I try instead to keep my eyes closed, to absorb all the sensations.

He runs his fingers up and down my arms, kissing my throat as he enjoys my body. He knits his fingers through mine and his tongue is back in my mouth as he lies completely on top of me, his erection pushing against my belly.

He lowers his body and tugs down his long johns. I look down and bite my lip when I see how hard he is. I wind one of my legs around his buttocks and it gives him leave to push between my thighs and enter me.

"Oh god," I yell. "Oh my god!"

I thought there was already a fire inside me, but whatever was there, he just lit up for real. He rocks into me until he's able to fill me full and I groan, holding onto his brown hair as he rests his cheek against mine. Underneath me, his hands clutch my shoulders and he rocks into me in long strokes, gasping with each move he makes.

He kisses me but this time, it's different. His kisses are sloppy and rich and luxurious. He bunches my hair in his hand and tugs on it.

I slide my hands down his body and enjoy the smooth skin of his back and behind, kicking down his long underwear with my feet. He growls when I squeeze his buttocks in my hands.

"Fuck, I wanted you the first moment, the very first moment, baby," he groans.

"Me too. I want you so much." I place my hands on his chest and feel his thundering heart beneath—and through his manic beats, I know all I need to know.

I begin lifting my hips into his and rocking with him, my hands on his shoulders. I tip my head back and he rests his nose and mouth against my throat.

"I'm gonna come, Nate. Gonna... come..."

We keep the rhythm going and I hold his cheeks, my head tipped right back. My back aches and my thighs begin to tremble, wildly. Inside me, he feels like burning desire stirring the very guts of my soul—awakening every part of my body.

"Don't stop, Nate," I beg, my voice not my own.

"Beatrice..."

He cries out first, moaning, grunting, yelling. I keep thrusting in time with him and I pummel all around him and shake beneath him, my whole body in spasm. When I feel him flood my womb, I gasp, both pain and happiness overwhelming me, my cries loud and unabashed.

I love him—and it hurts. This love hurts, because it's real.

We cling to one another, trying to catch our breath. I stroke my hands through his hair and slap his arse when he tries to suck my nipple again.

"Don't you dare. I'm unbearably sensitive all over."

He has the cheekiest look in his eyes. "Any nastier and I'd be hard all over again for you, Beatrice."

I laugh my dirtiest laugh. "Maybe I'm done being nasty, you beautiful man, you."

"I'm glad," he purrs, biting his lip as he sneaks a good look at my tits.

Then he leans up and kisses me. Little presses and tiny nips, a little tongue. I purr in response to his touch and he smiles against my mouth, provoking extreme happiness in every corner of my being.

He rolls off me and moves me around the bed until he's spooning up behind me, the sheets around our bodies. He wraps his arms around my shoulders so tight, I know that I'll never need anything else.

"You're safe, Bebe. Don't worry about a thing. I've got you safe and sound." He kisses my shoulder and buries his face in my hair.

"Bebe?"

"Yeah, it suits you."

"Does it?" I laugh, and he laughs.

"What? I'm sticking with it. My, Bebe."

"Bebe... huh."

He makes his little noises, curling himself even tighter around me, his legs nudging against mine. My stomach is still on fire.

I turn my head and cup his cheek, my other hand clutching his forearm. "Nate?"

"Yeah."

"Can we stay here? Just me and you. If something comes of the trouble earlier, we'll go, but otherwise I just want to stay. For now, anyway. I know we'll have to go one day, but for now I'd just like to stay here."

He leans in and we stare into each other's eyes as we share a soft, tender kiss.

"Sure, Bebe."

"Okay? Yeah?"

"Yeah," he groans, kissing me again.

I wriggle back into him and sigh, beginning to finally relax, exhaustion sweeping over me. I stare at the stars outside the window and eventually, my lids fall shut.

Chapter Twenty

I'm in the cupboard again. It's cramped and stinks like sweaty socks. It's the only place in the trailer where I can escape... where I can't see anything. There's really no place else to hide in this tin can.

She shrieks and it's piercing. I have to put my hands over my ears.

"Stupid bitch, shut up!" he yells.

It's the guy from the bar. He drops round every Thursday night, bringing chaos. He's just one in a long line of guys Mom sleeps with for cigarettes and booze and whatever else they've got.

No matter how hard I press my hands to my ears, I can still hear every word, every slap and punch against her skin. She tells me to never intervene, but I'm getting bigger and it's getting more difficult to hold myself back. It's not right.

"Stay still," he demands.

She always tells me afterwards that it's what she wanted, that it's nothing, but the black and blue marks across her arms and legs tell me otherwise. Unless this is what people really want...

Is this love?

If it is, I don't want it.

"Ahhhhhhhhhhhh!!!!!!!!!" she screams, and my heart almost stops.

I'm eleven but I know that it's not a consensual scream. It's not a cry of passion.

It's a genuine cry of horror and pain and torture.
Why does she continually torture herself like this?
I wrap my arms around my head, but it changes nothing.
Tears rack my soul.

I'm in the cupboard but the smell of his cigarette meeting her skin is unmistakable as it drifts between the cracks, because as small and contained as this space may be, what's going on outside the cupboard door is truly inescapable.

This is the only place I can hide in the trailer, but that doesn't mean to say I have to stay here, does it? I can leave my mother. I could. It's just that I won't. I can't. She'll die if I leave. Surely, she'll die. Right?

"*Now Claire-Anne, how does that feel?*"

"*G—g—g—good,*" *she manages, struggling to speak even one syllable.*

"*You know I only do this to punish you for your misdemeanours, right?*"

"*Y—y—y—yes.*"

"*Good. Now it's time to gag you.*"

What follows are the sounds of flesh being broken and him doing things not right. Not good. While she's gagged, all she can do is gargle. She cannot scream to protest. She has to take it all. I can only imagine what he's doing now she's gagged.

I push my fingers as far into my ears as they will go, but the problem is, in my heart I feel the suffering and the pain she's in and I can't just close my heart, can I?

What feels like hours... days... weeks later, the whole trailer shakes as he slams the door behind him, finally leaving. I remove my fingers, hearing an engine start and after that, complete quiet.

I don't want to leave the cupboard. I want to stay here and never leave. Each time this happens, I want to pretend this has never happened, and yet I'm put through this again and again, just as she is.

I need a pee however, so I use the bathroom and try not to stare at the pile of bones lying in the centre of her bed, buried beneath sheets, but barely masking the ugly truth she cannot hide.

I feel the truth in my heart, just as she does, and that's why she needs the drugs.

I'm not going to go the same way. I see things. I know things. I can escape this.

I will escape.

"Nathan, I need you," she cries.

I go to her, just as I always do.

I rub cream in her wounds. I ice her cut lip. I shake from head to toe, terrified out of my mind as I witness what that man did to her.

"It's okay, baby," she whispers, stroking her hands through my long, unruly hair. I can't remember the last time I got a haircut.

"Don't say that to me, I'm not stupid."

"No, I mean it. It's okay."

I remain silent because she will continue to argue her case, even when we both know it ain't right.

When she's like this, I can't tell her what is plain. She has herself convinced this is the only way, when it's not.

"I'm going to bed," I growl, storming through to the living room, where I sleep on the pull-out every night, even though it stinks of piss.

I'm a pathetic bedwetter.

I hear her light up a cigarette and a minute later, I smell it drift through. "It's really okay, Nate."

I put a pillow over my head and try not to leave.

I could leave... anytime... but that way she'd die.
I know it.

Chapter Twenty-One

Nate's the one normally setting up the fancy coffee machine every morning because he's usually first up. I'm here struggling to work out where to put the water and beans, when he comes up behind me, sliding his hands around my body.

"Why did you leave my bed?" he demands, holding my stomach and my breast, my body immediately responding to his touch.

"I'm making you coffee."

"I don't need coffee, I need you."

I turn around to discover he's entirely naked. "I'm not here just to service you, Nate."

I hate the words as soon as they're out, but instead of recoiling, he breathes deeply and demands, "What's wrong?"

"Nothing." Except that I woke up beside the love of my life this morning and now I'm shit-scared.

"It's not nothing."

"I can't take you seriously. You're naked and standing with your hands on your hips." I try to avert my eyes, but I can't. It's that thick v-shaped wedge of muscle between his hips. It's glorious.

"I'm sorry. Shall I grab my jeans so I can thread my thumbs through my belt loops?"

He starts laughing and I can't help but laugh, too.

I can't resist him when he pulls me into his arms and holds me close. I wrap my arms around his neck and murmur against his chest, "I've been in so much pain."

"I know, Bebe." He strokes my hair and kisses my cheek.

"This doesn't seem real," I say, beginning to cry against his chest.

"It's real."

"It hurts, Nate. It hurts so much."

"That's why I'm here, to make it all go away. Let me take it away for you," he murmurs, softly.

"I'm scared." I burst into tears and wrap my arms under his, trying to hide myself away against his chest. The lump in my throat hurts so bad, I can hardly breathe.

"I'm scared, too," he whispers. "In fact, last night, I was terrified. I've never been that scared in my whole entire life. I knew in that moment, as he held that weapon against you, I'd do anything for you. I knew it there and then and it frightened me because I don't think there's anything I wouldn't do for you."

I pull back, tearstained and afraid. The look in his eyes is one of vulnerability and love.

I stare up at him, pleading with him, earnestly begging with my eyes for him to tell me how he feels.

"Is this more?" I beg, feeling sick for having to ask, the lump in my throat still there.

I just need to know. I'm so raw right now.

He cups my cheeks in both of his hands and using his thumbs, he wipes away my tears. He leans in and presses his delicate lips to mine, once... twice.

There's a smile in his eyes when he tells me, "I love you, Beatrice. I knew it the moment you first spoke my name, your voice like a dagger to my heart. I'm falling more deeply in love with you every day and I want you to be mine, as I'll be yours. No in between. Just you and me, baby."

My chin wobbles and I can't help it, more tears fall.

"I need to be inside you again," he begs.

"Yes."

Nate steers me until my back is against the kitchen wall. His body presses against mine as we kiss, my hands tugging his hair, our tongues duelling even as my tears are still drying.

"Hmmm," he groans, "you've got the same inside leg measurement as me."

"Oh...?" I try to seem as light-hearted as he is.

"Yeah..."

"How do you know that?" I beg, as he cups my breasts over my nightie and massages them.

"I checked your jeans. I had to know all your sizes to buy you clothes." He's breathing heavily and I can feel how ready he is for me, his erection pressing against my belly.

"I should get you arrested, you pervert."

"Oh god, it wouldn't matter to me—because I love you—but please tell me you're a bad girl, Bebe. Please tell me."

"For you, I reckon I could be persuaded into anything."

"Oh god, I knew it. I'm such a lucky fucking prick," he groans.

He presses me hard into the wall and lifts my silk nightdress until he's exposed my lower half. He encourages me to spread my legs and he slots between my hips, holding himself to my entrance before pushing inside.

For a brief moment, I stand almost on tiptoes as he enters me without the same resistance he experienced last night, when he first pushed inside me. He moves slowly, wedged tight, his length snug against my clit.

"Okay, Bebe?"

"Yes, yes... don't stop, Nathan. God, don't stop. Keep moving, just like that." If he keeps rubbing his dick along my clit like this, he's going to make me come in no time.

Nate holds my back as I lean in to kiss his chest, working my way up to his throat, licking his jugular. He rocks his hips slowly, enjoying my kisses, his moans of approval encouraging me.

I love the stubble decorating his jaw and as we kiss open-mouthed, his bristles bring heat to my skin. Just his nose turns me on, as it brushes my cheek or rubs against mine as we kiss.

I love his mouth more than I think I'll ever love anything else.

He holds the back of my head, my hair held tight between his fingers, as he becomes more forceful and needy. My head tips backwards as he kisses my throat, my blood boiling, my cheeks fiercely hot all over again. The thin strap of my nightdress falls and he leans in to kiss my nipple as I bury my hands in his hair.

He gasps against my ear, "I could do this forever."

"Me too."

He pulls back to look at me, my sex so full of his, and in the daylight, I'm dazzled by all the blueness of his eyes.

"I love you. I love you."

"I know you do, baby. I know," he acknowledges, a sweet smile on his lips.

He takes my hands and pushes them above my head. He fucks me harder and I have the urge to wrap one of my legs around his hips, so I do.

He buries himself deeper inside me and I feel my taut nipples sting each time they brush against his chest, cutting into his skin.

His thrusts grow longer and deeper and I wrestle my hands out of his to hold onto his shoulders instead. He tears the night-dress off my back and throws it away. I wrap both of my legs around his waist and he holds my bare buttocks, squeezing my body closer to his, always closer.

"I need you," I groan.

"I need you, too."

We push back and forth against one another until I feel the build-up inside me of unbearable pleasure, as my muscles begin to contract and pull him into me. Nate can barely hold on, and when I come, he bursts free in my arms, his cries loud and unashamed, turning me on even more. I too sound like I'm disconnected from myself, screeching and yelling with joy.

I pant against his throat as he pants against mine. We're locked tight together, because there's no other way for us to be. He licks the sweat from between my breasts and shows me his satisfied expression. He nips my bottom lip and gives me the sexiest smile, making my heart purr. I rub my hands through his beard and kiss him, my entire being filling up with happiness. The way he looks at me is the way I've always wanted a man to look at me—and I never knew it until now.

He carries me back to bed and I lie in his arms, staring into his eyes, stroking his skin. It's all we do all morning, and it's all I want to do forever.

Chapter Twenty-Two

Within two weeks of us becoming lovers, we're experts. We've done everything. Enjoyed everything. I know every scent of him now. Every taste. We go to sleep wrapped up in one another and we wake up having rolled around the bed all night, still together. I love the feeling of when his body connects with mine and we melt together, like we were made for one another, a perfect fit. Whenever he kisses me I'm instantly wet and I only need him.

It's September now and the onset of autumn always makes me contemplative. I feel restless and ill at ease. He's everything to me, but as I lie here in his arms, watching the sun rise outside the window, I feel like there's still some kind of itch to scratch. I don't know what it is. Maybe I'm bored of being his lover 24/7. Maybe it's not even that. I don't know.

Nothing seems to have come of the mugging debacle. Nobody's been and knocked on our door. When we've been into town, nobody has pointed at us and whispered anything. Hopefully the mugger took off to the next town, who knows?

As much as I want this to last forever, I know that it can't. If we stay cooped up, we'll end up hating one another. Eventually, real life will go on, and we'll go back to the real world—maybe together, maybe apart.

"You're awake," he says, stretching behind me, his grip on me tightening as his muscles awaken.

"I am. How can you tell?"

"I can feel your heart beating harder. It's those cogs turning, right?"

"Well, my mind does seem to need a lot of fuel."

"Go back to sleep, gorgeous," he groans, kissing my back.

God, I do love him. Very much.

"I'm restless, Nate."

"I know. Perhaps if we make love, you'll fall back to sleep again."

"That's not what I meant, and you know it."

"I know," he whispers, his breath skating across my skin as he kisses my shoulder.

I roll onto my back and fold my arms, looking up at the ceiling. He props himself up on his elbow, and using his other hand, he draws circles on my stomach.

I look over at him and curse, "Stop being so utterly gorgeous. You're distracting."

"Oh, let me rectify that." He sits up and mangles his face with his hands, going cross eyed and making horrible noises with his tongue sticking out.

I hold my stomach, I'm laughing that hard. I throw the pillow at his head and then put it over my face, cursing, "For god's sake!"

He takes the pillow from me and strokes all the hair away from my face. He deposits a tender kiss on my mouth and murmurs, "Okay, okay. I'll make the coffee and we'll watch the rest of the sunrise in the hot tub and talk."

I frown at him. "We never talk in the hot tub. Nice try."

He pouts. "But you love the hot tub."

"I do, darling, I do. But we never talk in the hot tub and right now, you know I need to talk."

"I know you need to talk," he groans, exiting the bed and pulling on his long underwear, which never stays on for long. He scratches his wild mane of hair as he walks to the doorway, flicking a grin over his shoulder before heading for the coffee machine.

When he comes back, I've pulled on a t-shirt and some knickers, and I'm sat cross-legged on the bed. He nuzzles my neck after he bends down to place my mug on the nightstand and I turn into him, kissing his jaw.

I love every inch of his body and I've already decided he should be my husband, but...

"So, tell me what's going on in that beautiful brain of yours," he asks.

He sits opposite me, his legs crossed too. After I take a sip of my coffee, I capture his hands in mine and hold them, gazing around the room as I search for the right thing to say.

As is usual, though, words rush out of me... "I hated my old life, but the thing is, now all this has happened, it's kind of made me want it back."

He stares, confused. "Okay..."

I keep trying to avoid his eyes. "So, I don't mean like going back to modelling. Not that. But like, living an ordinary life. I mean like, I don't know, being purposeful. It's weird how because I've been forced to hide for the past few months, it's made me yearn to live again. It's weird, but I like really want to live again." I find myself saying 'like' a lot when I feel nervous.

"Well, we've discussed this. We don't know who had it in for your father. Aside from the incident with the mugger, Montreux is so fucking quiet. It's safe and there's no drama. In Edinburgh, there are CCTV cameras on every corner."

"Yes, I know..." I feel and sound dejected.

"I just don't know what I can do..."

"Me either," I groan. "I should be happy. I have a load of money, a man who loves me, a ton of books to read and my days are mine. I love that we can go for a hike whenever, eat whenever, do whatever, but I just... I miss routine, you know? I'm used to routine. It's bizarre and I never thought I would say this, but I want a boring life. I do. I want a boring life with you, baby." I want to wash his clothes and make sure I get the nice shampoo he likes and the food he enjoys. I want to take care of him.

"You say the nicest things to me, Bebe."

I climb onto his lap and wrap my body around his, nuzzling my way into his embrace. "You should take it as a huge compliment. I never wanted domesticity before now."

"Me either, but..."

We stare at one another because there are still so many questions hanging over us.

"Can we just live?" I ask him. "Can we? Or does this have a shelf life?"

He pulls me tight into his arms and kisses my hair. "We can live quietly, Bebe. You could go back to school. You could do anything. Just not modelling. Too much like attention seeking."

I pull back and search his eyes. "It's like you see right through me."

"Yeah, well. I'm going for a run, will you be okay?"

"Sure I will, honey."

He studies me after he's pulled on his shorts, trainers and shirt. I prop myself up in bed with my coffee in my hands and just stare at all that is mine. He's my dream come true.

"Bebe?"

"Yeah..."

He looks all serious, while I'm sat here drooling over those calf muscles.

"I know you're not used to being happy, and I'm willing to work through this with you. Eventually, you'll get used to being at peace, you know?"

"I know." It's like he can read my thoughts.

"You've had a few months of being on edge, afraid, scared. Not living in fear is going to take a lot of getting used to, but we have time. At the very least, we should stay in Montreux until Christmas. It's gorgeous here at Christmas. You'll love it."

"I know, Nate."

"Keep the bed warm, angel. I'll be back soon, all sweaty and in need of some warming down."

I smile in his direction. "I love you."

"I love you, too."

Chapter Twenty-Three

Three months later...

It's December 23, which is my birthday. Nate has prepared dinner and we're sat eating it at the kitchen island, on two high bar stools. We've sort of avoided meals out since the whole mugging thing, but I don't really mind. He's a good cook and I also know a thing or two, as well.

Since we've been in Montreux he's introduced me to a lot of new foods, including many different types of fish. I've always been a fish-eating vegetarian, but I was never adventurous before, probably because my mother never cooked fish. She and my father were vegans. Phoebe wasn't into any of it and ate meat, but I was something of the middle ground between my parents and her. It always made for interesting meal times, and my mother always used to visit the supermarket with so many different lists. As a family we rarely ate out, especially with my parents being vegans... in Scotland.

Dad used to say the planet was going to die from people eating meat and that's how he convinced my mother not to eat anything remotely animal—especially nothing that had emitted gases into the air to increase the greenhouse effect. They also never bought leather or animal fur.

Of course, my lover looks gorgeous tonight. He's combed his hair. He's put on cologne. He's wearing a check shirt tucked into his Levi's. It's winter so he's swapped his cowboy boots for snow boots. With sheepskin. He bought me a matching pair and I almost said something, but I didn't. I love him way too much to deny him the happiness of buying me a gift—even if he doesn't know how those sheepskin boots get to us.

"Is your dinner okay?" he asks.

He wants this to be perfect and I am feeling quite contemplative tonight, it being my birthday and all. My first one sans family. Now Nate and I are both 25, except he'll be 26 in February.

"It's beautiful. The fish tastes great. Did you steam it?"

We had a crayfish starter and the main we're eating now is dover sole, perfectly seasoned with a lemon sauce and lots of parsley. It's melt-in-the-mouth good. He's served it on a bed of quinoa and spinach and we're drinking some of the nicest chardonnay I've ever tasted. He had it delivered from nearby France, especially—a whole case of it.

"It's roasted," he replies, proud of himself.

"Well, it's gorgeous."

"You seem far away," he says.

"Hmm," I muse. "Just thinking about the MA."

I've applied to study for an MA in Art History at the John Cabot University in Rome. I should find out in the new year whether I've been accepted, and if I have, then Nate and I are going to move to Rome in the spring to get used to living in the city. We've both decided that we have to try to live out in the real world, then see how it goes.

Since we came to Switzerland, apart from the mugging, there hasn't been any trouble and we don't anticipate any in Rome. Nobody seems very interested in us anymore. Nate does a bit of work on his laptop sometimes. He says it's just to keep the cash flowing in. I try not to ask too many questions and let him do his thing. I just pray whatever it is that he does isn't going to bring trouble to our door.

In preparation, we've both started learning Italian. There's a language school nearby we've both been attending and we have the CDs at home to work from, as well.

"You'll get in, Beatrice."

"It's not my credentials I worry about, it's that we doctored all that stuff."

My degree certificate and everything blew up with the house, so I had to get Nate to forge a degree certificate for me in the name of Annalise Williamson, because I got my degree from St. Andrew's under that name. It's not like I haven't got a degree, I have. It's just that it all feels false, because I'm not Annalise. Nate only ever calls me Beatrice and *I am* Beatrice. I was never Annalise. We just have to hope the university in Rome is more interested in taking my money than calling up St. Andrew's to check up on me for references. I fear they might speak to Arthur and he will tell them I'm dead and it can't possibly be me who's applying—because Annalise wouldn't have left him without a word—so it must indeed be some imposter applying for graduate school in my place. (It all sounds as ludicrous in my head as it is in reality.)

"Think of it this way, the worst that could happen is they turn around and say no—and so what if they do? You've still got me, you've still got your talent. The personal statement you wrote clearly shows you know your stuff and you have your specific interests. Please Beatrice, try not to let this dampen our Christmas or your birthday. I'm sorry this has happened to you, but I love you so much and I can't bear to see you sad like this."

I nod rapidly. "I know, I'm sorry."

"Finish your dinner and I'll get the cake ready."

He takes his empty plate away while I finish the last crumbs on mine. I should be so happy. I've got this beautiful man cooking me dinner. We've been out and bought so much food for Christmas, we won't have to leave the house. I'm warm and safe and cosy. I'm in love. I should be so happy, but I guess it's hard not to think about what might have been. Then again, I may never have met Nate if tragedy hadn't struck. I may never have left Arthur, who wasn't good for me. I may never have realised the error of my ways.

He takes my empty plate away and I eagerly await cake. He makes a mean cake, too.

"I'm going to blindfold you," he says, "otherwise this won't work."

He's been possessive of the larder all day and I've not been allowed to go anywhere near it. I'm wondering what he's gone and done... when I notice the familiar smell of my own perfume as he wraps my own silk scarf around my head and covers my eyes.

"Oh my god, what's happening?" I beg, desperate to know what he's got planned.

"Be patient. I'll be back in two ticks. I just have to light the candles."

I hear him go into the larder, taking the two steps down into the naturally chilled room. He returns a few seconds later and warns, "Don't move a muscle. There are 25 candles on this sucker."

I feel the heat as he draws near and places the cake in front of me on the counter.

"Are you ready, Beatrice?"

"I suppose so!"

He moves behind me and unties the blindfold. I blink rapidly and look down. It's a circular chocolate cake, my favourite. It's maybe only eight inches in diameter, but there are words spelled out in white icing:

Will you marry me?

I laugh hysterically, not getting it at first. In fact all my laughing near enough blows out all the candles.

"Nate, what's going—"

He reaches around me and positions a ring, right in front of my eyes.

"We don't have to do it this year, not even next year if you don't want to, but I just wanted you to know that I'm yours and I'd like to call you mine, all mine." I take the ring from his fingers and stare at it.

He spins me on my stool to face him. With his hands around my cheeks, I look up into his sparkling blue eyes, not sure if this is real.

"Will you marry me?" he asks, as though I didn't get it the first time.

Maybe I did need to hear it from his lips.

I say only what my heart is screaming for me to respond with: "YES!"

He picks me up and spins me around and around. I can't believe he did all this without me suspecting a thing. He laughs, seemingly relieved, his face buried in my hair.

"God, I love you, but you sure know how to keep a man waiting."

"You were waiting, what? Like a few seconds?"

"They felt like an eternity," he complains.

He puts me back down on my feet and takes the ring from my clutches, sliding it onto my finger. It's a platinum motif ring like something a medieval princess would be given, with diamonds and rubies. It reminds me of a secret garden with an iron gate before it, carved in the same swirling pattern. It dominates my hand, it's so chunky. I love big pieces like this. I would have chosen this if I'd been there, for sure.

"I absolutely adore it, Nate. It's so beautiful."

"I knew you'd like it."

"I love it. I love you."

We slam together, kissing. I ruffle his hair, needing him close, his chest pressed tight to mine. He's vital and strong, smells great, and I feel safer with my fiancé than I have ever felt in my whole, entire life.

"You're a sneaky, sneaky man Buchanan."

"Yes, I am."

He lifts me into the bridal hold and takes me to the bedroom, the one we share nowadays. The other one has become my dressing room, aka my dumping ground for clothes.

He puts me back on my feet and by the foot of the bed, we hurriedly undress one another.

He tugs my dress over my head and pings my bra open before I've even got his shirt undone. I fling him towards the bed and kiss his mouth wildly, making him groan beneath me as I break open the poppers on his shirt.

He wrestles with his buckle and untucks himself. I lean back and pull my thong to the side, sliding down onto him.

"Oh baby," I groan, my body humming in response to his.

"I want to watch you," he calls.

I squeeze my hands around his pecs and throw my head back, grinding into him, taking myself to the root of him and shifting against his pelvic bone. I moan deeply, enjoying him.

He rubs his thumb over my clit and I shake my head, "No, let me. Lie back and relax. Let me pleasure you, Nate. Let me."

We lock our hands together and I throw my head back, wild with abandon, his body filling mine deliciously. I like to wear woollen hold-ups in winter and Nate likes to stare at them as we fuck while I'm still wearing them. Tonight is no different.

"For a second, I thought you'd say no."

"I never thought I'd be asked, let alone that I'd have the chance to say yes."

"God, I want to fuck you Beatrice."

"Lie there and be a good boy."

I grind down onto him, taking him deep, rolling my hips and swirling him inside me.

I've got to go and get my hormone implant replaced soon but I'm thinking that I might not. I'm thinking that I might let nature take its course and make a baby with him. I could still study. He could take care of the baby while I go to my lectures.

"You're thinking again," he groans.

"About having your baby. It'd be a beautiful little thing. A designer kid. Your tan and my red hair. Poor kid."

He laughs, and I whimper, as I feel him vibrate inside of me. He feels the same thing as I laugh along with him.

I settle my hands on his chest and grip firmly, riding him hard, the bed bouncing along with us. I rock in long strokes, taking all of him, until I can't take anymore.

"Oh god, Nate," I gasp, as I sit up and take him as deep into me as I can.

I pull at my own hair and bite down on my lip, my head tipped all the way back, my spasms shaking my thighs as I come around him and tense up and down his length.

I have my eyes closed and my head is still tipped back as he sits up and sucks my breasts, his beard savage against my skin. Once he's feasted on me, he rolls me over and pins me to the bed, kissing me deeply as he rolls his hips, tipping himself deeper and deeper until I'm gasping for breath, trying to indulge him in his excessive need of me.

"My wife," he groans, "my love."

"Please, Nathan. I'm gonna come, again. Please, come with me. I can't—" He knows that after the first orgasm, I'm always super sensitive and can practically keep coming on command. If only it didn't exhaust me so much.

"Because it's your birthday honey, you get exactly what you want."

I lock my ankles around his buttocks as he bites and sucks my mouth, licking tempestuously too.

"I need you," I groan, and our hands above my head tighten together, as he speeds his thrusts so that the headboard is banging against the wall and I can't see straight. Light explodes across my eyelids and I shatter in his arms, screaming for him to come.

He cries out loudly, repeatedly, as he empties inside of me. He collapses on top of me and I couldn't be happier to feel him spent and weak, crushing me in his arms.

We kiss each other's necks and mouths and hands until I get dazzled by my ring again and have to stare at it.

"Would my lady like cake and coffee in bed?"

"Your lady now remembers why she said yes, oh cake and coffee bringer of mine."

"I don't want to talk in medieval tongue again, Beatrice. But thou art a naughty little wench, aren't thou?"

"Talk dirty to me, servant man of mine," I growl.

"Milady likes what she likes," he says with a wink.

He leaves the bed and grabs a robe, knotting it at his trim waist.

I can't believe how happy I am, still staring at the beautiful, chunky ring on my finger.

Chapter Twenty-Four

On Christmas Eve, it's just after the sun goes down that we head into town to enjoy Montreux Noel, where the festivities are. The local Christmas festival has been abuzz since November and we've been and visited a few times since it got started, but the atmosphere tonight is a little bit more pumped than usual—and that's saying something. Nate and I weren't planning on coming down tonight, but I can't resist. I adore everything to do with Christmas.

In the distance the castle looks adorable covered in snow as the Ferris wheel takes us on another lap. Nate likes to make the seat swing and I'm constantly slapping his shoulder for making me feel even more sick than I already do. Maybe I ate too much sugar…

He's busy eating a giant pretzel and he whispers in my ear, "This thing is so delicious, I'm gonna keep this paper bag, and when we get home I'm gonna smear all these loose bits of pretzel salt all over you, then lick them all off. Slowly. Until you whimper."

I giggle mischievously. "You're not right in the head."

"I'm gonna take that as sarcasm. Good, Scottish sarcasm."

"Take it how you want, laddie." I put on the accent and he loves it, nuzzling my neck and growling.

After the Ferris wheel, it takes us a little while to get our legs back, so we wander aimlessly for a little while, staring at the goods on sale at all the little wooden huts that form the huge open market here. There are piles upon piles of chocolate goodies and so many other sweet things on offer. If only I'd known, I'd have bought my stash tonight and not last week—everything seems to be half price on the last night of the market.

Tonight though, everything glitters and looks just that bit more magical, lit up against the night sky.

People here are happy and carefree, they're completely without burden. Visitors come from far and wide to enjoy the delights on offer in Montreux and I can see why. It's a magical place, not only because it's so close to the lake, but because the belle époque houses sit like they've always been here, like they will always be here. It feels like tradition has a tight grip on Montreux and its niche could never be overshadowed by developers sweeping in and changing everything. Montreux could never be transposed either. This place is who she is and I envy her. I envy Montreux. She knows who she is. She knows where she belongs. She knows her place. Even with the dominating mountains surrounding her, she shines bright enough to hold her own against their majesty. She's not shy or reserved. She's putting herself out there.

Sometimes I wish I was more confident of myself, but I'm not, not quite yet. What I do know is that this man by my side makes me very happy, happier than I've ever been, and I'm going to stick with this because it feels right.

It feels like a hidden corner of the world here, built just for me and Nate and these other people who could be movie extras, just decoration to maximise the experience. All these people with their easy smiles and rampant chatter, their shopping bags brimming, their hats pulled down over their ears and their children squealing at their feet—they enhance everything about Montreux. It's too perfect.

"You look happy," he says, pulling his arm tight around my shoulder and kissing my cheek.

"I have a little thing to buy," I say, kissing his lips, "would you go and get me some more of those lebkuchen I love? I'll catch up with you."

He wears an inquisitive smile. "Don't buy me anything. I told you I didn't want a thing."

"I won't," I lie.

I already have three gifts at home for him, and I'm about to purchase one more.

He'll have to deal with it.

He wanders off, shaking his head.

I spot the stall selling caramel churros and make a mental note to visit that one more time after I've got this thing I want to get for Nate.

The market is a treasure trove for those seeking knick-knacks or crafts, Christmas treats or street food—but I want a little something different for Nate. I wind my way through the stalls and head for the one I hope is still here. Some have already packed up and gone home, but...

I find it, thankfully open.

I greet the seller, "Good evening."

"Oh, wow, a Brit."

"You got me." I stare at her beautiful silver pieces. "You travel all the way from New Zealand for this, every year?"

"Yeah," she replies, in her thick accent.

I bow a little, ducking to inspect some rings.

"I want something for my fiancé. I think silver would suit him."

"Ah, well I have some titanium pieces under the counter. I don't keep them out because they're worth a bit more."

She goes behind the counter and produces some rings.

"You make these yourself?" I hold one up to the light to inspect it. It's got a single diamond in the centre and is a chunky band. An engagement ring for a man.

"Yeah, using old-fashioned forging methods. All of these are unique. I don't replicate. They're all one of a kind. I can take dollars or pounds or euros, whatever you have."

"Yeah, how much in dollars? I've got some to offload."

"A thousand," she says, and I stare at her, studying her closely. She keeps her lips pursed, showing no willing to back down.

She knows I have money from the way I'm dressed. She would probably sell these to other people for half the price. However, that amount of money could make her entire day. Hell, her entire week.

"Throw in the butterfly necklace on the jewellery tree there and we've got a deal."

"Deal," she says, grinning.

I know the butterfly isn't worth much, but when I see Nate, I can say that's what I've been buying, and not a secret ring for him. I'm just hoping it'll fit now! He does have big fingers but then the ring is good and big and I'm betting she's used to making rings for big guys back home.

"Thanks a lot," I say, turning and walking right into my love as I leave her stall.

"What did you get, honey?" he asks, having somehow found me in this maze of a market.

"Oh, just a necklace. I'll show you when we get home."

I stuff my wallet back into my handbag and pull my gloves back on as we walk away.

I look over my shoulder and see the stallholder I just spoke to starting to pack up. Sometimes it's nice to help those people out who really need it.

"I'd like to go and watch the projection show on the Palace once more, and then we can go home," I tell him.

"Oh, I got you lebkuchen, and these," he says, pressing a brown paper bag full of churros into my hands.

I grin wildly and say nothing, passing him one before I wolf them all by myself.

He takes my hand and walks me towards the hotel where they have the big light show with Christmassy images projected onto the main façade.

I am so in love with this man.

AT MIDNIGHT I SNEAK out of his arms and leave the bed, heading for the living room in my thick towelling robe. I grab my handbag from the coffee table and dig into it to remove the ring I bought him tonight. I pull open the drawer of random stuff in the kitchen and discover there is still some ribbon left. I grab the scissors too and head back to the seating area. By the coffee table, I wrap the jewellery box in ribbon, tie it in a bow and curl the ends of the ribbon with the scissors. I write out a tag:

For my husband-to-be. A ring of your own. A promise.
Until we become one, you'll know my heart's yours.

B x

I knot the string of the tag underneath the ribbon and tie it tight.

Sneaking over to the real Christmas tree in the corner, I stack Nate's ring on top of the little pile we have under there. I bought *Death Note* for him off Amazon, both the book and DVDs. I also bought a very sexy baby doll with red see-through material and white trim, but I doubt it'll stay on long once he dresses me in it.

I look in on him in bed. He's lying face-down, tired out. Once he got me home earlier, he did pour salty leftovers all over my stomach, then he slowly sucked them all off, gave me oral pleasure and made love to me up against the wall of the shower.

I don't really feel tired yet. I'm too excited for tomorrow, so I head back to the living room and switch on the TV. *Home Alone* is showing with French dubbing. I keep the sound down because I don't know French well enough yet and anyway, I don't want to wake my love. He tires himself out, endlessly working to keep me happy.

As the film plays, memories enter my mind... Family Christmases. Again, as with any gathering, we all ate different meals around the dinner table, even at Christmas. Mum and Dad would eat nut roast. Phoebe would warm up a microwave Christmas dinner from Marks and Spencer, and I would have salmon with all the trimmings, also from M&S.

I smile to myself as Macaulay Culkin finally makes friends with the old guy who lost the favour of his family.

I'm astonished when my phone vibrates in my handbag. At first, I tell myself it's just a noise on the TV. It's nothing. Then I hear the noise again.

I pick my bag up off the floor by my feet and inspect the phone. Only Nate has the number of this phone.

Maybe it's just one of those things? Maybe a wrong number?

The screen says I have two new messages, which read:

Beatrice, Merry Christmas.

I'm just outside, by the way. I couldn't stay away.

There used to be only three people in the whole wide world who still called me Beatrice.

I doubt Nate is sending me these texts. I leap up and check the bedroom again anyway.

Nope, he's still fast asleep.

Another text comes through:

I'm by your boy's car. Come out and see me.

I gulp down my horror. *Your boy.* Familiar language.

I tiptoe to the front door, still determined not to wake Nate, and as I look through the decorative glass behind the door curtain, I spot a figure stood by the Ford Focus. It's a figure I know.

It's a figure that can't be real.

I'm imagining this.

My phone pings again.

It's me, Beatrice. It's not a hallucination.

It's him.

I fall to my knees, shaking all over, the phone slipping out of my hand.

Chapter Twenty-Five

I become hysterical in the moments after. Things start to whirr and spin. There's this echo around me, and noise, so much noise, and I don't know where it's coming from. There's the space I'm in and then there are three other versions of reality, all whirling around me, converging, spinning, trying to suck me into some sort of vortex above. Is this a panic attack? Or something else? Shock? What is going on? I'm trapped in my mind while my body shakes uncontrollably, cries of despair wracking my body.

I can feel hands on me. Nate's.

He's by my side, kneeling.

"Beatrice, Beatrice... what happened?"

I'm shaking all over.

"Beatrice, calm down! Speak to me."

I'm scared, so scared. How can this be?

"Outside... out there," I say, and manage to point, even though my hands are trembling, and I can barely extend my finger.

"What's out there?" Nate peers behind the curtain and I try to take a hold of myself.

I keep swallowing, and swallowing, bile rising in the back of my throat. I need to focus and breathe, but I can't.

"It looked like my father," I manage to say, and Nate's head whips around.

"What?"

"My father."

"There's nobody out there, Bebe. Nobody. Are you sure?"

I pick the phone up, but it drops from my jelly fingers and he takes the hint.

He looks through the messages.

"There was someone out there and he was a dead ringer for my father. I swear to God."

"Okay, all right," he says, and leaning down, he picks me up in his arms and takes me to the bedroom.

Nate tucks me in bed and strokes my hair. "Keep breathing, beautiful. Breathe."

I nod.

He leaves the room but comes back with whisky. I knock it back and vaguely watch as he gets dressed, pulling on clothes. He pulls on his running shoes and I start to question why. How could he leave me at a time like this? Is he intending to go outside and see if it was really my father? Doesn't he believe me? Has he a death wish? What?

There's something about this that isn't right. I mean aside from the fact that my father is seemingly walking and talking, why has he shown up at this ungodly hour, on Christmas Eve night?

Nate leaves the room for a moment and comes back with his winter coat added on top of his jeans, jumper and trainers.

"I'll be back as soon as I've checked outside, I promise. I'm just going to see if he's gone, okay? If he isn't, I'll ask him what he wants. I'll invite him in. Is that okay with you?"

"No, Nate." I'm shaking my head wildly. "Nate, don't go. I don't trust this. It doesn't feel right. Don't leave me. I'm frightened! I'm scared, baby. Don't leave me!" I scream.

He comes to the bed and rocks me in his arms as I cry, my head in my hands against his chest.

"Maybe he has some explanation, Bebe."

"Nate, I'll come with you. Please. Don't leave me on my own," I beg. "I'm telling you, I don't feel right. I can't explain this... I can't... but don't leave me in this house alone, not right now. Not after— How is— I don't understand!"

He takes my face in his big hands. "Bebe, you're going to go around and close all the curtains. You're going to lock the door and you're not going to open it unless I come back and ask you to, okay? You'll be safe."

"No, Nate, no!" I beg, swinging my arms around him and kissing him, even as tears roll down my cheeks and my nose runs. "Please, honey. Don't leave me. Stay."

"I have to know why, Beatrice. I have to know."

"I do too, but please Nate. You have to listen to me. Please. Something inside me, something terrible, is warning of something. You don't know what it's like being me. You don't know, okay? He raised me to know things. He raised me to see. I know that there is something terribly wrong with his appearance tonight, if indeed it was him. I know that this is all wrong Nate, and you can't go out there. This is a trap, believe me. It's a trap. You have to believe me, baby. Don't leave me. I can't live without you. Please, don't go now. In the morning. In the morning."

I cling to him tight. His face contorts. He's torn between going out there and finding out the truth, and staying in here with his crazed fiancée.

"Nate, in the morning, when it's light, we can track him. We can do it then."

"Beatrice, what is he going to do to me?"

I feel wide-eyed with terror. I must look a fright. "I don't know Nate, that's the thing. I don't know. It could be him, or there could be a dozen other people out there with him, making him do this. Something must have happened. Tonight. Maybe we were spotted at the market. Maybe our photo was taken when we weren't looking, I don't know. But they've found us. Whoever they are, they've found us, and they've chosen to arrive at this time of the night for a reason. They want to do this when every one of our neighbours down the road is out for the count, sleeping off their eggnog and all their treats from the market."

Nate looks like he's having a moment of clarity. "There were reporters there tonight, interviewing for the local news. We could have been photographed in passing. The crowds were thick, but... it's a possibility."

"Yes." I nod rapidly. "See. They've found us. And if you go out there, there's going to be hell. You can't leave without me, Nate. I won't let you go. I love you too much, don't leave me. You don't know my father like I do. If it is him, if he has survived this, then there's a reason—and it's most likely not a good one."

We both almost leap out of our skin as my phone pings again. Anxiety rides through my veins in a fresh wave and I can barely work my fingers on the screen. Nate takes the phone from me and I watch over his shoulder as a new message is revealed:

Let him out, Beatrice. Let him come to me.

"No, no, no, no, no," I'm screaming, as Nate stands, turns and looks at me, his face one of staunch resolve.

"Beatrice," he says, in a stern voice.

"NOOOOOOOOOO!!!" I scream.

"I'm coming back," he reminds me, "just lock the door after me. Set the alarms for the living areas. Close the curtains. Don't let anyone but me in, and if necessary, call the police. If the burglar alarm goes off, that will trigger their presence anyway."

All the way to the front door, I try to pull him backwards, but he's stronger than me. I try to wrap myself around his leg but he's having none of it.

"Beatrice, if I have to chain you to that bed, I will. Stop this. I'm only going out there to speak to your goddamn father."

"You're not listening to anything I'm saying!"

He raises his hand and holds his fist out angrily. It's the first time he's ever been angry with me. "You are the one *not* listening to me. We've waited months for answers, maybe now we'll get them."

I find myself on my knees, begging, the cold floor beneath me. I'm only wearing my robe.

"I swear, if you go out there, you'll die Nate. Don't ask me how I know, I just know. This is all wrong, it's just all wrong. You have to believe me. You have to stay with me. I know what I'm talking about. Stay with me and love me, that's all I'm asking."

He presses his lips together, still determined to take his own route. His jaw sets and he looks exasperated with me. He has his hand on the doorknob and begins turning it. That's when I start screaming, over and over, as loudly as I can. I shriek and I shriek, as if I'm being attacked. My throats burns and my lungs ache so badly, but I can't stop. I can't lose him.

Nate takes me over his shoulder and carries me in a fireman's lift towards the bedroom, shutting us both inside and locking the door.

"They will think I'm hurting you! Goddammit."

In the bedroom, I cling to him, hanging onto him like a small monkey to its mother.

Once I've calmed down and got my breath back, I ask, "Wait, wait."

When nothing happens, when nobody comes running to rescue me, I look him in the eye, "Whoever that is out there, it is not the father I knew. It could be him, but if it is, then that is not the man who I thought would storm a building to save me. That's the man who faked his own death because he's a bastard and he will kill you. That's the man who knows I never sleep well on Christmas Eve because I'm always too excited. That's the man who knows my habits inside and out. He's playing us. Just trust me. Trust my gut instinct."

My phone pings and we both look at it at the same time.

You'll have to come out sometime.

In the distance, we hear a car engine start and speed off down the narrow track that takes you down to the road at the end of our driveway.

Nate runs for the door before I can stop him. It's like my father's words are too much of an enticement, too goading for him to ignore. It's like there's something here I didn't know about—something between my father and Nate. Some history. Something.

I can't stop him. I can't catch up to him. His mind is set. By the time I make it to the open doorway, he's already in the car. He looks so blank, I can't read him at all, but I guess the urge to chase our enemy is greater than his urge to stay with me.

Nate starts the engine on the vehicle and my every sense is assaulted as a blast rings out.

Heat.
Fire.
Dust.
Whooshing.
Whistling.
Screeching.
High in the sky.
A ringing in my ears.
I'm knocked backwards, right off my feet.
I told you.

Chapter Twenty-Six

H*e's left me, he's left me.*
        Survival mode kicks in.

I crawl on my belly towards the bedroom.

The fire in the sky will soon attract attention, so I don't have long.

I have to go.

I make it to the bedroom and even though I'm numb and jellified all over, I find knickers and a bra. I pull them on. Woollen socks next. Two pairs. It's going to be a long night.

Undershirt. Jumper. A Hoodie on top. Jeans. Beanie.

I grab my rucksack and stuff my handbag inside it.

I can't even kiss him goodbye. He's being incinerated in the car. I can't even...

I can't think like that, not yet... I can't think. I have to act.

I have to escape. I have to know things. The only way I can know things is to stay free, to stay out of the way of interrogation, or capture. I can't get caught. Not by anyone.

I crawl on my hands and knees to the cloakroom.

Hiking boots.

I manage to loosely knot the laces. I can tighten them later.

I remove my sim card, wrap it in tissue and flush it down the loo. As I'm staring into the toilet bowl, vomit surges up my oesophagus and I puke for a good five minutes straight. After my

176

guts are evacuated, I throw the phone at the wall and it smashes. It was cheap. A crap model. Just a phone.

I don't need a phone anymore.

I don't need anyone.

I have me.

I'm the only one I can rely on.

I can't rely on anyone else.

I think of the ring I wrapped only a little while ago, sat there under the tree. His other gifts too...

A hole inside me begins to grow, rooting itself, a black nothingness. Swallowing me. Nothing left. No hope. No love. Nothing. But I have to know the truth. I have to know. *There's no time to cry, Beatrice.* There's no time to go and watch as the love of your life rises into the sky in ash. The ring under the tree never meeting its owner...

I dig into the cloak cupboard and pull out my winter coat, fastening it up tight.

Back in the bedroom I see his laptop, sat there charging on the nightstand. It may hold some answers. Perhaps I could find someone to hack it and tell me what it contains. I unplug it and shove it into my backpack. I throw it over my shoulders and I'm ready to go.

As I chase down the corridor to the other side of the house, I see there are already flashing blue lights heading this way.

I don't need anything but my money and my passports and myself. I have every single one of those things. So, that's it, right? I have to go. Nothing else. No... mementos of our time together. Not his ring... the one he'll never wear, not now...

I can't.

I can't even...

I leave the house through the patio doors out back, my whole body shaking. It feels like I'm leaving him behind and I'm having to force myself to make every move. How could he leave me when, even now, for me, it feels like hell just walking out of the door?

The icy cold blasts my face as I make it outdoors, awakening me. Reminding me.

I stop and think for a moment.

What would my father do?

What should I do?

My father will know I don't have a vehicle. He'll know I'm on foot. He'll be waiting for me to make my move. He'll want to speak with me, I know it. He'll want to twist words and make me see that he's innocent. When I know that he's not.

I need to be cleverer. I need to think outside the box. My father presumes me weak. I'm not. I'm strong. So far, I've defied him at every turn.

I make a decision. I need to stay close. Until I can make some other escape.

I see the hot tub to my side, the winter cover on. I slide it off and climb into the empty tub, pulling the cover back over, curling up into a foetal position. It's not a stormy night, it's calm, if cold. The cover won't blow off even though the toggle is not attached at the corner at the back, which nobody will notice unless they inspect it carefully, which they won't. Why would anyone imagine a girl like me hiding in a hot tub for the night? In the middle of winter?

Well, for starters, because I want to solve this whole damn farce.

And because unlike Nate, I don't leave the people I love.

I'm not ready to leave his side yet.

Chapter Twenty-Seven

The night is spent listening to people moving about inside the house, rifling through our belongings. Clothes and books; cupboards opened and closed; Swiss voices mumbling about how we were a private couple, never any trouble. Nobody among the police can understand why a car exploded, on Christmas Eve too. They find nothing with my name on it, nor anything with his name either. I'm still not sure if this house is in his name, or a fake one.

At around six in the morning I hear a tow truck taking what remains of the car away. About an hour later, there's silence. There may be a police officer standing guard out front—I can't be sure—but neither can I stay here a second longer. My legs are screaming for relief, to stretch and flex. I need to straighten my neck and get out of here. I need to go somewhere and regroup.

My head pounds as I start to move around. I feel truly drained. I don't have much energy. I need a vehicle to get down the hillside because I won't make it on foot. I need to get to the rail station and then the airport. Or maybe I should avoid those altogether.

So, okay, I just need a vehicle.

What would Nate do? Throw money at the situation, probably.

If there's no other way... then I will have to get down the mountain on foot. Unseen, too.

Quietly, I slide the corner of the cover off the hot tub, peeping my head out and sensing the same damp air I've been breathing in all night, the sort of air that's kept me awake and chilled to the bone, so that I'm now completely exhausted.

I have to use my arms to haul myself from the tub and it's an effort. I get myself standing by the tub and wait a few minutes for all the blood to start circulating properly again, pins and needles wracking my limbs.

After a few deep breaths, I test the patio door. It's open.

I walk into the house and discover chaos. They've tipped everything upside down in their bid to discover more about the former occupant(s). I reach behind me and into my backpack for the small handgun Nate bought me a couple of months ago. It's a simple gun, easy to use. I stalk through the house and hear nobody else, but I can tell the front door is open because there's a draught. Someone must be standing guard out front.

I stalk towards the Christmas tree, which has been treated with more reverence than the rest of the house. Still, all the presents have been ripped open and there's the tag lying on the floor that I wrote last night. I can barely breathe as I bend to pick it up.

Where's the ring?

I search around my feet and it's nowhere to be seen. Someone's probably taken it. They didn't think I'd be coming back. I take the tag and nothing else. I can see from the nonsense strewn around the floor that most of Nate's presents to me were lingerie and chocolates. He'd already got me everything I needed for my birthday. I open the pantry door as quietly as I can and start packing my backpack with as many supplies as possible. Then I prepare to leave this beautiful house and all my happy memories behind. It was always too good to be true, wasn't it? It was the way we met. There are still questions I have about the way he and I met. Questions I still need answered. He's a part of this thing with my father and I need to know more.

With the gun held out in front of me, I approach the doorway cautiously. As I get closer, I sense someone outside. A lone figure, keeping guard, as I imagined. Just your ordinary Swiss guard. I won't kill him, but I won't let him take me either.

I wait until he makes a move, crossing the porch in front of the door, doing his standard march to keep his legs warm. As he makes a second pass, I throw my leg at his head and knock him out.

After he's on the floor, I check for a pulse. He's going to be okay.

I drag him inside the house and grab the duct tape from the kitchen drawer. I tie his wrists and then his ankles, and I hoist all his limbs together and hog-tie him. Then as he starts to come around, I clock him once again and put tape over his mouth.

I peer outside the front door, edging my way onto the porch. There's nobody else around. The policeman has a car parked by the hedge, well out of the way, so anybody approaching wouldn't see it. I go back to him and rummage his pockets for the keys. *Bingo.*

I chase to the car, going around the cinders left behind, jumping straight into the vehicle.

I hit the gas and speed off down the lane towards the road, trying to calm myself down.

It's okay, I'm just stealing a police car. I just hog-tied a freaking officer of the law. I laugh manically because if I didn't, I'd cry.

I take the vehicle down the lane and thankfully encounter nobody as I do. I pull onto the road and head towards town. I need to dump this car as soon as possible.

I head for the nearest parking bay and leave it. I don't need it anymore.

What next?

It's Christmas day and I need to leave this place.

I need to escape.

I look around me on the street and don't see anyone following me. That's not to say there won't be anyone. They have eyes in the sky.

I look up and don't see a satellite shimmering above my head, but I don't know, do I? I don't know a thing.

I need a car. Any car. I can't get out of here without one. It's not like the showrooms will be open today, not even for someone with as much money as me.

I start walking down the promenade, hoping an idea will present itself.

Maybe I should go back for the cop car? Stupid idea.

I keep walking and walking, until it feels like I might walk right out of town and right into the middle of nowhere.

I hear a truck heading my way and I have an idea. I hold my thumb out and he whooshes right past, but then stops.

I run towards the vehicle and he winds his window down.

"English?" he asks in a Polish accent. I nod. "Where you want to go?"

"Out of Switzerland... I don't know. I'm backpacking."

"On Christmas day?"

"I'm... Jewish? Plus, I have money."

He looks at me suspiciously. I don't have a very big backpack, after all.

"I'm going to Paris. Any good?"

"Perfect!"

I hop into his truck, trying to mask my disgust at the combined smell of farts and cheesy crisps.

And just like that, I'm free again.

Chapter Twenty-Eight

We reach Paris very late at night, though it's not proper Paris, but the outskirts. The truck driver is stopping at a huge distribution centre up ahead, before going off on another adventure of his own. I've listened to him talking about his six kids and his ex-wife, his current wife, and this woman who wishes she were his wife (the woman must be a lunatic, much like all of those women in 'Allo 'Allo, always after René). I've been nothing but polite, nodding along, gasping, "Never," or "You're joking," or, "Poor, poor you!" I haven't told him a thing about me because that's too dangerous and anyway, I'm in survival mode and I don't have time to process what's happened—not just yet.

I'm dropped near Charles de Gaulle where I'm told there will surely be a hotel for the night. I'm half tempted to go straight to the airport and buy any ticket I can get, but I feel sick and tired right now and if I were questioned prior to boarding an international flight, I might not answer very well.

I walk into your usual budget hotel, cheap and cheerful and no-nonsense. I check in using one of my many fake passports and pay in cash.

In the room, I'm desperate to get rid of the smell of that truck and I dive straight for the shower, in dire need of getting clean.

I realise as I'm washing that I'm also washing the last of Nate from my body—and I hate it.

I hate that his scent on my skin is disappearing, that his kisses against my throat are lost. I love him so much. How bitter the reality is: to have love snatched from you when it's in its prime.

I sit on the edge of the bed in my towel, watching planes taking off and landing out of the window. You wouldn't think it's Christmas day.

I open my rucksack and tip some whisky down my throat before smashing open a box of pretzels. Even as I eat them, salty tears stain my cheeks, but I have nothing else to eat, just what snacks I quickly gathered this morning.

When it becomes too much, and when the pain is unbearable, I roll into a ball and sob into my hands. My Nate. My love. My life. Now that I'm away from Montreux, I'm desperate to be back. I'm missing it unbearably. I fell in love there, with him, and with the life we were beginning to establish together.

I cry endlessly, thinking I'll never feel his arms around me again. I'll never feel any of those feelings—ever again. It's too much to bear.

When a knock comes on the door, I'm surprised. I know the walls are thin in these hotels, but I've kept it down, crying into my hands.

Feeling terrified, I wait. The knock comes again, soft this time.

I swallow thickly and pad quietly towards the door. Could it be my dad? At the peephole, I stare through.

When I see who it is, I stagger back—terrified.

Only the thing is, I want it to be true—and I want to know for sure.

I swing open the door and Nate rushes at me. He throws his arms around me and crushes me against his body. He smells the same. Maybe this is true. Maybe...

The door slams shut and he drops all his things before kissing any breath I had left away, so I can't breathe at all. My towel falls and he sucks my breast into his mouth.

"I'm sorry, Bebe. I'm so sorry. Forgive me," he begs, as he madly rushes kisses all over my skin. "I'm sorry. I'm sorry. Forgive me. Forgive me, Bebe. I love you so much."

I slap his face hard and gasp, horrified. After I realise I'm naked and there's not as much privacy here as there was in Switzerland, I slam the curtains shut and throw back the bedcovers.

"God, I thought you'd gone. Come to me. Please, right now."

I lie back and open my legs wide. He quickly sheds his clothes and climbs between my invitation.

He enters me in a hurry and I cry out in pain and longing. I squeeze myself around every inch of him I can hold, kissing him wildly, our tongues out of control. We hold one another so tight and I beg, "Harder! Harder!"

"Bebe, I'm so sorry, forgive me!"

"Harder, I need to feel you, I need to know you're real."

I'm not crying anymore, but he is. He's sobbing in my arms as I lick his throat and inhale him deeply; scrape his skin under my nails; absorb his fluids into my body. I need to lace him around me and lock him tight inside me. I need him buried within me, always.

He fucks me until I see spots, until our neighbours will be in no doubt of what we're doing in the bedroom next door.

I scream, in agony, as he pours into me and holds onto my breasts so tight at the same time, his hair mangled in my tight grasp.

My chest heaves up and down as he rests his cheek on my breasts.

"I realised it was a hologram, Bebe," he says, puffing and panting, "your father. It was a hologram. They were trying to coax us out. When I realised it was *them*, I knew I had to act. To take myself out of the equation. It was me they were after. Me."

"My father's not alive?"

"No baby, how could he be? They're just fucking with us."

"How did you find me?"

"My laptop, you took it. Clever girl. I knew you'd do fine. I knew it. My clever girl."

He lifts his head and kisses me all over my face, my neck, desperate to show me how much he loves me.

"Oh god, Nate. Oh god. I couldn't have lived without you. I couldn't have lived," I gasp, as he licks wildly at my throat. "All I wanted was answers. I wanted answers. I wanted to know why. Why. After I got the answers, I couldn't have lived. I'd have gone right back to how it was before."

"I know angel, I know," he says, brushing his nose along mine and sinking back inside me again, our bodies one, our kisses softer and more tender, more sensual this time.

I slide my hands all over him. "I love you, Nate. I love you. Don't you do this to me, ever again. You hear me?"

"I hear you. I love you so much. I love you." He clings to me hard and weeps with me as we make love.

Chapter Twenty-Nine

S o, I've gathered what really happened. The Ford Focus he had was a uniquely upgraded car, programmed with special features, one of which was a hologram in the driver's seat. Nate used it that night and when I thought I saw him in the driver's seat, it wasn't actually him.

Nate knows the tactics of the Collective and he knew that one day, they might try to use the car to blow him sky high.

He used the remote ignition key to start the engine and of course, that triggered the explosion.

After the car went up in flames as predicted, Nate did a runner down the mountainside to make it look like he'd been killed—see if that couldn't satisfy the Collective's bloodlust.

He thought I would do the same—chase down the hillside. However, I had a different tactic and when he realised I wasn't coming, he went into the woods near our house and picked up the emergency kit he had buried there. He spent the night in a tent in the woods and intended to find me the next day. When he saw his laptop was on the move from the tracker he had embedded in it, he went to a car dealership, rang the number and told them if they wanted to sell him a car today, he would pay double the asking price. They opened the shop especially for him. I should've thought of that.

Nate tracked me all the way to Paris and here we are, still wrapped up in each other's arms. I have never been so grateful in my whole life to be alive. I can't take my hands off him. I won't ever let go. Not ever again. I can't. Not after all this.

Never.

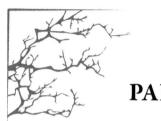

PART TWO

MARRIED IN TEXAS

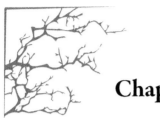

Chapter Thirty

Six months later...

"It is now my honour and privilege to pronounce you husband and wife. You may kiss your bride," the courthouse official announces, and Nate draws me towards him and kisses my mouth, embracing me. My hands rest on his chest and I allow him to envelop and kiss me deeply. He moans his approval and then pulls back.

"Goddamn, I'm a lucky guy," he states, his smile so wide.

"I'm the lucky one."

Oh man, he's gorgeous. We're in Texas so he's wearing a cornflower three-piece suit, white shirt, pencil-thin cream tie and matching pocket square. His body fills his outfit cleanly and his hair is golden from all the sunshine. His eyes are piercing and make me weak at the knees.

It's only a courthouse wedding but I decided to wear a big dress anyway. I found a website selling failed garments and I picked up an Oscar de le Renta for cheap. Not because I'm cash-strapped, but because a discounted dress by the great Oscar was never going to arouse much suspicion. If I went to his people direct for a wedding dress—Annalise, the model, that is—I'd certainly never escape being photographed, or something. Anyway, it's champagne in colour, just beautiful. It has floral appliqué around the bust and so many ruched layers that the dress weighs a whopping amount. The only fault I could find was that the patterns didn't quite match up at the back, but that doesn't bother me, nor Nate. He couldn't care less.

Nate leads me out of the courthouse with a bright beaming smile and directs me towards the exit. His mother and his ranch manager Eric follow behind us and we exit to no fanfare whatsoever. I'm not surprised when he doesn't allow his mother to congratulate him. Her presence is more of a formality, I guess.

Once we're out of the courthouse, his mother shouts after us, "Let me take a damn photograph!"

Nate tenses beside me; I can feel it in his fingers and in his tight smile as we pose for a photograph, which she takes on her phone. I'm not entirely sure how her pictures will turn out.

Eric, who's a little more sober, takes some on his phone too.

Eric's ten years older than Nate and basically takes care of the ranch full-time. Nate bought the ranch and his mother lives in the main house free of charge. Eric manages the place, but Nate owns it outright.

It's June now but we came back to Texas in January. He ventured home first and I followed him, after he knew it was safe.

I don't know how, but I've taken my life back. I'm no longer on the run. Nate says that we're safe now, that our enemies won't bother with us anymore. A part of me wonders how the threat we once lived under is now suddenly gone. A part of me just wants to grab this happiness while we still have it. We're going straight, or at least I think we are. I don't want to ever repeat that night when I thought he was dead. I don't even want to think about how I felt that night, so I'm embracing every minute I get to be with him, and now I'm his wife, I couldn't be happier.

We jump into the back of a chauffeur-driven 1960s Rolls Royce he has hired especially for the day. His mother and Eric throw cheap confetti at the windshield as we pull away.

"Now we can relax," he says, as we drive away from the stately courthouse of Del Rio and head out of town.

Ever since we've been in his home state, I've had to behave a certain way around his mother. I've been warned never to ask Claire-Anne about Nate's father. I've been asked never to mention her drinking. I've also been told to go along with whatever she says, and also to keep up the ruse of me being Annalise.

Around his mother, Nate calls me Bebe, but he says it's just a cute nickname.

On the backseat, he holds me close as I rest my legs across his lap. We start kissing and I don't want to stop. The taste of him makes me hungry for all of him and even as he begins to slide his hand up my stockinged leg, edging towards my panties underneath, I push him away, smiling as I do.

"Later, husband."

He groans his annoyance, but I flick my eyes in the direction of our driver, who would see everything, it being an old-fashioned car and all.

I hold my left hand on top of his and admire our matching platinum wedding rings.

"I've never seen anything sexier than a wedding ring on you," I tell him.

"The sexiest thing for me right now would be you, stripped naked already. Wearing only your rings."

I bring his palm up to my lips and kiss it, then place his hand over my cheek, my eyes shut as I rest my head on his shoulder—completely in love, never happier.

"Soon, my love," I coo, "soon," I promise, and he grumbles as he wraps me tight in his arms.

It's not long before we're out in the countryside, the vast landscape whooshing by us. The driver is taking us straight to the nearest airport and then we're flying to Hawaii.

I'm glad I didn't have a big wedding. It would upset me if I had to think about what my mother and sister have missed out on. This way, it's simple. I've married the man I love and that's all that matters. Nothing else does. Not table settings, not menu choices, bridesmaid dresses or music or drawing up a gift list. No, this way I get exactly what I want: him.

I SHOULD'VE GUESSED when he said we were flying from a local airport—he's hired a private jet for us. When he helps me out of the Rolls, I recognise that look in his eye as he smiles and takes my hand. He wants us to consummate as soon as possible.

After we've boarded the jet, we have to take our seats for take-off, but Nate asks the air stewardess, "May my wife change in the bedroom? She hardly wants to arrive in her bridal gown."

"As soon as the seatbelt light switches off. If you wish, I'll vacate the cabin and give you two privacy."

"Thank you," I tell her, shaking my head at Mr Prim and Proper, who doesn't want to admit he hired this jet just to join the mile-high club.

"You are so transparent, Buchanan."

"I'm was just trying to be a gentleman."

"You're so sweet." I turn and kiss him as we make our way towards the runway, the small jet bouncing along the tarmac.

The lady returns with menus for us, handing them out. "If you'd like anything, perhaps Mr Buchanan might write a list and I'll prepare you something, say... in an hour?"

I love the way her nose wrinkles, trying to be polite.

"Make it two," Nate almost growls. "I'll leave ticks next to what we want, and leave them on our seats."

"Very good, Mr Buchanan. You'll find there's already champagne and strawberries in the bedroom. Please be careful when popping your cork, if there's turbulence I mean."

She swiftly turns on her heel and I have to hide my sniggers against his lapel.

I look up and see the huge grin in his eyes. I think it's even funnier because the stewardess is British, so it sounds like we've just dropped in on a James Bond movie set or something.

"You British..."

"Aren't we disgraceful?" I ask, nibbling his ear as the airplane judders, picking up speed.

"Terrible," he murmurs, turning and kissing me hungrily as we take off, climbing high into the sky.

Once the plane levels off, he puts his hand under my dress and I spread my legs in readiness. He presses his thumb over my clit, my knickers already drenched. He takes his hand away and sniffs his thumb, growling, making me sniff it too.

I'm more than ready for him. He could bend me over right now and I wouldn't complain, if only it weren't for the other people on the plane and the seatbelt light still being on.

"When that light goes off Beatrice, you're going to visit the bedroom and get out of this dress. You'll be spread naked, ready for me when I walk in."

I shake my head. "No can do. It has hooks. I need some help."

He frowns. "Way to ruin my big bad wolf routine."

"Hey, just unhook me and we can still do that."

He presses his lips to my throat and I run my hands through his hair, tipping my head backwards.

"I love you," I groan.

The seatbelt light goes off and we look at one another. It's almost like we can't believe that we finally have the freedom to make love as man and wife. But we do.

"Unhook me here and I'll go get ready for you."

"Sure?"

"Sure."

I sit on his lap and feel his erection brush my backside as he unhooks the full length of my fastenings, then pulls down the zip underneath, his fingers moving slower than slow.

Nate kisses my back and whispers against my skin, "I'll be there in two minutes."

"You better be."

Chapter Thirty-One

I'm on the bed, my hands above my head, my body stretched out for him. He walks into the room, quickly closing and locking the door behind him.

Blood rushes into his face and he looks mad with lust when he sees me, wearing only my rings—oh, and my wedding stockings, the ones with extra big white bows on the garters.

"I want to see you play with yourself. No self-administered orgasms," he demands, as he stands by the foot of the bed, worrying his lip and watching with an urgent desire to see me touch myself.

I bring my heels up to the backs of my thighs and spread myself for him, barely a whisper of my fingertip down there, in case I come without him.

Nate angrily unknots his tie and throws it to the floor. We have a change of outfit in the overhead lockers out in the cabin, but god knows which of us will be going out there later to retrieve our other clothes.

"Harder, Beatrice," he demands, as he shrugs out of his jacket and tosses it towards a chair in the corner.

"I can't. I'll come."

"Harder," he demands.

"Nate, I'll come," I plead.

"I said, harder, Beatrice. Are you going to defy me?"

"Baby, no, I'll never defy you."

I press my finger harder to my clit and my back arches, knowing he's watching me, knowing he wants to see me—just like this.

I increase my ministrations, but not enough to make me come.

My back begins to stick to the bedcovers and I open my eyes to see Nate finally has his shirt off. He recently stopped shaving his chest and now it's covered with hair... I can't even put words together to describe how much I love his chest hair. The thought of it makes me want to...

I snatch my hand away, pressing my lips together, desperate to control myself.

Nate is working open his pants and spots that I've stopped.

"Beatrice, I told you..."

"No, I won't touch it again. I'll come and I don't want to, not without you."

"You must resist. Touch yourself and resist."

"I can't resist."

"You must."

"I can't."

"Lucky for you, I'm ready for you now, anyway."

He crawls up the bed and covers my body with his.

I give him a dirty laugh as he licks the finger I was just using to play with myself.

It's been filthy like this ever since that night in Paris, when he showed up after I thought he was dead. I don't know why the dynamic changed that night, but it did. He's changed, too. Something happened that night I'm still not sure of, but he's a lot more open about what he wants from me sexually these days—and I'm totally into it.

"Wrap those fucking stockings around my butt," he says, and when I do, he grins and runs one hand along my leg, grunting.

I impatiently wait for his next instruction.

"Take me," he says, while kissing my nipple.

I wrap my fingers around his length and guide him towards me. I can already feel my walls pulsing, my entrance opening and closing, my body constantly on the edge of orgasm.

As he enters me, it's unbearable.

"Oooh, oh, oh," I cry, unable to help it.

Nate takes both of my hands in his and holds them above my head. He tips deep inside me and halts, as I wait on the precipice, my pelvis gripping him tight.

He licks my throat and between my breasts as he makes me wait for his body to pleasure mine.

I hear a little snicker break loose of his throat, right near my ear, and then he pulls out slowly, oh so slowly, before ramming into me hard.

Waves of pleasure cascade up and down my body, waiting for more—for everything.

"Beg me for it, baby," he asks.

"I need to come, Nate. Please. I need you."

"Say it, Bebe. Say. It."

"I need your cock to make me come. Please. Please."

"No. Say it, baby," he begs, panting against my chest, because his need is just as great as mine, if not greater.

"I need your cum inside me. I need you inside me, baby. Deep, deep inside my body."

I'm quickly flipped over and brought onto all fours. He grunts as he enters me from behind.

The power of his body always astounds me. It shouldn't anymore, but it still does. He's fucking me into oblivion.

Since arriving in Texas, I've watched him throw around big bags of grain and huge bales of hay like they weigh nothing more than a feather pillow. He's powerful and I love how safe he makes me feel—except at times like this—when I feel like I might murder him if he doesn't make me come soon.

His chest sticks to my back as he rests his weight partially on top of my body. He strokes long and deep, so deep I have to keep breathing heavily to take him like this.

When he reaches underneath me and strokes my clit with such tenderness, such delicate touch, I can hardly bear it and my shoulders flop down onto the bed, raising my ass higher, giving him all of me.

As I begin milking him, I realise my cries of passion will surely be overheard, but I can't help it—this is too good. He takes his hand away but holds my hips, savagely thrusting through my contractions and making me spurt everywhere.

"Uh, uh, uh," he cries, louder than usual.

He doesn't withdraw immediately, he works us down, and even after he's worked us down, he stays within me and turns me gently until we're spooning on the bed. He holds me around my belly and drenches my arms, throat and shoulders in kisses. I know he wants a baby as much as I do, but I want one so that I always have him with me. I think he wants one because it's the last thing I can do to prove I love him. I've come to realise it's hard for him to believe my love sometimes. I've already forgiven him for not believing me. I've forgiven him because of Claire-Anne... because of the things he won't tell me. I just know he's experienced a lot of hurt in his life and it only makes me love him even more. It's just an instinct I have. It's never said.

I turn my head and he leans over and kisses me. His tongue does wicked things to me and before I know it, we're gently writhing together, our legs and arms entwined, our minds lost to this undeniable sexual energy between us.

"I'm so in love with you," I gasp, holding onto his buttock as I near orgasm again.

"I love you more," he growls, squeezing my breasts in his tight fists, his body lord and master over mine.

Chapter Thirty-Two

The flight, plus all the lovemaking we've done since we arrived in Honolulu have tired me out, but for some reason I'm still wide awake. Maybe it's the excitement of the day, I don't know. Maybe I'm overtired. I can't keep watching Nate sleep so I leave the bed and knot a flimsy robe at my waist, padding over the cool, tiled floors and towards the kitchen, which is down the corridor from our bedroom. Nate's rented a house for us on Waimanalo Beach and it's gorgeous here. Earlier, I dug my toes into some of the whitest sand I've ever seen.

I pour some milk into a mug and put it into the microwave. Never will I heat up milk in a pan, not ever again.

I take my warm milk out onto the decking and sit and watch the night sky. There are a billion stars up there and I feel uninhibited here. You can see satellites skimming the night. You can see everything. Constellations. Shooting stars. You wouldn't think so many stars existed.

It's beautiful in Honolulu. Clean. Free. Unpolluted. I feel like I could stay here forever.

The house is typical Hawaiian style, very rustic and homely, but beautiful nonetheless. We have someone who comes and cooks our meals and we don't have to do anything else much.

So, why then am I still finding it hard to sleep?

It's been like this ever since the night I thought Nate had died. Sometimes I do manage to sleep, but that's usually after a lot of whisky. Something tells me we haven't managed to fall pregnant yet because of my sleeping problems.

Nate has suggested I try sleeping pills, but I don't want to become reliant on them. I'd rather seek homeopathic methods. Anyway, if I did fall pregnant, I wouldn't be able to take medication after that.

A sigh leaves me, long and laboured, not the sigh of a young woman who just married a beautiful, intelligent man, and certainly not the sigh of someone who's honeymooning in paradise.

Maybe I know what my problem is, but maybe I just can't admit it.

Chapter Thirty-Three

The next day, we're swimming in the sea together and he can tell I'm tired. It's like my mind races at night, but during the day it all catches up with me. It's not just the time difference, either.

"Let's go back to the house," he says, and I hang onto his shoulders as he swims us back to shore.

I'd love to stay out in the blazing sun and swim all day, but I'm exhausted.

It only takes us a few minutes to get back to the house and by the time we're back, I'm all dried off again. In the bedroom, I strip out of my black bikini and leave it on the tiled floor. Nate shakes his head at me as he picks it up and throws it towards the laundry hamper.

I crawl into bed and Nate pushes down his shorts and crawls in with me.

"Are you tired too?"

"A little," he says, "but I just don't want to spend a moment apart."

His declaration of how much I mean to him touches my heart.

I roll into his arms and our cool bodies touch, but we soon begin to warm through with the contact.

"I could give you an orgasm. It might help you sleep."

"I've had lots of those, and still... I don't sleep."

"It couldn't harm, though."

"Go on then, but I may taste of the sea."

He grins. "Even better."

I MANAGE TO SLEEP FOR about an hour, before I'm woken abruptly from a nightmare I don't want to live anymore. It's the image of my father, standing there like a ghost. It terrifies me.

That night has played on a loop ever since—haunting me—following me like a shadow.

I know Nate said it was a hologram, used by the Collective to fuck with my head, but it's left doubt inside my mind. Is my father really dead?

Nate's here to cuddle me, murmuring, "Another nightmare?"

"Yeah," I mumble.

He holds me even though I'm clammy and I could do with a shower.

Everything that happened last year hasn't left me and I'm not sure I will ever get over any of it.

"I'm here," he barely whispers, his arms tight around my shoulders.

He *is* here. I can feel his body surrounding mine, his strong arms and thick thighs, delicately muscular calves and big feet. He's kissing my throat, his long neck stretching to reach mine. I have my hand reaching back to stroke my fingers through his silky mane of golden hair. His hands are bliss and his lips are better. I can feel he's here and what's between his legs is heavenly.

He's everything a woman could ever want in a man—tender, sexy and kind.

But there are still parts of him I'm missing. Parts buried deep inside.

Even as he begins making love to me, I have a question on my lips. A big, burgeoning question:

What happened to his mother?

Chapter Thirty-Four

It's on our last day of the honeymoon that I realise I'm a couple of days late for my period. I'm never late. It's as I think about it more and more, I can't deny what I'm feeling any longer. If we're to bring a child into the world, then there are things that need clearing up.

He's packing our cases, ready to go, when I circle the bed and stand and stare at him.

I realise as I'm leering at my own husband that I'd rather not argue with him—not here, not now. I don't want to do this now. I'd rather ask him to come and hug me.

"Nathan, leave it and come and give me a kiss."

He looks up at me, as I stand by the bed naked. He doesn't hesitate. He comes and kisses me.

In just his shorts, he takes me in his arms and wraps me in his love, kissing and holding me close, his love unquestionable. He does that little groan in his throat I love and his arms feel warm and strong, comforting me.

"I might need to buy a pregnancy test when we get home. It's a possibility," I reveal, between little pecks of his mouth.

The biggest grin lights up his face, the twinkle in his eyes blinding me.

He hugs me so hard, so tight, I can't breathe. I'm pulled up onto him, my legs around his waist.

"Oh god, Bebe. I pray it's true, I pray it's true!"

I breathe in the scent of his neck and kiss his strong muscles, feeling his throat twitch beneath my touch as he gasps on air.

"I love you so much, Nate."

"Me too. I want this, more than you'll ever know."

When I see a tear in his eye, a part of me thinks my only job in life now is to love him and care for him; be here for him and bear his children, surround him in comfort and safety.

His mother's an alcoholic, and I didn't know until we arrived in Texas. I didn't know the extent of it. I still don't.

What I do know is that it's bound to have affected him, but he won't say. He won't tell me how much it hurts, but I know it does. So, my job is to love this man as fiercely and as passionately as I can.

Because I really do love him.

"Let's stay another week," he says, walking backwards until the bed catches us, so I'm sat in his lap with my legs around his back.

"Can we do that?"

"We can do anything, you and I," he says, and I swing my arms even tighter around him.

"I wouldn't say no! Oh, really?"

"Yeah, I'll make it happen."

"Hmm, but... we don't know... we can't be sure, Nate." I keep my arms tight around his neck, needing his chest against my own. "Let's not celebrate until we know."

"I don't need to know, I just know," he says. "I know you're going to have my baby. Okay, perhaps not now... I mean, hopefully now, yes to now, but even if it's a false alarm and isn't now, I know that one day we will have a baby and for me, that's enough.

It's enough that I want to lock you inside my arms for just one more week, before we go back to the real world again. Okay?"

"Okay."

I hold his head tight to my chest, my arms wrapped around his hair. I know what he wants next because his breathing changes, and his hands are groping my bottom and not holding my back. I'm not sure I want sex, though. Not the sex we've been having anyway...

"Nate..."

"Uh-huh..."

He's trying to get out of my tight embrace so he can kiss me, suck me... but I hold onto him, not letting go.

"It's all been so tortured since Paris... I don't want it to be like this anymore."

His head flies back so he can study me, and what I see in his eyes takes me aback.

He's suspicious.

"What are you saying?" he asks, and behind the suspicion, I see fear—and doubt.

I need to erode all that.

"I want it to be like it was in the beginning, when we'd just lie cuddling and kissing for hours on end, when it was tender and gentle and soft, when holding hands was enough and sitting on a mountainside with our arms around one another was beautiful. It still can be like that. We can go back to basics. It doesn't always have to be tortured like this."

He looks down at his lap and tucks his lips inside his mouth, rampantly biting them—a habit he has, when he's nervous.

"I just thought this was what you wanted. You wanted me to be so rough that night and I was and it was... you liked it so much, and so did I..."

I take his cheeks in my hands and make him look up at me. "Nate, it was a situation of extreme emotion. I thought you were dead, baby. I thought the love of my life was dead. I needed to know you weren't dead anymore. That's all. I don't need freaky stuff... I mean, I'm not complaining, I'm really not. I'll take you any way I can get you, but in the beginning, it was just so tender and I really want that again. If I'm going to have your baby, I want us to be gentle and tender once more."

"In case we hurt it, you mean?" There's a flicker of light back in his eyes now, as he begins to understand.

"There's that, but no. I'm asking for that tenderness back because I need it, because this might change us, and we need to be strong. We need to be close and I don't want anything between us anymore. I need you to let me in. I need to be right here, with you. Just you. No games. No wild sex. Just you and me and our babies."

He runs his hands up and down my back and looks up at me as if he's worshipping a deity.

"You just don't know how much I love you," he says. "You don't know. I'd do anything for you."

I lean in and kiss him, but it becomes passionate very quickly, and I have to pull back because I have more to say.

"Nate..."

"Oh, what now?" he asks, impatient.

I chuckle. "Nate, you have to let me in."

I must be feeling braver today than I imagined earlier.

"You have to give me time," he asks, tugging me closer, our noses brushing. "You have to let me tell you in my own time."

I nod, and I can't help it, but my lip trembles.

"Bebe, no..."

"I'm sorry."

"There is nothing you will ever have to be sorry for. I will love you no matter what."

I rest my cheek on his shoulder and weep a few little tears. He strokes his hands up and down my sides and I can tell behind his concern, his mad passion is still simmering, still needy.

Maybe a part of me enjoys making him wait.

"Answer me one thing," I ask, my lips pressed to his throat as I speak.

"I'll try."

"Were there others? Before me, I mean. Lovers? Women? Anyone?"

Eric, the ranch manager, once told me that Nate never brought a girl home before me.

I wait on tenterhooks for his answer.

I'm desperate to have it confirmed: what I think to be true.

"No," he whispers.

"Okay," I reply, shaking, because his confirmation means he's only ever loved me, and I've only ever loved him.

I take my time kissing his shoulder, my fingertips tracing where I kiss. My touch against his skin makes him relax and his breaths become deeper, more even. I kiss along his collarbone and his sternum, loving him. I dig my fingers into his hair as I kiss and lick his throat, tasting sweat and the salt of the sea, from when he went swimming this morning.

Beneath me, Nate unzips his shorts and lifts slightly to tug them away.

We move so we are sitting up in the centre of the bed, his legs crossed, mine still wrapped around his back.

Our mouths brush and my heart soars, my stomach tips upside down and every inch of me belongs to him, that's all I know.

I hold his face in my hands as he wraps his arms tight around my back, holding me close. Our kisses are deep and tender, tongues caressing, teasing. I can feel how heavily he's breathing as his breath skates across my upper lip, his nostrils working hard to take in oxygen.

He yanks his face away to catch his breath and stares into my eyes.

"Do you know what you do to me, Beatrice? I can smell every scent of you. The scent of your nipples. Did you know they have a scent? Musky and sweet. You're perfect." He leans in and surrounds himself with my breasts, his head buried between them. He groans loudly as he finally sucks on first my left breast, then the right, drawing me deep into his mouth.

"They already taste and smell different. You're having my baby, Beatrice. My baby."

He tips me backwards onto the bed and I lie beneath him, his long, lean body stretched out over mine. I bring my legs up, wrapping them around his sides, hugging his body to mine.

Nate holds me and kisses me, eventually slipping into me.

I watch his eyes as he makes love to me, as he watches mine.

"I love you," I groan.

He kisses my mouth tenderly, as though to ingest my words, and I hold his hair and the gorgeous nape of his neck as he rocks into me, slowly and without hurry.

"You don't know how much I love you," he repeats.

"I do. I know. I can already feel you inside me. It's the greatest love I'll ever carry, holding your lifeforce inside of me."

Nate buries his face against my neck and shoulder, but I feel his tears as he cries, his gasps against my skin.

"Oh, baby," I groan, as his thrusts become clumsier and my thighs start to shake. "Baby."

He shows me his wrecked heart when he lifts up and displays tears, pouring from his red, bloodshot eyes. He tries to blink fast to get rid of them, but they keep coming. I hold my legs tighter around him and bring his palm up to my cheek. I shut my eyes and revel in the touch of his hand to my face. I turn my mouth and kiss the inside of his palm.

"Oh, Nate. I'm here, baby. I'm all yours."

He wraps his arms underneath me and we rock together as we kiss, deeply sometimes, then playfully, a little brushing of lips, then deeply again.

As my pleasure grows, I let go of all my worries and fears. I let them die.

Nate has never been with another woman. He's only ever been with me. I know that there's truth in that. I know that he was traumatised at some point, but that our love overcame whatever it was that had happened to him. I know that our love is undeniable because he's risked everything to be with me.

I cling to him as he grows thicker inside me. His kisses have less rhythm and he closes his eyes, our mouths brushing but nothing more, as we both pant heavily.

I cry out, my orgasm growing, the heat and the powerful milking of my core making him shake in my arms. He growls against my shoulder and does that thing he does, when he lets his first spurt pump deep into me, holding himself there, before slowly and tenderly emptying the rest of his cum into my body.

He rolls to his side afterwards and I pull his head onto my chest, throwing my leg over his body, clutching his mid-to-lower back. I feel cold as my sweat dries, but soon it's gone, and the sea air brushing through the room warms us again.

"Do you think I'm pathetic?" he asks.

"I love you more than I thought I could ever love another living thing. I love you more every single day. I love the way you hurt, the way you cry. I love the way you smile. I love the way you look when you wake up and see me. I love it when you try so hard to make sure everything is perfect, even when perfect is not what I want. I just want you so much. Just you."

He bursts into tears and I hold him close, hushing him as he cries, but at the same time encouraging his tears.

"It's all right, baby," I whisper, and he cries some more.

Suddenly it all seems so clear.

Love is the answer, it always has been.

Chapter Thirty-Five

Three months later...

One thing I never realised was how big the world really is. In Texas, it's become apparent to me just how big. The land Nate owns is hundreds of acres but then there's all the wild surrounding the sprawling farmland.

Growing up in the UK, you think you know what big is. You think standing on a Scottish mountain that you've finally discovered big. You haven't. Until now, living in Texas, I didn't know what big meant. I now understand why Americans all need cars, because it takes you three days to travel anywhere. The land is so vast and so sprawling... and different.

The house on the ranch is beautiful, wood everywhere. It's just amazing. It's almost as if he took the design of the log cabin in Montreux and transformed it into a three-storey house here.

Our life here isn't perfect, but we're happy, I think. The honeymoon was so very beautiful... and then, yes, okay... it was back to the real world.

I guess the trouble is, he's never been on a cattle drive that's lasted so long before now, and I'm left wondering if he's okay. I can't help but worry he's got something else on his plate. Without the ability to call him, I don't have a clue what he's up to day to day.

I'm lying in bed, its vast comfort soaking me into its depths, and I'm wondering if I should even leave the bed today. Should I bother? He's been gone three weeks now, and I don't know when he's coming back. Since we moved to Texas there have been absences, but not one as long as this. He said he'd be gone a while, but seriously, can't the cattle get grass nearer home? Without him here, I feel like there's no point to anything. Plus, it doesn't help that I'm three months pregnant and feel sick as a dog. This bed is my whole world right now. Partly because I want to vomit every time I leave it, partly because I'm missing him so much and I'm bereft.

I roll over and have a little cry, then I start to fall asleep.

THE MAID, MARTHA WAKES me at midday with a tray of food. She throws open the huge red drapes and tucks them behind the antique brass holdbacks at the sides of the windows. She spends a few minutes making the curtains look neat and tidy, arranging them just so, before she comes back to the bed and looks down on me.

"Mrs Nathan needs to eat."

"Mrs Nathan is called Bebe. We discussed this."

"Mrs Nathan needs to eat to feed baby Nathan."

"The baby will eat me, the doctor said so," I grumble.

"And there's barely anything of you," she complains.

I let her help me to sit up in the pillows. I shouldn't complain really. I'm lucky she allows me to sleep until midday, but she only does that because Nate told her to let me sleep in. I'm lucky in a lot of ways, it's just that for some reason, I have to keep reminding myself of this.

Martha arranges the tray of food before me and suddenly hunger grips my stomach and I grin. She relents and grins back. She opens the drapes at the other side of the room and the master suite is bathed in so much sun, it's blinding. She pulls the blind down on the window at that side and I breathe a sigh of relief. It's so hot in summer, it's unbelievable.

"Anything else, Mrs Nathan?"

"Yes, call me Bebe," I demand, but she smiles and leaves me to it.

Martha's old-fashioned, but I think she keeps calling me that because she's trying to remind me I'm the lady of the manor and should act like it, instead of slobbing about all day. Maybe I should get a set of dungarees and a long piece of grass to chew on, set myself up on the porch like Claire-Anne does every morning at daybreak.

On my tray there is ham, eggs and grits, which I love.

I gobble it all up, swallowing it down with warm milk and a hunk of homemade rye bread.

There's orange juice on the side and a couple of ginger biscuits.

Everything's demolished within five minutes.

With my stomach full, I head for the window which looks out across the farm. All the dogs are running around, chasing one another between the stables. Nate has two shepherd dogs which go driving with him, but three others have been left behind because they're too old now. Claire-Anne has a Boston Terrier, Fifi which sleeps forever at her feet and Martha always brings her Pitbull, Burt with her whenever she's working. Burt's as daft as a

brush and follows the other dogs even though he can't keep up
with the retired shepherds. Nate asked me if I wanted a dog of my
own. There's plenty of space and he looked like he wanted to buy
me another gift. Not that I haven't had enough gifts already—a
truck of my own, a horse, a lot of new clothes, countless jewellery
pieces and a membership to a spa nearby, where I can get the
works whenever I like. I'd only ridden horses occasionally before
I moved to Texas, but apparently you have to know how to ride in
these parts, so Reg, one of the hands was teaching me—but that
was until we knew I was pregnant.

I don't know how many horses they have here. I know there
are a lot. I know Claire-Anne used to have a horse of her
own—Jinny—until Claire-Anne was thrown off and didn't ride
again. I think Nate might have had a say in that. Claire-Anne was
no doubt riding drunk all the time. I stand watching the world
outside, thinking I might like a little dog. Maybe a spaniel, something sweet. We never had pets growing up. Too much like making roots, I suppose.

I walk into my closet and shed my nightshirt, walking around
naked between the rails and shelves. I tug on some comfortable
underwear and a maxi dress on top, slipping my feet into some
sandals. I used to love a flipflop, until I lived on this farm. Now I
need big sandals to protect my feet at all times.

In the bathroom I splash my face with water and do a quick
teeth-cleaning. I can't stand deodorants or perfumes right now,
so I leave the room, taking the tray down with me.

Martha's in the kitchen and turns red-faced when she sees me
carrying the tray. Sometimes she clears it before I can, most times
I clear it to piss her off.

"Give me that," she chastises.

"Wonderful breakfast by the way."

"It'll soon be lunchtime," she says, one eyebrow raised.

The three shepherd dogs of Nate's come running towards me, plus Martha's Pitbull.

I kneel down to pet them all and they buss their noses at me constantly, seeking more and more affection. I walk out onto the porch and sit in the swing seat. The dogs consequently sit around me, waiting for more affection.

Martha brings out a tall glass of ice water and puts it to my side. She stuffs my sunhat in my hands and I reluctantly put it on. She thinks I'm going to get brown blobs on my face otherwise. I'd like to tell her that I don't need a mother—that I had one—but I'm not up for talking about my mother, nor what happened to her—nor why.

The dogs eventually tire of me petting them and they all lie at my feet. The Pitbull goes back inside to follow Martha around as she busies about, doing her thing.

Claire-Anne is at the other side of the porch, where she sits every day. I've never seen a bottle touch her lips, but I know she's constantly drunk. It evaporates as it leaves her pores, but the stench of alcohol lingers all around her.

I sit thinking about what I could do today. I could go up to the sun house out back and read for a few hours. I could drive into town and look around all the knick-knack shops. I've already bought quite a few things and we're running out of space in the house, so maybe not. Plus, the handyman always gives me a look whenever I ask him to put more holes in the walls.

I could go back to bed and do a little more crying over Nate not being here. Since being pregnant, sleeping isn't a problem for me anymore, and in fact I seem to be catching up on years of lost sleep.

I could send Martha home and tell her I'll be in charge for the rest of the day.

Or I could just sit here cooking Nate's baby a bit more and wait for Martha to tell us lunch is ready. I think I'll do that.

AT THE BACK OF THE house, Martha serves us lunch on the patio, which you can get to through the dining kitchen. The back doors open on a slider frame so the whole house can be opened up at the back. The dogs have been locked up in one of the barns to have a proper sleep before they're released again. Also, there are three parasols sheltering us from the relentless sun and there's not another invention I've ever been more grateful of.

Claire-Anne picks at her egg salad, while I wolf mine. Martha can cook and I love her rice dishes. Our egg salad has rice and beans and all kinds of sauces, such as fresh sour cream, home-made mayo and guacamole. My vegetarianism didn't stand a chance, not once I showed up here with Nate. Martha bade me 'just try' her signature rack of ribs with the Jack Daniels sauce. I was converted.

"It's been three weeks," Claire-Anne mumbles.

"I know."

I'm surprised she's been counting. I didn't think she even knew what day of the week it is.

I mix some of my sauces together and clump a load of rice up, eating it all down in one, delicious mouthful. Claire-Anne looks barely interested in the food. She's only sat here with me because it's the routine. Nate is insistent on me having three meals a day.

Normally after lunch she retreats to her room for her afternoon nap. I wonder how much drink she has stashed under her bed. She has a vehicle of her own but Enrique, one of our other farmhands, always stops her from driving away alone and takes the wheel for her...

"He's gone again," she mumbles.

At first, her words mean nothing. She's stating the obvious, right?

Then I ask, "What do you mean, *again*?"

"He tells y'all he's driving, but he's actually doin' that other thing he does," she drawls, in an accent that is much deeper than Nate's. I have myself convinced Nate speaks differently because he's more educated, but I think I know deep down why he sounds less Texan than his mother.

"What *other thing*?"

I watch as she actually eats a slip of egg, but it curls her lip. She rarely ingests food. Her diet is the liquid one. Come to think of it, I've never seen her drink water. Or coffee, either. I've never seen her drink anything. All her drinking's done when nobody's looking.

"You know... that other thing." Her head's waggling in the way it does.

"So..." I stare into space, wondering how I can approach this without upsetting her. "Before he married me, he would be gone, for long stretches like this?"

"Yeah. Regularly. He'd be gone... for months... and months."

"And he'd be... driving."

"Sure, he'd say he was driving, but the other guys would be back before him. He must have thought I was the dumbest mother who ever lived if he thought I believed him, and when I told him as much that one time, he realised he couldn't lie to me. Now he don't even try to lie, but he continues to hide the truth. All that happens different is the guys all go hide up at the lodge in the wilderness and stay out of the way, watching over the animals during summer before they're driven back towards home in winter." She notices my aghast expression and continues, "Nobody drives for months at a time anymore. Nate thinks I've lost my mind, but I ain't. I know what century this is. I know things, see things he don't want me to. I always knew he was fixin' to escape someday, but... the way he does it ain't right, you know? It's like he's got something big to hide, so he uses this ranch as... I don't know... some kind of legitimate front, like a gangster, with something unsavoury on the side."

She sniffs, indifferent, as if she's not shattering my world with all this new information...

And then she continues her barbed assault...

"Eric told me he confronted Nate this one time, but Nate turned doggone crazy and told Eric all he needs to know is he has other business that takes him away. I know nothing about that other business because when I ask my son, he says he's been over yonder settling monetary matters—and we both know that what he says amounts to little more than a hill of beans. He says he's driving, but he ain't driving, girl. Problem is, he's too darn pretty, right? He don't seem at all capable of doing bad shit."

My heart starts banging against my ribcage and I have to calm myself down. I can't get like this, not when I'm carrying a baby.

"What the hell is he off doing, then?" I ask, even though I have a pretty good idea. I just don't want Claire-Anne to know that I do.

"Beats me," she says, chewing a lettuce leaf, even though she still has that look in her eye, like food disgusts her to the point of utter revulsion.

My food is no more appetising to me now than hers is to her, but I eat the rest of my lunch for the baby's sake. After Martha collects our dishes, she returns with dessert for me—apple pie and cream.

Claire-Anne never takes dessert and instead, she moves away from the outdoor dining set and takes one of the benches further afield as she puffs on a cigarette. She only smokes after eating—if half a boiled egg, a couple of forkfuls of rice and some salad leaves can be classed as 'eating'.

"Claire-Anne?" I ask, and she turns her head slightly towards me. Her withered face looks hollow and lifeless, but I can see she was once beautiful.

"Where's Nate's father?"

"He ain't never had no father," she says.

"What?"

She shrugs. "I reared him myself."

"You mean, you can't remember who you slept with? Who the father was?"

She turns and continues puffing on her cigarette, so I can't see her eyes. "It's not like I'm the only one in the world to bring up a boy without a daddy."

If she thinks I'm judging her, she's mistaken. Sometimes, when I was a teenager, I used to wish my mother would leave my father, just so we could have a normal upbringing. My mother would have done all right on her own. It was just that she loved my father all too much.

"It's just... I must have misheard Nate... he said his father used to bring him gifts."

Claire-Anne turns and stares at me, as if I'm crazy. "You must have heard him wrong, sweetie."

"And what about the ranch? Who does it belong to? Who bought it?" I ask, trying to figure out her motives and why she's saying all this.

"Nate bought it darlin', why you talkin' so silly?"

"You're the one who said he's not out driving?"

She looks at me over her shoulder, from where she's sat with her back to me, on the bench.

"Darlin', my Nate is the cleverest boy you'll ever meet. I don't pretend to understand him, but I know when he says he's driving, he ain't driving girl. He's doing his other business, the one that pays the bills. Ain't no real money in cattle, darlin'. Surely ain't enough to be buying you no fancy diamond bling. I thought you would've figured all this out already. Maybe you ain't as clever as he said."

After I've eaten my dessert—again, to feed the baby, not me—I excuse myself from the table and wander back into the house. I grab some books from the library and don my sunglasses and hat, taking myself down to the sun house at the bottom of the garden, which is long and has at least 30 perfectly mowed stripes running down its length. Enrique always looks like he's in love when he's mowing it on his ride-on.

In the sun house I lie out on one of the fainting couches and switch on the fan by my side, letting it blast cool air over my sweaty face.

Even when you leave the doors open and wind swoops through, the fan's still needed. Someone wafting a palm leaf over my head would be just about perfect right now.

I start trying to read my book, which would usually require no effort at all, but his mother's words have left me confused, and I realise—in shock.

Yes, I'm in shock.

I lift my hand up and it's shaking.

Firstly, according to Claire-Anne, he's never known his father. Which means he's a liar. He told me he and his father got to know one another, and that his father was the whole reason he joined the Collective. I don't find it hard to believe that Claire-Anne was wasted one night and never saw the father again. There are hundreds of thousands of men out there who don't even know they're a father. So, the truth is, Nate lied to me... and he lied for a reason. The thing is, he must have always known that I would eventually meet his mother and discover the truth... or maybe he never expected me to meet his mother at all. Maybe he didn't think what's between us would last. Maybe lying to me was a part of some act, or something. I dread to think... I can't think... I can't allow myself to become worked up right now.

Secondly, Nate's still working for them, isn't he? He must be. This ranch is his cover for what he really gets up to. He's not a cattle driver. He's *one of them*. In the early days, he told me he was a 'cleaner', then changed his story, explaining he was a 'high-level hacker', as he termed it. I've turned a blind eye to so many things, because I love him—and he's the only family I've got.

I slam my book shut.

If I was feeling vindictive right now, I'd leave the ranch, take myself off and get good and lost. See how he likes that. See how it makes him feel. Maybe then he'll know what it's like for me, left behind while he goes and does what he wants.

Thirdly, Claire-Anne is a drunk and a fool, but she's not stupid. She wanted to upset me today. She *meant* to upset me. Maybe she doesn't want me here. Maybe she doesn't like the fact that I see right through her, that I don't have as much tolerance of her lifestyle as Nate does.

I look down and rub my tiny little bump. At least he or she will have me, and that's all that matters. I've just got to take care of us two.

I'll figure out what to do about Nate later.

Chapter Thirty-Six

Three Years Later...

T   The room's spinning as I wake. It takes a while for me to realise why I'm even waking up. My body certainly doesn't want to wake, but my daughter is crying. I can hear her down the hall.

True to form, once Lola's crying, Seth's crying too.

My body is destroyed. I've been up half the night cuddling Seth as he copes with a chesty cough. Lola's slept fine, but now she's awake. And wanting me. And Seth's awake, too.

I pad down the hallway in my t-shirt and shorts, feeling zombiefied.

Martha's rushing up the stairs as I'm moving towards the nursery and we almost crash into one another.

"I'll take them if you like," she says.

"Seth's poorly, he won't let anyone else cuddle him."

"Oh, what's wrong?" she asks, fearful.

"Just a cold, Martha. Nothing to worry about. He only seems to want me for some reason."

I go into the room and grab Seth first. He silences as soon as he's in my arms, sucking his thumb. Two and a half and still a thumb sucker, but only when he's feeling poorly like this. Martha picks up Lola from her crib and Lola is consoled for a minute or two before she holds out her arms towards me. I take Lola and carry both children back to my bedroom.

Martha looks upset. She's been a great help, but she can't do everything. She's not a mother herself so she doesn't always understand.

"Can you bring breakfast up to the bedroom?" I ask Martha. "And then I'll try to get some more sleep with Seth. If you could push Lola around in her buggy for a while? She'll be fine with you, won't she?"

From her facial expression, you'd think I'd just offered her the crown jewels.

"Sure, Bebe. Sure." She busies away, ecstatic that she's going to get to push Lola around the grounds. I think Martha would have made a terrific mother, if she wasn't barren. Apparently, her ex-husband left her because of it. Poor lady.

I love that she's so caring and attentive to the kids, but I also sometimes have to subtly remind her they're mine and Nate's.

If only Nate was home, though...

IN THE NIGHT, SETH'S not sleeping—again. I'm at my wits' end. I'm tired and so is my son. I've tried giving him infant suspension, but I can't give him another spoonful until four hours has passed since the last lot—two hours ago—and he hasn't stopped crying in all this time. If I could just go back to how it was before, when Seth was a tiny baby and I could bring him to my breast for relief, I would, but he's bigger now and he knows when his father's not here. Nate always manages to calm Seth down, but my affection is only a temporary salve it seems.

With only myself and the children in the house during the night, it's a lonely place when he's away working. Incredibly lonely.

I try rocking him in my arms and he quietens for a while, but then he starts up again. I console myself that at least Lola is asleep down the hall, tucked up nice and tight.

Eventually, I feel so tired—and so unbearably hopeless—that I lie down in bed and tuck him against me tight, so he can't keep thrashing. Eventually Seth settles down and his breathing changes from heavy pants, to deep sighs. He curls up against me and falls asleep, tucked into my chest.

ANOTHER MORNING, AND I feel like death. It's nothing new.

This time, I ask Martha to take the kids with her to town. Seth always behaves when he's in his stroller or the car seat. It's just with me he misbehaves, because he knows he can get away with it.

I lie down to sleep but it's strange, even though I'm dog tired, the house is too quiet for me to sleep. I try but fail to take advantage of my empty house.

Instead, I find myself wandering.

I wander down the hall and stop at the door to Claire-Anne's old room.

I turn the handle and twist it.

I walk inside and stand in the same surroundings she lived in. Dust floats up into the air as I disturb the sanctum that's now never touched.

She died two years ago, not long after I had Seth. She was still cold and distant, even after I gave her a grandchild.

She died of liver disease. It suddenly crept up on her—and that was it. Dead at fifty-nine.

She was lucky to have survived so long.

Anyway, she died, and Nate dealt with it in his usual way—stiff upper lip, "I've got a life to live", sort of thing. He never cried, or he never cried in front of me anyway.

Whatever it was between him and his mother, I know it wasn't healthy—or loving.

Martha's been more of a mother to Nate than Claire-Anne ever was.

Anyway, I have no need of this room and Martha doesn't have the heart to take out everything that's in here. I think the truth is, Nate doesn't want this room clearing properly—afraid of what we'll find buried in secret places.

I leave the room and head downstairs, fixing myself breakfast in the kitchen—just coffee, toast and some fruit and yoghurt. I'm sitting out on the patio scoffing it, when I hear the front door bang open and shut.

I wait for the confirmation it's Martha, back to pick up something she's forgotten, but I don't hear her voice or the kids either. I hear heavy footsteps.

"Anyone home? Bebe!" he shouts.

"In here," I holler.

He strolls into the kitchen, his tired eyes seeking me and finding me outside. I watch his body move as he heads towards me—his sleek legs in long denim jeans and his ripped torso cuddled into a thick flannel shirt. He looks relieved when he finds me.

"Are you okay?" he asks.

"I'm fine. What's wrong?"

"I don't know," he says, coming to kneel by my feet. "I just had this feeling, and it made me come home. I felt like you needed me. It was an instinct. I was scared."

I put my face in my hands and cry. The tears I've been holding up a barrier to begin to slide freely, the dam breaking, all my walls falling down.

He winds his arms around me and I snake my hands into his hair.

"I need you so much," I say, gasping. "I haven't slept. Seth keeps crying. Martha tries but at night, he won't settle and there's only me... and..."

"I'm sorry," he says, and he picks me up and carries me upstairs. He slides me into bed and undresses, crawling in beside me. "I'm sorry. I shouldn't have been gone so long."

Once we're cuddled up and I'm warm and safe between his arms, all my exhaustion collects like a heavy mass inside my head, and I start to fall asleep.

I HEAR HUSHED VOICES in the evening. Martha's talking with Nate, out in the corridor, as I begin to stir. "Yeah, if you could just stay over, this one night," he whispers.

"You know that's no problem, Nate. I'll take the spare room, the one next to Claire-Anne's."

"Thank you."

She hurries off and I hear her return to the nursery. Lola is squawking while Seth is in his father's arms, babbling wildly, so happy to have his father back.

I should be happy he's home.

It's true that whenever he comes back, something inside me lights up. Something dead comes back to life, but with that renewed love always comes the reminder that he's been gone too long, and I don't know where he's been or who he's been with.

Since his ma died, he doesn't even try to hide the truth anymore. When the guys go off to drive cattle, he waves them off. When he has to work away, he merely tells me, "I've got to work, honey. I'll be back as soon as I can."

It's this unspoken thing, because he doesn't want to worry me, and I don't want the truth to slap me in the face.

When Nate walks into the room, he says to Seth, "Let's see if Mommy's ready to get up yet."

I shut my eyes firmly and remain in the exact same position. I sense Nate lean over to inspect me.

"She needs more sleep, baby boy. C'mon, let's leave her to it."

For the first time since I met Nate, I really wish I'd never stepped into that grocery store. With this love thing comes so many blessings—like the life we share and our children—but it's also brought me endless pain, not knowing who my husband is, beneath.

Who did I marry, really?

I just don't know.

I guess I know what it feels like to lose him—and that dreadful night I thought he'd died is never far from my thoughts.

I never want to feel like that ever again, so this for now, is better.

Chapter Thirty-Seven

Past

After we moved to Edinburgh, my father used to be away for weeks at a time, then he'd come home out of the blue. He'd also be home for weeks, then he'd be gone. Similar pattern. I never imagined then, that one day, I'd end up like my own mother—endlessly waiting around for her husband to return home.

One Christmas, we were all particularly happy and it was probably because he'd been home since the beginning of December and it didn't seem like he'd be going away again anytime soon.

He and I sat by the great fire in the living room, in the two hefty leather chairs he and my mother usually favoured, together. They were wingbacks and smelt of Dad's cigars, which he would only ever smoke after Phoebe and I were in bed at night. The thick, indestructible leather chairs were deep mahogany and studded front and arms. Mum collected porcelain pigs and the fireplace was covered in them. Above the mantelpiece hung an original Vettriano, my mother's favourite artist. Our house in Morningside was so much grander than the one we'd had in Yorkshire, where we lived on the Moors like the Earnshaws, content in our simple existence. It really was as though we'd swapped one life for another when we left Yorkshire to move here. We certainly never bought expensive paintings to decorate our old stone cottage, where we had a snow tractor and an ancient stove in an ancient kitchen, which didn't even have a radiator to heat it.

Mum and Phoebe had already gone up to bed. It was the day before my birthday and I felt like I was being accorded a great honour—not only staying up really late, but it also being just my father and me. The past year had tested us all—my mother more than any of us. It was rare she would allow Dad to spend time alone with his kids whenever he came home, because she wanted all his spare time for herself, but like I said this Christmas was different for lots of reasons.

"Would you like your present now?" he asked.

"I don't know. Will I sleep if you give me it? Or is it too exciting?"

It was my sweet sixteenth.

I would lose my childish outlook soon enough, once I discovered boys and cigarettes, booze and pot. Whenever Dad went away, Mum always let us get away with murder. She was only concerned with her own depression.

Even as I was being accorded this honour of getting to stay up late with Dad—and asked if I wanted my birthday present early—all I could think about was our beautiful old, rickety cottage in Yorkshire with the crooked chimney pots and the snow tractor always there, should we need it. Mum took us for rides on the tractor in summer, up and down the lane, just for fun. It was always like this, late at night, that I started missing our old life... our old house...

Me.

"You're right, you won't sleep," Dad said, seeming to read something in my expression.

"So, we should retire, right Dad? And then I can wake early and have my present then?" I started to rise from my chair, stretching. He reached for the remote and turned off the TV, which had been playing a Christmas carol service quietly, hardly noticeable in the background. The fire had dimmed and would be safe to leave as was.

"Sure, Beatrice."

I looked down on him, sensing something. "What is it, Dad?"

"It's about my job," he said.

"What about your job?" I had no idea what job it was he really did. All I knew was that he worked for 'the Collective'—and I only knew that from earwigging.

"Sometimes, when I'm away... there's danger." His eyes told me that what he was saying was true.

"Because you're abroad? And it's not safe in other countries?"

"Yes," he said, nodding fast, as if he was pleased he didn't have to expand any further. "And so, now you're older, perhaps it's better that you know..."

I sat back down and gave him my full attention. "Know what?"

"If something were to happen to me..."

"Like, illness? Or... death..." Oh, my younger self, how much more outspoken she was...

"Either," he said, his eyes dark and focused on mine.

"Okay..."

"You and your mother and sister will be provided for, you don't have to worry."

"We don't care about money, Dad."

He nodded. He looked maybe a little guilty, too. In the back of my mind I wondered whether his death wouldn't be better for Mum's mental health. Maybe I was young and topsy-turvy with my emotions, but... it would be years until I realised the full extent of the harm he caused not only Mum, but us, too. Deep down, I loved my dad, but I was torn. I wanted to respect him and a part of me did, but another part of me knew he didn't deserve my respect. Anyway...

"But if you ever needed anything more than money, say... I don't know..." His hands were held tightly in his lap, like this was difficult for him, uncomfortable. "If you needed some help, of any sort, there is a way..."

I rubbed my forehead. I couldn't understand what he was saying. Was he saying we were still in danger? That transposing our entire lives had all been for nothing? Was he saying his job was going to get him killed one day? Was he telling me he was a spy or something? All kinds of thoughts ran through my head that night.

"What do you mean, *help?*"

"I mean, Beatrice..." He leaned forward and looked ever more sincere, even though I could tell he didn't want to burden me like this, not really. "If money isn't enough to help you out, there is someone you can go to. He's a secretive person but I trust him with my life. If you ever need to contact him, it's easy. You just have to do exactly what I say."

"Okay." I tried to control my tears. I could go from hating him one moment, to contemplating the finality of his death in the next and feeling torn. There was also that continual, bitter resentment—at him piling even more weight on my shoulders. "Tell me what to do then, Dad."

He looked so relieved when I seemed to have accepted that measures had to be put in place should anything happen—like the unexpected.

He asked me to sit on the arm of his chair and he stroked my hair as he explained, "I'm telling you because you're a very sensible and capable girl, Beatrice. I hope you know this."

"I know. Thank you, Dad. For trusting me."

He kissed my temple. "I do, I trust you."

"Then, go on..."

And so, he told me what I should do. He told me every single little thing, from beginning to end. He made me remember every instruction I should take if the time came.

It was the only night I ever felt close to my dad, and I only felt close to him because he was afraid, and he'd never been afraid before.

After that night, I tried everything not to be afraid too, but my dad had burdened me, you see. I was always afraid after that.

I'd known there was always danger, but until then, I'd never seen my dad scared of it. I knew things had got serious. I knew I wanted that old, scrappy cottage back for one reason and one reason alone: I had never felt frightened there. I wanted ignorance back. I wanted my old self... but she was gone.

EVENTUALLY, I FORGOT he'd told me all about the man who could help me. Dad was soon working away again, and then he came back. And he went away, and he came back. And I thought his warning had all been for nothing—or maybe whatever it was he'd been scared of had all blown over.

Maybe my dad chose death the day he started working for the Collective. Death was always going to catch up with him, wasn't it?

He probably knew that even if it wasn't then, I would eventually need that friend of his to help me out.

I just forgot for a while what he said, like I forgot what my sweet sixteenth birthday present even was.

Chapter Thirty-Eight

N ate's been back home for a few days now. I feel refreshed. I've slept. I've even washed my hair. We also finally made love last night. Frantically. We miss one another dreadfully when he's gone. It was perhaps our lovemaking that rocked me into a deep sleep last night, a sleep deep enough that I dreamt.

I dreamt about the night my father told me about his friend. I haven't thought about that night in years. I forgot all about it, but I still remember every word he said. Even if I buried it, I stored it away somewhere safe—deep inside my mind.

I trusted my father and my father trusted his friend.

All I know is that my husband would rather be here at home with us, but he's being forced to spend time away.

There are also huge gaping holes in what happened to us the year my family got decimated. There are answers I need, and I'm too scared to approach my husband, because I think he's embroiled.

I need outside help.

Nate walks up behind me, where I stand in the kitchen, chopping vegetables. It's Martha's day off. I love it when it's just us and we can stay in our sweats or PJs all day. The kids can make a mess and the dogs are packed off with one of the guys for a couple of days.

"My beautiful wife," he says, sliding his hands around my waist and kissing the nape of my neck. "I love you. Don't you forget it."

Perhaps he senses my mind is elsewhere today. Nate is perceptive and emotionally attuned, when it comes to me anyway.

I turn and offer him my mouth, which he takes with gentle kisses. We stand nudging our lips into one another's for a while, before he takes off to check on the kids, who are in the playpen in the sitting room.

He returns to the kitchen, excitedly telling me, "They're both zonked! You should see Lola. It looks like she fell flat on her face. She's good though."

"Wow. See, when Daddy's home, order is restored."

"I do wish it could be like this all the time, you know."

"I know," I say, my voice soft.

"We're okay, aren't we?"

"We're fine. It's just that I need to leave the house sometimes, you know? And I can't."

"We've talked about this before. You said you didn't want a nanny."

I turn and find him staring at me, chewing his lip. He only ever does that if he feels threatened.

"I don't want a nanny. I've seen the bank accounts, Nate. We're loaded. You don't need to—"

His face crumples. "We're not talking about this, Beatrice."

It forever goes unsaid. Always.

"I think what's happening is unfair, is all. The dynamic of me being home, you being gone. We need a better balance. It's not that I don't want to be a stay-home mother, I do. I don't want to miss a thing, it's just I'd rather you were here sharing all of this with me."

"You're right, but I can't help it."

"So, what if I were to seek work, how you would feel knowing that I don't really need work, but I'm seemingly doing it to get out of the house?"

He throws his hands up. "I guess I'd have to deal with it. Maybe, work keeps people sane, I dunno."

"So if I did some modelling work, you'd be all right with it?" The idea just came to me. Maybe I'll call his bluff. "I mean, would it be safe? Could I... what do you think?"

He sighs, nodding his head, because he knows I'm right. "I know you've already been emailing your ex-agent. I monitor everything you do for your own safety. And don't give me those eyes..."

"First of all," I rail, "she and I communicate about personal stuff, not work. And how dare you?"

"You know I'm not controlling, you know that Beatrice. I do it to keep you safe."

"Ah yeah, only someone controlling would say that, though. Wouldn't they?"

"Call her up, then. Say you're good to go. I can be here another couple of weeks. Do it. If that's what you need, do it."

I almost don't believe it. How have I managed this? "You mean it? I can go."

"Sure, go. Get out of the house. I hope serenity will be restored on your return."

"Thank you."

"You're welcome."

I smile before returning to my vegetable chopping. I'll call Stella later and tell her I need a job. She'll have something for me, she always used to. People might be shocked to see me back on the scene, but hey...

"I'm taking Spartacus out for a ride," he says, referring to his horse, "you'll be okay?"

"You go enjoy yourself, big guy."

He kisses my cheek before he leaves the room.

"Won't be long. Back in time for tea and crumpets," he says, putting on a British accent.

I giggle and get back to it. Once he's left the room, I let myself sigh and breathe out all my tension. It occurs to me that a guy who can choose to come home whenever he wants—might be the boss of whatever it is he gets up to when he's away. Also, he came home because he knew I was having a meltdown, so is he watching me, even while he's on a job? What doesn't he know about me? Probably only what's inside my head, but even then, he appears to be something of a mind reader. Maybe it's a trick of the trade he's in...

Anyway, I've just set myself up with the perfect opportunity to call up Dad's friend, haven't I?

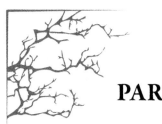

PART THREE

ANSWERS IN VEGAS

Chapter Thirty-Nine

After standing in a car park behind the Aria in Vegas for hours on end, wearing barely anything but bits and pieces of material strategically placed, I'm more than ready to hit some shops, blow some money and get a spa treatment or two. Me and the other girls have acted our arses off as Amazonians in the concrete world. While the cameras have been off, we've been dashing in and out of the hotel to take advantage of the aircon and to replenish make-up rapidly dripping off while outside. I must look so glamorous right now. I can't even remember who I'm modelling for, or how much this gig is paying, all I care about is that I've got two whole days where I'm me and I can move around freely and do what I need to get done.

Tabitha, who's to my right mumbles, "You seen her husband, Sylv? Has she shown you a pic?"

I know Tabs from way back, and Sylvia from later on. The top models all know one another. I may have gone right to the top of the plus-size lists if I hadn't dropped off the face of the earth during those months Nate and I were in Switzerland, hiding. The fashion world loves it even more, now that I've emerged as a natural redhead. With freckles.

Sylv, to my left, whispers, "Why, is he hot?"

"The man is sick. I've only seen photos on her phone. In real life, damn, I bet he's jaw-dropping. Mind you, Lis is slaying, right? Even two kids later, SLAY-ING," she says, dramatically.

"I live on a farm," I explain, through partially closed lips. We're not meant to be talking because we could ruin the shot, but the photographer is having a thing with his minion over there. I think they've run out of water mist. "I don't have it all, trust me. But it's true, he's damn fine, girls."

"FINE? FINE?" Tabitha exclaims. "That man is some sort of dangerous narcotic, woman."

I giggle. "I know."

"Right ladies," our British photographer says, swaggering in the way photographers do, "blue steel with a side of evil. And... go."

IT'S MIDNIGHT WHEN I get off the phone to Nate. Over FaceTime, I've been telling him about my day—the shoot, eating sushi with the girls afterwards, having mani-pedis too and blowing a load of money in Gucci. Just because. He seemed to believe everything I was saying. I dramatized a few things from the shoot, just to make him laugh. He showed me the kids, who were both fast asleep.

I walk to the window of my hotel room and look down on the Strip, from some several storeys up. Nothing's sleeping, at all.

I walk back to my bed in my robe. I need to rest well tonight. We're doing reshoots tomorrow, just to make sure they have everything they need. Problem is, I don't know if I'll sleep at all.

I play with the burner phone I have in my hand. I picked it up as we were passing through Caesar's Palace. While they were buying more shoes, I slipped into a phone store 'to get a new cover'.

It's more than a decade now since my dad told me about his friend, the one who'd help me no matter what. It's a long shot this guy will still be contactable in the same way my dad told me about, all those years ago, before all this happened and shit hit the fan. Still, I didn't come all this way just to stand in the boiling hot sun partially nude all day long. I came here to get answers, because I'm sure not going to get them from Nate, am I?

My finger hovers over the screen. As terrifying as this is, I must do it. I need to know how to extract my husband from the Collective. My life can't go on like this. What if, one day, Nate doesn't come back? What if my entire family blows up, too?

I take a deep breath and do what my father told me to do. He said that if ever I needed help, all I had to do was make sure I was in a room alone. Make sure I had a phone not attached to my name—so buy it in cash and make sure I'm not caught on camera buying it (which is why I told the store I was buying for a VIP and they took me in the back). He also stated I should contact his friend without using my name—just codewords.

I punch in the number I memorised all those years ago and write out a text, the same one my father told me to write all those years ago:

It's Snow White. I ate the poison apple.

My heart's thudding as I send it.

I wait to see if it sends.

It sends.

The phone lets me know it's not pinged back. It's bloody gone through.

Now, the waiting begins.

Will the recipient respond? Have they kept the same number all these years? It was a strange number, with a hell of a lot of zeros in it, and a strange code I googled which belongs to no country in the world.

Anyway, the phone says it sent, so it couldn't have been all that duff, right? Right?

My mind's racing. I'm wondering if Nate will find out. Does he know? How could he know? All I've done is send a text.

I almost leap out of my skin when a reply arrives. I work my fingers on the screen even though they're shaking.

I read the reply through bleary eyes:

Fremont Street. 30 minutes. I'll find you.

I dress quickly in jeans and a plain t-shirt so I won't stand out. I don my sunglasses—because everyone wears glasses in Vegas, even at night—and leave my room carrying the phone and a roll of notes stashed into a small purse.

Whoever just contacted me, they know I've come to Vegas for a reason. They know this isn't normal behaviour for me. I haven't modelled since before the tragedy.

My stomach's a little looser around the front than it used to be, but smart dressing works around that. Besides, bodily changes aren't why I don't work anymore. It's my kids. I'd rather be with them.

Somebody's watching. Somebody knows.

Somebody has answers for me.

They must.

Or otherwise, I'm heading into a trap and the man my father trusted isn't to be trusted after all. Either way, I jump into a taxi downstairs and tell them to take me to Fremont Street.

Time to find out what I'm dealing with.

Chapter Forty

The taxi drops me outside the Golden Nugget and I'm absorbed into the crowds as I start walking down Fremont Street, Downtown Las Vegas. This older and smaller version of the Strip has a huge video screen erected above the street, making it feel like you're in a tunnel, with its convex shape. All kinds of images play out on the screen, from music videos to psychedelic floral patterns, to light shows out of this world.

Even plainly dressed, I get touted immediately by people trying to get me to gamble in their casinos, with free chips and drinks galore on offer. Vegas has no shame. There are places with the windows all blacked out, but the doors are open and streams of men in single file shuffle indoors, welcomed by a scantily dressed hostess holding a tray of free cocktails. Walking by at the same time are families pushing children, just out for some dinner and a walk.

On the other side of the street—as I'm continually assaulted by the ceiling light show and all the lights of the casinos and stores and restaurants all around—I spot a camera crew filming something. Maybe a TV show, maybe a film. They could be filming anything. They would be lucky to ever get permission to shut down Vegas, even this part.

I have no idea what I'm meant to be doing, or where I'm meant to be going. I was just told to head for Fremont Street, wasn't I?

The lights, the crowds and the noise—as I approach the stage where a band is playing loud rock music—have my senses on overload. I suppose if someone wants to meet me here, it's because there are so many sights and sounds, and so many bodies, we can easily get lost and we won't draw attention to ourselves, at least not here anyway.

Then I begin to fear all sorts. If I am being followed by someone whose intent is to harm me, or worse, kill me, how do I know they're following me? I'm being pushed and shoved around by so many people right now. How can I tell if someone is following me when there are thousands of people all around? How do I know if someone has malicious intent?

The phone in my little handbag vibrates and I open the drawstring and look down at the screen without taking the phone out. The message reads:

Head for the Chinese restaurant up ahead. Don't search the crowds. Head right there.

I look up and see a rather minimalistic Chinese restaurant up ahead, to my right. I start pushing in the direction of the other side of the street and get elbowed one too many times. It's lucky I'm tall and can see over the crowds.

I stand outside the Chinese restaurant looking through the glass windows, trying to find someone familiar inside, when a hand grabs my elbow. Beyond my own reflection, I vaguely catch sight of a tall guy stood behind me, wearing a baseball cap. It's just an outline.

"Let's go," he says, directing me away from the window and swiftly into the Chinese. I'm forcefully walked through, right to the back of the restaurant. A waiter sees us heading towards him and pulls away a curtain, allowing us access to a backroom or something. I could be heading for death, but somehow, I know I'm not.

I know the voice.

I could be hallucinating. There is a lot of noise, and I may have misheard, but that voice...

We enter a dark corridor and then turn a corner, and after that, I hear clinking of forks and knives on plates. We're shown to some seating right at the back and some privacy curtains are drawn around us.

Once we're alone, he says, "You can turn around now."

I turn slowly and catch just a glimpse of him as I begin to take in the whole picture. I hear myself draw breath so audibly, it sounds like I'm catching a breath after being under water for more than three minutes.

I slap my hands over my mouth in response, because we may be shrouded by curtains in what is obviously the VIP section, but people would still hear my scream if I allowed it to escape.

"Calm down, Beatrice. Please," he begs, pulling out my chair and encouraging me to sit.

He pours me some water and sits opposite me. I keep blinking, and blinking... and blinking... trying to make sure it's him, and not some imaginary version, like the one I saw in Montreux.

"Dad?" I gasp, tears streaming down my face. "Mum? Phoebe?"

He shakes his head, regretful. "It was just me who survived."

"And me!" I exclaim, but he leans in and implores me, "Hush, Beatrice, hush."

"Why? How? When? I can't... it *was* you, in Montreux. Nate lied to me."

He nods slowly. "It *was* me."

I'm trembling wildly, so when the waiter comes over for our drinks order, Dad asks for a bottle of whiskey. It has an 'e' in it over here. In Scotland it's just whisky.

Once the whiskey's here, Dad orders food, just to be polite. I'm not hungry. I couldn't eat a thing. I do partake of the whiskey however.

"Tell me everything," I demand, once the waiter's gone and we're alone. He sits forward, looming over me. He's six-foot-four and redhaired. He couldn't ever hide in a crowd.

"What did *he* tell you, Beatrice? Before I tell you my side, what's he said? What's he made up?"

I shake my head. "Oh god... he said he was the cleaner. And then he said he was sent to kill me, to make sure there was no trail. He said he couldn't do it. He didn't want to. He couldn't kill me. So, then, we were hiding in Montreux. Suddenly, after running for so long, we were safe, and it was lovely... and then I saw your image and... the car exploded... and I thought he was dead, but he was alive... and I don't know what to believe or who to trust... or what to think, or how to feel. YOU'RE HERE! For Christ's sakes, you're here!!"

He absorbs all I've told him and reaches his hands out towards me.

"Beatrice, you remembered what I told you when you were just sixteen?"

"I remember!" I nod wildly. "Even twelve years on, I remember, Dad."

"Working for the Collective, it wasn't like my old job, the one I had before. It was different, so much more dangerous. I thought I would have to disappear, and that's why I gave you those instructions, just in case. The reason I didn't disappear is because I somehow managed to hold it all together, albeit by a thread, but I held it together for your mother's sake. She wouldn't have been able to go on without me, it's why she could never let go, even when she knew you'd all be better off without me."

I swallow hard because I feel the exact same way about Nate. I can't let go.

"The truth is, a friend of mine helped us all disappear that time, and that's how we got away to Edinburgh. My friend was called Horace Chichester, a guy I knew in the Special Forces, back when we were young together."

"I never knew."

My father shakes his head. "I was retired because of a thing... a mission gone wrong. Your mother knew, but she wasn't supposed to know. I shouldn't even be telling you right now, but I am. I've got nothing left to lose, have I? Except you, maybe."

"SAS...?" I'm shocked.

He nods his head. "After that, I didn't know what to do with myself. I'd been brought up by a military father—he was Army too—and it was all I'd ever known. Don't ask me how, because I don't even remember now I look back, but I somehow got myself involved in paid killing."

"So, you were an assassin? I always thought so..."

He doesn't deny it. "And this one time, I fucked up a job. I fucked up big style. And because of my previous in the SAS, there was a price on my head. A big one." He leans in and looks anguished. "You have to understand, I was young in the SAS. I made a mistake, and that mistake came back to haunt me. People make mistakes when they're young. So, okay, the second time, it was bad luck, but the two instances together made me a wanted man with not just my employers, but with the government, too."

"So, that was when we had to leave for Edinburgh?" I think I'm following him now.

"Yes, and Horace was willing to help get me out. The one caveat of him helping us however, was that I join the organisation he worked for. The Collective. Only working for them would enable our escape from our old lives, to begin again. Horace was retired from the Army after he developed type one diabetes—that's how he came to work for the Collective, as an analyst. I knew it was a risk banking on him. I knew it, but I didn't have any other choice. I knew once he died, I wouldn't be protected anymore. The Collective is dog eat dog and I wouldn't have any friends after he was gone. I'd be done for."

"So... he died? I'm guessing..."

He's nodding fast. "Four years ago, when our house blew up, that was because he was gone, and they'd found us. The agency I'd worked for before the Collective found out where we lived," he repeats, trying to hold back his emotion. "By stroke of luck, you were in Florida, but we were all home. They came with guns. They shot your sister first, in the head. They shot your mother while she was in the shower. They shot me in the chest as I sat behind my desk downstairs. An inch from my heart. I once told you, do you remember? My heart isn't situated where it should be."

"Oh my god." Tears rain down my face.

"The killers left but not before setting the house on fire. I tried to crawl up the stairs, to... I don't know..." He can barely speak. "...to rescue them, check they were... I don't know... say goodbye... something... but then the shower upstairs exploded, and the roof blew off. I managed to crawl back down the stairs, but there was someone watching. His eyes caught mine through the window. He stood outside the house, on the pavement. Staring. He had a choice: risk shooting me through the window and being seen, or enter the house and potentially be blown up with the rest of us. He chose to leave. Anyway, I crawled to the cellar and escaped through the small window that looked out onto the alley. I went to the neighbour, Joe. He's a doctor. I told him I needed to leave, quickly. I was lucky. The wound wasn't deep and he dug out the slug okay. He wrote me a prescription for penicillin and gave me a big bag of painkillers, and I left. I left and I've been underground ever since. I hoped, I prayed, you'd be okay. Somehow, I knew you would be."

"And Nate?" I ask.

"He's waiting to see if you've heard from me. It might be why he chased you."

Food is delivered, piles of it in fact. Noodles and special fried rice and shredded duck and spring rolls and fat-cut chips and curry sauce and sweet and sour balls. The smell of it all makes my stomach gurgle, and Dad says, "I knew you'd be hungry. You always were."

I start tucking in, putting various things on my plate. Dad doesn't touch the food, he dines on whiskey and watches, unsurprised, as I tuck into meat dishes—having already somehow acquired the knowledge I'm no longer vegetarian. Has he been watching me, then? If so... why?

After I've eaten a bit of food, all the pieces of the puzzle begin to stack up inside my head, when for so long they've all been floating around up there, with no real formation.

Everything Nate did that year we met was to make me trust him. The grocery store stick-up. The hotel room shooting. Arriving in Montreux and hiding, in order to 'stay safe', when all along, I was with the real enemy. Now I'm married to him.

"Do you love him?" my dad asks, without any emotion. It's just a question.

I stare into his sharp, green eyes. "Very much."

His lips purse. "There's nothing we can do, then. I can't kill him."

"I know, but this is the thing, Dad. My gut tells me he doesn't want to work for them anymore. He's trapped. That's why I used the number. I want someone to help me free him, before they kill him too."

He condescends to eat a chip and a forkful of rice, swilling it down with whiskey. I spot a bullet wound scar beneath the open-neck shirt he's wearing, poking out. So, he *was* shot.

"What does he specialise in, do you know?" he asks me.

"He's a hacker."

"Even worse," he says, "he's indispensable."

"And what was your specialty?" I look down my nose, awaiting his answer. I've always wanted to know about his job, and now I'm finally getting the answers.

He captures my eyes with his for a brief second of honest exchange, before he says, "Interrogation."

Everything about our conversation tonight has been transactional. There's been the odd reassuring hand touch from him, but what about a hug? Kiss? I've always known my dad loves me, but there's something cold about him sometimes, something distant.

With Nate, all I feel when I'm with him is warmth. He holds me so tight when we lie together in bed at night and makes me feel more loved than I've ever felt.

"You've got two grandchildren," I remind him. "I'd show you pictures but they're on my other phone."

He winks. "I'm sure they're as gorgeous as their mother."

"Thank you."

He polishes off the last of the chips and scrubs his hands clean afterwards, downing a hearty amount of whiskey to wash it all down. "Now, Beatrice, was that all you wanted? A way out for him?"

"Yes."

"He's not mistreating you?"

"No, no, in no way has he ever, will ever... no," I profess, because that's not Nate, not at all. "He's a wonderful dad to the kids, wonderful. I just... I want him free."

"People make their choice, Bea," he says, "and I made mine, like he made his. Once you've made it, you can't go back on it."

I frown, not sure I like what he's saying. "So, why did you make the choice?"

He holds his chin up on his hand and tells me, "Because I wanted an exciting life. By the time I met your mother, I was already in too deep. If only I'd known before I signed my life away, that there was something more worthwhile in existence than chasing an adrenalin high."

I look down at my hands, because there's not much in it between my father and my husband, but there is one little factor that separates them.

"I think Nate joined because he grew up struggling. He's mega clever. I think that's why he did it."

His brow furrows deeply, making him seem his age suddenly. "If I tell you something, you have to promise me you won't tell him it came from me."

"Okay?"

"After I found out you'd married him, I looked him up. His background, I mean. He and his mother used to live in trailers."

"Go on..."

"She was a prostitute."

My heart clenches, thinking of Nate going through that.

"To pay for the drink," I say.

"She had a lot of charges against her. Theft. Public indecency. Drugs. I hardly think that was any kind of childhood. You don't need me to say it, but I'm going to say it anyway. You need to be careful. If he thinks you know something about me, he will not only pick up on it, he may turn nasty if he thinks your loyalty is with me. I know the type all too well. He'll be good at hiding his inner torment, but it's there Bea. It won't have left him. It'll always be with him. That life, it affects people, you know? He's probably had to do some things to survive."

"I guess, but haven't we all?"

He gives me a look full of regret. "Some more than others."

"Doesn't it bother you? That we can't bury them?"

"Sometimes," he says, "but they're never really gone, are they? They're still in here."

He pats his heart, and for the first time tonight, he looks emotional.

"What did you do? For them to warrant killing your family," I ask, trying to avoid his steely stare.

"I didn't do anything. Horace was the best analyst they ever had, and they couldn't touch me while he lived, because he would have revolted otherwise. But when he was gone... well... they didn't have use for a washed-up piece of shit like me anymore."

I don't get that. I try not to let it show that I don't get it—but I just don't get it. Why not just kill Bill Fleming and toss him in the river? Why did they have to kill my mum and sister, too? Does he think I'm stupid? There are rules, even for monsters, and there had to be a reason for them to do away with my mum and sister—and for my father to get free.

"Listen to me, Beatrice. Nobody ever escapes this life, nobody. Even if he wants out, there is no escape. Do you hear me?"

"So..." I run my hands over my tired face, wishing I could be back home, where I could just crawl into bed with my husband and never wake up. "You're saying there's no escape for Nate, right? There's no getting out? If there was, he would have found a route out already?"

"There's no escape for him, but there could be for you. If I were you, I'd play the dumbest you can manage. Say nothing. Question nothing. Know nothing. Take care of your children and yourself. When the time is right, I could get you out, but not him."

"No," I assert, reaching over and squeezing his arm, "there must be some way. There must be. He has to get free, too. I won't leave him."

"He's a clever kid, so believe me, if there was an exit route, he'd have already thought of it. You don't escape the Collective unless you appear dead, like me. The house was too heavily obliterated for them to prove my corpse was there, yes or no. His boss trusts him because Nate told them I was dead, and I haven't surfaced since. If you and I were to be seen together, all of us would be dead by morning. Trust me. They are plugged into everybody. There's nowhere they can't get you."

"You've been watching me, or else how did you know I'd be in Vegas?"

"My daughter wouldn't come to Vegas unless she was looking for something. Plus, I knew if there was anyone you'd keep in touch with, it'd be that wicked old tart Stella. She got you this gig, right?"

"I see."

He stands up, throwing some $100 bills on the table. I rise from my seat, not sure I want to let him go.

"Can't you stay? A little longer."

"I've already stayed too long," he tells me.

"How do we stay in touch?"

"We don't."

"I can't believe this."

"I know," he says, pulling me into his arms.

He doesn't smell so great.

"You sent me the money, didn't you?"

"I did," he says.

"Do you have enough?"

"Plenty."

"Are you sure?"

"Yes," he says, "but I can't live in fancy hotels. It'll draw attention. I can't manage anything much, Bea. It's how it has to be. Knowing you're safe and happy is enough for me."

But I'm not happy, Dad. My husband still works for them. I want to say it, but I don't. If he wants to think of me being happy, because it makes it easier for him, then so be it.

"You'll be fine, Bea. You're strong. You've always been independent. You've never needed anyone to keep you upright. You'll do great. I know it." He kisses my forehead and leaves out of the back way. After he's gone, I don my shades and walk back out into the madness of Fremont Street, all while tears wash away the emptiness of my soul.

Chapter Forty-One

When I turn up for reshoots the next day, my hair and make-up girl holds up my photo from yesterday and compares the two. "Someone had a late night?"

"You could say that." I barely slept a wink, my mind on overdrive. What sleep I did get was plagued by various images. If I wasn't dreaming about my house ablaze on the Fremont Street video screen, I was dreaming about Dad floating around in hologram form, telling me we're all going to die eventually—which is true, but not what I wanted to hear from him, not in a dream. All my night-time rest ever gives me is night terrors, and for once, I'd prefer my dreams to provide some sort of reassurance, not constant anxiety.

"We're gonna have some trouble making you the same, but that's why you've got me," she says, as I sit in the chair and she begins her work, trying to make me look the same as I did yesterday.

I haven't been in hair and make-up longer than five minutes when there's a kerfuffle across the room.

"Security, security!" Ankar shouts, the photographer's number one assistant.

"Tell her to come verify me," I hear a guy shout, and I recognise that voice.

Rolling my eyes, I fold my arms and stay in my seat.

He's just ridiculous. I told him the whole purpose of this weekend was so he could take the kids for a change, not me. But oh no, he can't help himself, can he?

Nate marches through the cordoned-off sections and blasts into my section. He arrives big and tall, his chest puffed out, arms swinging.

"Well, hello husband."

Harley, my make-up artist, looks frozen to the spot when she sees him.

"Why don't these people believe I'm your husband?" he asks, sounding paranoid.

I keep my arms crossed and give him a filthy look. "Husbands stay home and if we let everyone in, how would that look, huh?"

"Well your friend... is it Tabs... she said she recognised me."

I clear my throat, trying not to laugh. "Yeah, I'm sure I'll be thanking her later. Don't stop what you were doing Harley, ignore this idiot."

She smiles nervously. I can tell she's intimidated by my guy.

"What's up, then? Where are the kids?" I ask him.

"Martha took them to her place. She's going to bring them back home this evening. I thought I'd fly in, take you to lunch and fly back with you."

"I'm not flying back till tonight, Nate. We discussed this. I'm working all day."

"Yeah, well... you still eat lunch, right?" He's fidgety and he's jittery. This is how he gets, and I've only been gone from home for one day and night. Doesn't he know what it's like for me when he's gone for weeks sometimes?

"We normally nibble on the buffet, but I can't eat a proper lunch, I'll bloat."

"Okay, well then, can I just stay and watch?"

"Fine," I answer, sounding aggrieved.

I'm not unhappy to see him—well, I am a little—but he has left our kids alone with Martha in another state. It's not ideal to leave them without a legal guardian when they're so young.

He watches Harley adding a base to my face and tries to look interested.

I start worrying about why he's here. Does he know about last night? Has he heard something? Seen something? Does he sense something?

"I love you Nate, but you look really out of place round here. Everyone's starving and you just look like a great big hunk of steak, or something."

He manages a smile. "I'm sorry, I shoulda called."

"Yeah, you shoulda."

He winks. "I'll go do... something. Gamble. Shop, I don't know."

"You do that."

He stands up and asks Harley, "Can I kiss her? Is that allowed?"

"Yeah, sure, just don't bruise or scratch her. I'm trying my hardest already here."

"Eh, less of the cheek," I chastise.

Nate leans in and kisses my lips softly. He holds my head, his hands in my hair, staring at my face as he hangs above me. "I just missed you so much."

"I know you did, baby. Come back for me at four, okay? We'll get out of here right away."

"I can do that." He kisses me again and leaves.

Everyone in the vicinity goes quiet as Nate passes by, making his way back out.

I hear the gasps of awe after he's gone.

Harley stares at me. "Oh my god, bitch."

"Yeah, well…"

If only these people knew the baggage he comes with.

Well, I can't talk. We kind of share the baggage now, don't we?

ON THE FLIGHT HOME, we're cuddled up on the seats, wrapped up together. We've got the window seat, the middle seat and the other one's empty. It's freezing on this tin can, but it's boiling on the land down below. Go figure.

There's so much floating around my head, but I know Nate's heart is in the right place. I know he loves me very much. I'm lucky to have found love at all, aren't I? I have to keep reminding myself of that.

"You feel so good," I tell him, my mind hazy, my body tired. His chest feels unbelievably comforting against my face.

"You too, Bebe. You're so beautiful, you know? I'm proud to call you mine."

"I know, big guy."

He presses a kiss to my temple. "Get some rest. We land in an hour. I'll wake you, then."

"Okay big guy," I reply, descending into sleep, where more dreams of terror await…

IT'S MUCH LATER AT night, and we've just made love. The beauty of our bodies, entwined, is something I always seek at times like this. Being with him makes me forget about everything else.

"Are you leaving me, Bebe?" he asks, still catching his breath.

I roll onto his chest and search his eyes, his body still covered in sweat. "What?"

"Are you leaving me?"

"I don't understand. Why are you asking me that?"

"It feels like you're leaving me. Don't ask me why, that's just how I feel."

"I don't understand what you're saying. We just made love. How can I be leaving you when I just had you inside my body?"

"Yeah, but are you leaving me? Inside your mind? Your body's one thing, your mind another."

I lean in and kiss his lips, kiss his cheek, his ear and his forehead. "How could I leave what I love more than anything else in the entire world?"

He looks assuaged and we roll so we're looking at one another, lying on our sides. He drags the sheets up to our waists and plays with my hair.

"I can't explain it, it's just a gut feeling," he says, "but I feel like you're leaving me. When I look into your eyes, there's something different. Martha says she's worried about you. She says I shouldn't go away so often. I don't want to, but—"

I roll onto my back and look up at the ceiling, my arm flung above my head. I figure he knows something's wrong, so I may as well just admit what I'm really feeling.

"I want you to leave the Collective and for us to leave Texas. I wanna go back to Montreux and live there. We were so happy there, weren't we?"

He lays his hand across my chest and my heart beats hard across the palm of his hand.

"You know."

"I know."

"And you're not leaving me?"

"No, but I can't help the way I feel. I want you to quit. It's how I feel. I know that it's probably impossible, but I want you to quit. I hate it when you're gone. I want to go back to Montreux and for it to be like it was. For it to be just us and our freedom. I don't want this. I don't want to be living on a cattle farm, when cattle isn't really your business. I don't enjoy the heat in summer. I don't mind a lot of things here, but I'm European Nate, and I want to go back home." I turn and find his eyes glistening. "We were so happy there, we fell in love there. It's not sweltering and it's fresh and pure. It was wonderful, wasn't it?"

"Of course, it was," he says, his breath catching in his throat, "but you know it's not as simple as that. We could go back there, but never to that same house. And if we went back, we could never leave, not even from out of our own front door. The children couldn't go to school. The life we have here would seem a holiday in comparison. We wouldn't be able to live out in the open. We would have to hide for the rest of our lives."

A tear snakes down my cheek. "Then we'll hide. We can teach the children ourselves. Once they're old enough, they can live out in the real world if they want. We'll continue to hide, but at least we'll have one another."

He tugs me close and holds me tight. "You really love me?"

"I never wanted marriage or children before I met you. Of course, I do. You're my whole world. I can't bear it when you're gone. It makes me feel so sad. When you go, it seems to get longer and longer. It hurts so much. I can't live like this anymore, but it's not that I don't love you. Even if I left, it wouldn't be because I don't love you. It'd be because I just can't take what it is that you do."

He holds my face in both of his hands. "If I could take it back, all of it, I would. I'd do everything differently, but then—"

"We would never have met."

He nods and his shiny eyes leak a tear. We kiss deeply and eventually, we cuddle up, ready to sleep.

"I'll find a way, Bebe. I'll find a way, for us."

"I trust you, Nate. I'll wait."

"I don't deserve you."

"No, you don't, but you have me. Till death do us part. Maybe even then..."

"I know, I know," he whispers, shuddering in my arms.

He falls asleep before me, as I remain awake, cuddled in his arms but still troubled.

I'm not going to tell him about my father being alive. My dad was right—Nate is incredibly insecure. He thinks even after giving me two adorable children I don't really love him? I love him ten times more! I just wish he was here, bringing up our children with me. I want more babies, too. I just don't want to do this all alone, with only a bereft maid for company. As lovely as she is, Martha's not family. She's an employee.

I shut my eyes and picture the house in Montreux. I can see me and Nate wandering around the Christmas market, eating lots of food and buying even more to take home. We're on the big wheel again, laughing and joking. He's swinging the seat more than I'm comfortable with. He has that pretzel in his hand and he's going to use the salt when we get home.

As I think more and more about that Christmas Eve night, I remember that Nate didn't seem at all different. He wasn't acting strangely. He didn't know that we were going to be set upon, so to speak, only hours later. Nate was himself. He knew nothing about my father turning up, unexpectedly. In fact, my father might have picked Christmas Eve to approach me, because I never sleep well the night before Christmas. I always stay up late, it's my thing. I still do it, even in Texas.

Still, there are things that don't add up. Truly, I don't know what to believe...

Nate allowed me to think he was dead for almost a full 24 hours. He dropped into my life under circumstances that weren't pleasant. He may have been my executioner, if he hadn't liked what he saw.

Also, there's the whole thing regarding Nate's mother. It's not hard for me to believe Claire-Anne was mixed up in all that stuff my father mentioned, but did Nate's childhood make him a monster, or is he the guy I know and love? The guy who buys me beautiful things, rocks my world in the bedroom and tries to make sure I'm always fed, warm and happy.

If there's only one thing I know, it is this: I have to trust myself.

I must remind myself that my children come first and through my love for them, my judgment trumps everyone else's.

I fall asleep with that image of Montreux in my mind—a snowy Christmas Eve, a new engagement ring on my finger, and a wonderful man waiting for me in bed. It was maybe the happiest moment of my life, and the most ignorant, because just minutes later, my strength was cruelly shattered as I watched what I thought was Nate go up in smoke.

It's time to regain my stoic resolve and help Nate figure this out. It's time to wind back the clock and bring back the woman I once was, not this one I am now, too afraid to tell him this life isn't for me.

It's time to make a stand.

Chapter Forty-Two

I've been all set to be strong, to resist; to tell him that's it—I'm done.

I can't do it, though.

Fuck this love thing. Fuck it. My love for him overrides all else. I can't help it. He started packing this morning and I'm too scared to ask him when he will be leaving again. Whenever he packs a bag, it's normally the next day that he goes, but I just can't bear to have this reality confirmed. I just don't want to face up to this ever-present reality we have going on here: he goes, and I stay behind, as ignorant as ever.

I'm preparing lunch with my back to the room, when he stalks up behind me, sliding his arms around my waist. I tense and he notices. He halts, not moving, unsure.

"Don't touch me," I ask, and he slowly retracts his arms.

He leaves the room and once he's gone, I cling to the counter and try to take a deep breath. The thing is, I can't. My breath is trapped inside me.

I rush from the house and dash across the lawn, heading for the summer house. Once I'm inside and the doors are closed behind me, I let go of all my pain, crying and crying. There's so much light in the room but I'd give anything for darkness right now, a cave, or a corner. Somewhere I can go to sleep and never wake up, willing the nightmare to fade. I lie on the fainting couch, letting go of it all. He's the man I love, but I don't think I trust him.

How can I?

SINCE LUNCH, I'VE BEEN out of action. I've made him take care of the kids. I've taken my horse out, which I rarely do. I've gone for walks, alone. I've not eaten. I've not changed, or washed, or anything. I don't care anymore. I don't care about anything.

In the evening, he finds me in Claire-Anne's old room. She used to sit up on the windowsill sometimes, watching the horses in the paddock to the side of the house. I'm watching the stars, or maybe nothing. Maybe I'm staring into space.

"I can't leave if you won't take care of the children," he says, his manner and tone short.

I know he doesn't like coming in this room; it's half the reason I'm in here, hoping he wouldn't cross the threshold to find me.

"What do you care, Nate? Just go. Get lost. Do what you want, you're going to anyway."

I can see out of the corner of my eye, his fists are bunching, over and over. He's tense and I'm upset. We're rubbish when we're like this.

"You know it's not what I want," he growls. "I have to go. I have no choice."

"Well it seems to me like you can't wait to get away."

I fly from the window seat and push right past him, leaving the room in a hurry.

I head for the bedroom and he catches up with me as I start undressing out of my sweaty clothes, which I've had on all day, not even changing after my ride.

"I can't stand to see you like this," he exclaims.

"Keep your voice down, you'll wake the kids."

"Oh, so you do care, do you?"

I walk towards him and smack him around the head. How dare he accuse me of not caring? Caring is all I ever do.

Pointing a finger at him, I warn, "I don't smoke, I barely drink, I cook them fresh food every day. They're always clean and tidy. I buy them cute outfits and things, all by myself. I never have anyone with me when I'm shopping. No husband. No grandma. Just Martha. They receive a hug and a kiss from me every night. I read to them, sing to them, play with them. Take them to the soft play. Take them swimming. Bathe them. Hold them as they cry. So fuck you if I decided to take one day off. Fuck you, Nate. Don't you ever criticise me. Don't you ever..."

I run out of gas and turn around sharply, giving him my back. I undress the rest of the way and storm into the bathroom, switching on the shower. I'm grateful when he doesn't follow. It's another opportunity to have a cry in private.

When I emerge in my robe, he's sitting in the wooden rocking chair by the window, looking out over the front aspect of the house, down onto the driveway.

In profile, he looks beset by anxiety. His jaw is set and he's biting his lip, over and over. My instinct is to go over, sit in his lap and wrap my arms around him, hold him close and kiss him. Say I'm sorry. Whisper I love him. I want him. I need him.

"I knew you weren't coping, but today showed me just how much," he says, bouncing his fist on his knee, "so, if you're ready,

I'll tell you everything. Once you have all the information, you can stay or leave, it's up to you. I just can't stand the thought of you—"

He can't say it, but we both know what he's thinking. He can't stand the thought of me going the same way as his mother—not caring about her kid anymore.

"Tell me everything," I beg, because even though I've buried the truth for so long, I need to hear it now. Just so I know I'm not insane, if anything.

"We lived in a trailer," he begins, his eyes still focused on the world outside, as if he's picturing the story as he's telling me it. "Mom was a wreck. I used to have this friend, Enrique, the same one who works for me now. I'd go to his trailer and eat with his family, otherwise I never would've eaten. When I was twelve, they discovered I had above average IQ. They sent me for more tests and I was offered a scholarship. When Mom found out we'd have to move, she said no. She was stuck, wrapped up in her own twisted lifestyle of drugs, booze, men. I'd hide in the cupboard whenever she had one of her boyfriends over. I wouldn't have to see it. I could hear it, but I couldn't see it. It wasn't... I mean, it was awful, okay. She was only ever into abusive men. It made me think sex was gross and it made me angry and vengeful. So, I was pretty mad when she said I couldn't go to this special school. I told my teacher about what she was like and I got taken away by social services. They put me in a foster home near the new school and my life got so much better. She would never have mentioned it to you because she blocked it out, like it never happened. Like I never went away and was still hiding in the cupboard. Then, when I was nineteen, someone approached me. Someone unfamiliar. He told me he recruited people like me. He knew I was gifted. He knew how I made money. He knew I was a hacker."

"So, that bit's true then?" I ask him. "You *are* a hacker?"

He opens his hands. "I had a sports scholarship but working for this guy would mean dropping out of college. My foster parents had encouraged me to get the qualifications, do everything right—delay the inevitable and stay on at college, to get the credentials, you know? Have the letters after my name. For me, studying at college meant I was on the straight and narrow, that nobody would suspect what I did behind closed doors... but what this guy was offering, it was *big*. Huge. It was virtually impossible to turn down. I knew it would mean leaving everything behind, but I looked at it like this... I could wait three or four years to leave college and start earning real money, or I could earn money straight away—and there was no competition, not for me. The Collective presented me with this idea of getting out—of having freedom."

"So, what happened?"

"I was nineteen and my foster folks weren't my legal guardians anymore... just people who thought they were giving me good advice. We were never that close, but that's not to say they weren't decent people, they were. So, I upped and went. I made the decision, and I was gone. I wanted something for myself."

"I get that."

"I signed up to become one of the Collective, though I didn't know at the time what I was getting myself involved in. I think that's why they choose people like me. People with a hazy family history. No real ties. A little rough around the edges, people who won't ask too many questions."

He waits. I can tell what for. He needs me to ask him the question, because it's too difficult for him to just come out and say it.

"What is it the Collective does?"

"If I tell you, it can never leave this room, Beatrice. I mean it. If they know you know, they'll kill you. Trust me, I know. They wouldn't hesitate."

"Tell me," I demand.

He turns his face and looks at me, shadows falling over his handsome visage now the dark is drawing in.

"We stage deaths," he says, in barely a whisper, "we extract people from their lives for a huge sum of money. They either go into hiding or they start again. It depends upon the reason for wanting to do it in the first place. Some are genuinely sick and tired of life and want to escape, some people just want to get away from an enemy, but the police won't put them in witness protection, or whatever. The reasons are always different depending on the person. For instance, a lot of famous people are now living on an uncharted island in the South Pacific. They just wanted out. My job has always been to hide all the digital evidence. Cut security cameras. Tamper with bank accounts, whatever. Make things look real, like with your father."

I throw my hands over my face. "Oh my god, what are you saying?"

He stands up and walks around, his fists still bunching as he moves. "Before I even worked for the Collective, your father approached them. It was a long, long time ago now. He wanted to die, said he'd got himself backed into a corner. He said it wasn't safe for him anymore and that he was putting your lives in danger—those of you, your sister and mother, I mean."

"Oh my god." My head starts pounding.

"He didn't have enough money, not to make a whole family disappear. We could make him disappear, but not all of you, so instead he sought the help of a friend who worked for the Collective, and that's how you all ended up starting again. You took on new identities."

A huge tear is poised on the edge of my eyelashes, but for some reason it's refusing to fall.

"I was fifteen," I tell him. "We changed our identities. Nothing was ever the same again."

"In the late 80s, before your mother ever met him, your dad was dismissed from the Army due to gross misconduct. The files are sealed. Nobody knows what he did. We only know it was bad. Given the things you've told me about him, I can only assume he began work as a contract killer after that. Maybe he did that for a while before he joined the Collective, which was when you all moved up to Scotland. A friend of his, a guy called Horace, swung it all for him—the new identities, everything—but Horace was one of the Collective, he couldn't be seen to be showing favouritism, so your dad had to make a deal, and in exchange for your new identities and our protection, he had to begin working for the Collective."

"So, before we all moved up to Edinburgh, why did he want to drop off the face of the earth and fake his death, as you say? Had he killed the wrong person?"

"We never knew, Beatrice. We never knew the specifics. We just knew he felt in danger and that's why he needed to leave you all."

"Oh god, so when the house blew up in Edinburgh... what was that? What happened?"

His eyes narrow. He's studying my reaction as he admits, "He could have staged it, just like we do all the time. Perhaps he took matters into his own hands, assembled a team of his own to manage everything. We don't know. We just don't know. The blast was so fierce, there wasn't enough evidence left behind. All we know is that given your father's history, it's not surprising he might try to evade the Collective and drop off the face of the earth off his own back, without any help from us."

"But why would they all leave me...? Why would Mum and Phoebe agree to it?" My heart starts racing so hard, I can barely breathe. My face feels like it's on fire. "Why not me?"

"My best guess is that maybe, he knew you wouldn't willingly go with them. Either that or too many people are familiar with your face. Your image is all over the internet, of course. It makes it harder to hide you from view."

I dig my hands into my hair and twist it. "They could be alive?" Phoebe and my mother, I mean. I'm still not sure whether it's right to tell Nate about my father...

"I personally think they are. I think they all survived. It's why I was put on your tail, to find out what you knew."

"So, while I was working away in Florida, Dad saw his chance?"

"Yes."

"And I was left wondering what the fuck had happened... I was left in the dark for three months, thinking I could be next? Because Dad didn't trust me?"

"Yes, I think so. It's the most logical reasoning, no?"

"And then you came along. Didn't you?" I look up into his eyes, where he stands in front of me, no longer tense but still unsure of my reaction.

"You landed in Texas, my old stomping ground. They sent me to that store, to find out where you were at, what was your mind-set. My boss thought you were acting odd. He didn't understand why you didn't just go home and continue living. He thought you knew something... he thought perhaps you knew about the Collective. He just wanted me to find out what you did and didn't know. To put his mind at rest."

I shake my head. Side to side. Side to side. It all makes sense.

"Was it ever real for you? Did you ever love me? I don't..."

He kneels before me, takes my hands and catches my eye. I see love in his expression, I see fear. "Montreux was as real for me as it was for you. I fell in love even when I didn't want to. I fell so hard and fast for you, Beatrice. I love you more than anything in the whole world. You and the kids are the realest things to ever happen to me. You're the only woman I have ever loved... will ever love."

He takes my hands and we slide our fingers through one another's.

"Why's he done this to me, Nate? Why?"

"I don't know." He shakes his head. "I really don't."

"So, after he paid his dues with the Collective, that was it? He just thought, 'right, time to die now'. Is that right? Was that what he thought?"

"I think so, Bebe."

"What about the hotel in Longlake? The shots through the door. The stick-up at the grocery store. The mugger in Montreux. The car explosion at the log cabin."

"Aside from the mugging, everything else was set up." He swallows hard. "My reaction that night, when that guy held that knife to you in Montreux, that was real. My fear that night was a hundred per cent real. I was terrified. The rest was to test your reactions, put you under pressure and then find out what you knew."

"Staged?"

"Yes," he admits.

I swiftly snatch my fingers out of his and push him away. This whole thing has been one big farce.

I walk away and stand facing the nearest wall, putting my head in my hands, hoping the wall might absorb me and I might become the same as it—nothingness.

I forgot my father's first lesson: trouble begets trouble.

I wasn't the trouble, though. It was the year I met Nate that it began following me around—because Nate is trouble. He's trouble! The only reason I didn't see it was because I was in love.

"What about my father? You said he wasn't there, the night the car exploded in Montreux. You said it was a hologram?" I turn and stare at him, aghast and numb, freed yet even more imprisoned. "If he's still alive, then... was it him?"

"It was a hologram, I assure you."

He sounds honest, but is he?

In Vegas, my father swore he was there that night in Montreux, so one of them is lying...

It's terribly difficult to process the reality... that Nate has been working for the Collective all this time.

"What have you been doing this whole time we've been together, Nate? Have you only ever been with me so you could find out if I knew about what had really happened to my family? I don't understand how you can say you love me when you don't even trust me. I told you over and over, I knew nothing and you still didn't believe me! Then there's Montreux... You fucking staged the car explosion to see what I would do, didn't you? You staged it all. You picked a night when I was the happiest I had ever been, carefree and recently engaged. That night, you crushed me, utterly and completely, all for the sake of your investigation into my father. Just how much of our life is real, and how much is fake, Nate? Because right now I'd bet on it being more fake than real. I cannot believe I ever trusted you. I've blinded myself to the truth. I must be mad. Of course you never, ever left the Collective. Of course they were never after you. YOU ARE THE COLLECTIVE, aren't you! You lying sack of shit! You broke me to the extent that I've been too scared to see the truth, but now I see it, oh now I see it all crystal clear. You broke me so you could control me. You're only now telling me the truth because you've got a guilty conscience, not because you love me and feel a duty to me. I'm right, AREN'T I?"

"BEATRICE!" he demands, standing at his full height, looking right at me from the other side of the room. "I was a teenager when they got me. A kid. I have no way out. You think you work for an agency like ours and ever escape? You don't. You don't get free. I was following orders. It's what I've been doing from when I was a kid. You follow orders; you stay safe. That's how it goes. Imagine if it got out that we exist, that we do this... what trouble would that bring? If people started thinking, 'Hey, did my favourite popstar really die in an avalanche, or did he go to the Collective and strike a deal, giving him a new life, one where he still gets to keep all his money, but there's now none of the stress or expectation?' You don't escape this. Once you're in, that's it. It's how it goes. Trust is everything."

I'm raging inside, but something about all of this still doesn't add up.

Does Nate know my father has been in touch? Or does he want to know?

What is happening here? My dad said he *was* in Montreux, but Nate's still saying he wasn't.

Who do I trust? My father or Nate…

"So, what? You'll die doing this? Is that what you're telling me? You'll die doing this. Because you'll never stop, and they will never let you go… is that what you're saying? I mean, correct me if I'm wrong, but you are claiming that my father was working for the Collective and then opted out, dying and taking my mother and sister with him. That's what you said, wasn't it? So, if he got free, why can't you? Hmm?"

He sighs, walking back to the rocking chair. He slams his arse down into it and runs his hands through his hair. "I'm too damn valuable, Bebe. I'm young, too. I've got years left in me. They won't let me go."

"Why can't you work from home?"

"It doesn't work like that. I work in an operations room, in Geneva, where the Collective is based out of. I head up a team. We have to plan the logistics months, sometimes years in advance. It's complex stuff. We work for hours and hours, for weeks on end, never sleeping. Have you ever wondered why I never sleep? I'm not trained to sleep, I'm trained to work."

"Well, this is bullshit. Total bullshit."

"Are you going to turn around now and tell me you didn't sign up for this, Beatrice? Is that what you're going to say? Because if it is, fine, okay. But you knew when you met me that I wasn't your ordinary guy. You've always known it. You know I'm not that different to your father. Aside from the killing aspect, that is."

I shake my head at him. If he wants to try a low blow, fine, but just because my dad was an assassin (perhaps still is), that does not mean that Nate can take the higher ground because of it.

"I'll tell you in what way you are like my father," I start, finding it hard to speak and not sound out of breath, because I'm that angry, "you're a very capable liar and I don't believe anything you say anymore. I don't trust you and I don't want my kids growing up thinking that lying is the way to go. You and he, you're the same in that respect. Look what he's done, making me think he's dead, when he isn't. My sister... my mother... I can't even think about that. I can't process it right now. You and he both want the excitement of *that life* and the indulgence of a family, too. Well, you can't have both. I've put up with this for long enough."

"And you wonder why I never told you," he shouts, throwing his arms around.

His anger is palpable as he picks up the ceramic plant pot off the windowsill, throwing it across the room so it smashes against the wall.

I sit on the bed and listen as he angrily grabs his stuff off the floor, flinging it over his shoulder. He runs downstairs, slams the front door shut and starts up his truck.

He tears off and leaves the ranch in a raging fury. After he's gone, I send a text to my agent:

Coming to New York. Line me up some work. Lis x

Chapter Forty-Three

ix Months Later

S After finishing for the day, I go to my booth and wipe off my make-up, peel off my false eyelashes and untie my hair from the various pins it's been pulled back against my scalp with. Rob, one of the lackeys round here, is around my age and sidles up next to me, staring at me through the mirror as I clean up.

"Do you want to catch a drink tonight, Lis?"

"No, no, I have to get back to my kids."

"Oh yeah, I always forget you've got kids. You seem so..."

"Young," I offer, before he says something daft.

"Single," he says.

"Well, just because I'm single, doesn't mean I once wasn't, does it?"

"No, but you know how it is... all these moms... they still have something with the dad, don't they? Someone told me that, Nate—is that his name?—doesn't even see his kids anymore."

I put down what I'm doing and turn and glare. "Fuck off, Rob. Before I kneecap you."

He burns bright red, not knowing what to do with himself. I don't think I've ever sworn at work, or threatened to kneecap someone before. Maybe he believes I would actually go through with it—because he leaves the side of my booth looking disgusted and afraid.

I just cannot deal with this nonsense anymore—guys coming onto me, when they don't even know the half of it. Maybe Rob didn't deserve the way I treated him right then, but people around here are treating me like I'm fodder for their watercooler gossip. Most people imagine it's great being hit on all the time, that it validates my beauty. Well, all it does is remind me that my heart belongs to one man—a man I can't have. I can't have Nate because of his profession, and because his profession puts my life and that of my kids in danger.

I drag on an oversized sweater and a wool overcoat, some shades and a beanie. I know I'll still get papped for the fashion columns, but I don't give a shit right now. Besides, I only took on the mantel of the new face of Estée Lauder because I need to feed my kids and property isn't cheap in New York.

I leave the tower block in Tribeca where I just had the shoot and snatch a cab outside without having to wait.

"Bleecker Street, please," I ask, and the cabbie says nothing. It's not unusual. Some are more talkative than others and I prefer no talk.

After he's dropped me off, I pick up dinner from my favourite vegan restaurant around the corner from home. I can't eat meat anymore—it only reminds me of him.

The kids are waiting patiently for me as I arrive. The nanny Tilly has them dressed presentably on the couch and she's ready with her bag—to get out of here.

"Thank you Tilly. I'm not late, am I?"

"No, perfectly timed, as always."

"You're too kind." I notice on the clock I'm a good five minutes late, but I'm a good boss in other respects.

"Hello babies," I yell, and they throw their arms up for me. I pick the kids up together and squish them tight. "Have you had your dinner?"

"We ate, Mommy," I'm told by Seth, and Lola nods along.

"Okay, Mommy's going to eat and then we're going to go play round at Aunt Mimi's, okay?"

They both scream with pleasure. They love my friend Mimi and her twin boys. Mimi's a designer I met and became very friendly with, as soon as I landed in New York. I'm the only model she wants to see wearing her stuff. Works for me.

"We'll watch some cartoons while Mommy eats her eggplant."

I PUSH THE KIDS TO Washington Square Park, nearby. It's nearly spring and so much nicer at this time of year. Everything suddenly seems to break into life.

Mimi welcomes us at the door, all smiles. Her house is just off the park.

She's a single mother, too.

"What's that face for?" she asks.

After the kids all rush into the living room to explore the toys Mimi has laid out for them, we congregate in the kitchen with two glasses of wine.

"This runner sort of asked me out for a drink today, but... he got stupid and I got stupid... and I told him I'd kneecap him. It sort of slipped out."

Mimi raises one dark eyebrow at me and runs her hand through her afro hair. "Say what now?"

"Yep."

"You're in real need of it, aren't you woman?"

"Possibly."

I can't even think about sex. Not now, not ever.

Not without Nate.

He's still my husband in every way, it's just that he's not here, not by my side.

"He said something like..." I try to remember exactly what it was he said. "He said I seem single, even though I've got two kids. He said I act like I never... he basically said it's like I cut off the father of my kids. Anyway, whatever it was he really said, or was intending to get across to me, it thoroughly pissed me off."

"Well, you are young to be single and separated, with two kids," she says, "and if he's a guy like any other, they just run their mouths off without thinking it through."

"Yeah, but... you should have seen his face."

"I can imagine. You do keep yourself fit and trim. You have a swimmer's body. Maybe he looked at you and knew you could do it. Kneecap him, I mean," she titters.

I slide her an evil grin, not saying it—but I could. I could actually kneecap the jerk.

"So, are you ever going to tell me what happened between you and Mr Buchanan?"

I shake my head. "It's complicated."

"So, we're still going with that, huh?"

"Yep. All the way."

Mimi is forty-two and divorced because her husband had an affair.

I'm separated because my bloke is involved in something called the Collective, which enables people to fake their own deaths and start a new life. Imagine if it got out...

I suppose everyone would like to start again if they could. Brand new. Shed everything that went before and start again. I guess that's maybe why people have affairs, because it allows them to be part of a fantasy for a while, even though the person they really love is getting hurt in the process.

So, that's why I won't say anything. It would open a can of worms.

When one of the twins starts crying, Mimi leaves the room in a rush. I stand alone in the kitchen, contemplating my predicament.

Since Nate left and never came back, I've received parcels without the sender's details attached, but I know they're from him. He sends toys and games he knows the kids would like. He even sends clothes, and every now and again, he will adjust what sizes he's getting the kids. It's like I can feel him watching me all the time, but I can't see him. He must be checking up on me to know what size clothes his kids need, or else he's good at guesswork, which could well be the case. Nate is the most intelligent man I've ever known. He can diagnose injuries in horses and he knows which areas of his land will be better for the cattle, from week to week. He plots the routes the cattle will take, even though he's never with them.

He's emotionally intelligent, most of all. He's the best at comforting the kids. I try, but Nate doesn't even have to, he's a natural. God, I'm still so in love with him.

A part of me thinks he told me the truth about the Collective to get rid of me, knock me out of the picture sort of thing. Like he picked a fight with me on purpose. With him being so clever, I know he doesn't do anything without a reason. On Valentine's Day just gone, I received an enormous bunch of pink peonies and there's only one person who knows they are my favourite flower—and he sends me them every year on the same day—this year being no different even despite his absence.

I know Nathan cares. I know he loves me. He even makes deposits in my bank account. I know it's him—so I also know he's up to something. I reckon I've just got to wait this out.

"Todd broke his train," Mimi says as she returns to the kitchen. "You look miles away."

"You wouldn't believe how modelling takes it out of you."

Chapter Forty-Four

We arrive home at eight p.m. The kids are almost asleep as I carry the stroller up six steps towards the house. To own a house in New York means prosperity, so they say. To me, it means a home for my kids. It's not even half as nice as our place in Texas, but this is where I can get work—and easily.

Getting the stroller up is no mean feat, it's a double, but I manage it because my kids are sleepy and I'm alone, so I don't have any other choice. A single mother, or so I pretend to the world. A single mother who attends Krav Maga and grew up knowing her father was an assassin. Somehow, I always knew. The words were never said, but I always knew—an instinct.

When I roll the wheels over the threshold, I instinctively know my house has been invaded in my absence. There's a scent on the air, but not only that, there's this feeling—a sense—that little things have been moved. The fridge has been opened—I know—because the stinky cheese has escaped recently, even though my nanny fed the kids hours ago now and we've been out all evening. I can also smell the fire has been lit in the living room.

I leave my sleepy children in their buggy and grab my gun from the hallway safe. I can tell from its hefty weight, it's still loaded. I take off the safety and hold it out as I peek around the corner of the door to the living room.

"Oh, it's just you," I whisper, signalling the children are sleeping.

"You all right, kid?" my father asks, as he sits by the fire, as if he couldn't be more at his leisure.

"What?" I wonder why he asks.

He nods towards the gun I'm holding.

"Oh. Well, I'm not in Kansas anymore, Dad."

"You certainly are not."

"Help me get the kids upstairs, will you? They're tired."

We last saw one another in Vegas months ago, and yet being father and daughter, we can slip into this easy exchange once more because of the fact we're cut from the same mould.

He meets his grandchildren for the first time as they lie sleeping in their pram.

I grab Seth first and hand him to my father, who looks more uncomfortable than I've ever seen Nate look while holding his own blood in his hands—and Nate never had a real family growing up. As far as I know, my dad had a charmed upbringing and a close relationship with his parents until they were killed in a car crash together, leaving Dad an orphan.

"You scored a good gig with Estée Lauder," he remarks, as we take the creaky stairs. Lola feels so warm and gorgeous in my arms.

"Ah, you noticed."

"How could I not? It's a big brand here. It's everywhere."

"It was meant to be, I think. Stella sorted me out not long after I came to New York. Right time, right circumstances. If I were younger, it wouldn't work."

"Don't remind me. The older you get, the older I feel."

In the nursery on the second floor, I show him where to put Seth and after the babies are down, I set about removing their clothes until they're just left in their baby grows. I had the forethought to put clean nappies on them before we left Mimi's, knowing they may both be asleep by the time we returned home—as is usual.

After I tuck the kids under their blankets, set the baby monitor up and kiss them goodnight, I leave the room and he follows. We head back down the creaky stairs.

"So, how come you're in New York?" he asks.

"Ah, well Nate left on a work trip months ago and I told him if he went, that was it. I'm done with him leaving me for months at a time."

"Ah, and there's nobody new?"

We arrive in the kitchen and I produce the whiskey. He helps himself after I shove the bottle and a glass in his direction. I boil the kettle for myself, pulling out my mint tea from the cupboard.

"Nobody new."

"Pretty woman like you? Surely you have offers," he says, and I pick up on his tell-tale interrogation, laced within seemingly innocent curiosity.

"Yeah, I got asked out today, as a matter of fact. Just a guy asking me for a drink. As I told him though, I have my kids. They're my priority."

"So Nate, he's not... he's not in the picture anymore?"

I look up from dipping my teabag and detect his nervousness.

"I haven't seen him in six months. I'd declare us separated but we don't really do things the way normal couples do. For a start I married him under a false name and he's not even around to contest it if I try to divorce him."

He looks at me, his eyes displaying regret. Then he looks down into his glass, swilling the amber liquid around the edges, coating the sides. "I'm sorry you're going through this, Bea."

"Me too."

I drink my tea, parking myself on one of the stools around the kitchen island, as he sits at his own stool on the other side of the counter from me.

"I did try to warn you, Bea. He had a disjointed upbringing. You do know he was fostered?"

I sense he's trying to dig deeper, to see how much I know. I can feel it—that he's eager to know what happened. The more I tell him about Nate, the more he'll imagine he can extract from me.

If there's one thing I've learnt, it's that I can't trust anyone.

"I didn't know that," I say—a lie.

"His mother was caught out," my dad says, "and Nate went to a school for the gifted, did you know that?"

I frown, as if it's news to me. "He never talked about his childhood. It was a no-go, I sensed, so I never probed him. All he told me was that his father got him into the work he does—and then later I discovered that to be a lie. His mother told me there was never a father; she said that she had a night out and ended up pregnant, and that was it. She didn't elaborate. I felt in my heart that there'd been trouble and I didn't want to dredge up the past."

I'm just making it all up, because fuck knows what the truth is. Maybe Dad will tell me.

My dad clears his throat. "His mother was on the bones of her arse when he found her, then brought her to the ranch. Did you know that?"

"I suspected as much," I say, because if I give my dad a yes or no, he'll be reading my face for how I look when I say yes or no, and that's a simple question we both know the answer to.

"He put a roof over her head, even after everything she did. He's a good kid, so why's he really gone and left you, Bea?"

I try not to seem intimidated as he keeps his eyes focused directly on mine.

"I told you already. He was going off to do another job and I told him if he went, that was it for us. I'd had enough. I told him it was all or nothing. I asked him to choose and he chose the job."

I take a deep breath to steady myself, but I can feel myself on the edge of what my nerves can take and beneath the kitchen counter, my knees are jiggling, and my hands are fidgety.

I have to hold my nerve because my father here might be the last piece of this puzzle. I think Nate anticipated that my father would eventually show up like this. It's too much coincidence that I cross paths with my father in Vegas and soon later, Nate spills his guts to me—then hotfoots it.

"No man just leaves the mother of his children. Hasn't he been in touch?"

"No. Not a word. I'm assuming he's on a job. It's not like he hasn't gone quiet on me before, it's just that this time he's been gone longer."

My dad pours more whiskey and takes a larger mouthful than before. He's getting impatient. He thinks I'm stupid enough that I'll spill everything—just because I'm lovesick and he's my dad. I think we're past the point of normal father-daughter interactions.

In my deepest, darkest imagination, I wonder if my father and Nate aren't enemies and I'm the pawn—and I won't be used like that, not by my husband, not by my father.

"Listen Bea, I'm not sure what he's told you, and because I don't know, I can't counter anything he may or may not have told you. So, I think it's about time I told you everything from my point of view." I detect the irritation in his tone, because he's being forced to let down his barriers, not the other way around.

"I'd like to hear what you have to say," I reply, putting the ball in his court.

"The Collective arranges for people to disappear. Sometimes they die, sometimes they just vanish. Mostly they die," he says, and I stare like I knew nothing, while really thinking, *So far, so good.*

"Okay...."

"If you've ever wondered why the rich won't be quelled in their pursuit of money, and why they want to become ever richer, I know the answer. Wealth can buy you anything, but only a serious amount of wealth can buy you freedom. Freedom comes at a cost. You're buying a cover-up. You're buying a way out. You're buying into the cover-up of the century. People accept that wealth and privilege is the reward for being a public figure, for being someone others look up to and idolise. Only, the drawback is your whole life is out there for scrutiny, but in exchange for providing entertainment, you get money. What if there's nothing at the end of all this, Bea? Maybe this life is all you get. There's nothing after. What if that's what people secretly believe and they're willing to pretend to be someone they're not for years on end, knowing one day they'll get their escape? Eventually they get the nirvana, they get life beyond death... they get a second chance...

they get to live like Adam and Eve, in paradise... where people live for 500 years because there's a cure for cancer, and there's technology for replacing and replenishing every part of the human body. There are ways to reverse ageing and all this exists, all while 97 per cent of the world's population still lives in poverty... 97 per cent without a roof over their head or a working toilet. Just three per cent of the world's population have a working toilet and a roof over their head, and still we're spoon-fed images on the internet and in the media, images of wealth and the American dream... all this is to aim for, right? Because there's this dream, and many are peddling it, it seems possible for anyone to get it. But while the 97 per cent know nothing but what they've always known, and the three per cent with a roof and a toilet get by, there is a tiny, tiny percentage, barely even calculable in fact. That tiny percentage has been groomed, from very young—told they can achieve anything, even eternal youth. All they have to do is agree to play by the rules—do as they're told, and they will become a legend, and even survive physically, long after they've left public life. The truth is out there Bea and they don't want you to know it. They don't want you to know about the machine and how it works. They don't want you to know about the chosen ones and why they're chosen, or how they're plucked from obscurity. The broken remain broken and the poor aren't given the cure for cancer, only the select are. The very fabric of our civilisation is held together by the dream—that if you keep trying, you can achieve it—that goals are a good thing, they keep you going. That capitalism is good, because it feeds the many. But it's all a façade, Bea. It's all fake. Backs break while the rich become richer and escape to paradise, all while the rest of us hold them up. Millions suffer and perish while the chosen ones are held up, aloft, high in the air. But the chosen are the only ones who flourish, all because billions are struggling beneath them. The poor remain pilloried, and the ordinary Joe dies so that the chosen can achieve paradise."

He takes a break from his mad musings and I remind myself that Nate's told me a few things already, but my father can't know what Nate's told me. I have to pretend to know very little because ignorance could save my life.

"I admit, I've made mistakes," he says, rubbing his eyes, "but your mother and sister's deaths... I cannot undo them, and it's on my head. They're the one thing I cannot atone for."

I swallow hard. I want to scream that he's a liar, but for all I know, Nate's the liar. I want to reject what he's saying, but it could all be the truth.

"I made a mistake, back when we were living in Yorkshire. I was seen. I was spotted. I was always meant to go unseen, but that one time I didn't manage to retain my invisibility—and then I knew the clock was ticking, that eventually they'd catch me. They didn't even have half the tech then that we do now, but I knew my days were numbered. Horace was the only light, he said he'd take on my case. He'd relocate us, new identities. He'd polish the trail behind us, clean the slate. He'd look out for people on our tails. He'd keep us safe, he said. He was the best hacker next to Nate I have ever known. The best."

I gulp down all the build-up inside my mouth, trying not to let it show that he's making me nervous with his chatter.

"With Horace dead, I knew I had to take action, so I started planning and I settled on the night we'd do it, but I couldn't tell you, in case one of you let slip and gave away our plans. So, I settled on Phoebe's birthday, just because I thought we'd all be home. We were all going to be home, I told myself. It would be easy. We'd just walk out of the back way altogether and never turn back. I was going to tell you that night about my plan. I knew it wasn't serious between you and Arthur, I knew he wasn't the beginning and end for you, so I knew you'd come willingly. If it had all gone to plan, we'd have been gone before it happened. We'd have been away before the place exploded. Trouble was, I fucked up. I let my emotions get the better of me. You didn't show up to see Phoebe, so I phoned you, and when you didn't answer—presumably because you were on an airplane—I left you a message. I don't know if you ever got it?"

"No," I whisper.

"They wiped it, then," he says with conviction, but we can all say things with conviction, if our ultimate conviction is to lie to get what we really want.

"In the message, I told you we'd had to leave... that one day you'd understand... but we'd be okay. And then I told you to take those passports we had gotten you, and to hide. I know that I needn't have bothered now. I know that you knew instinctively what to do."

Tears drip down my face and my father looks relieved to know that he can still affect me like this—that I still have feelings, even after all this time.

"My plan was to decimate the house, make it impossible to find any remains. I'd make sure we were seen before it happened, through the windows enjoying Phoebe's party, and our neighbours would tell the police we must have been home during the explosion, sadly. I thought my plan was ingenious, leaving it all up to interpretation. No evidence, but no denying the occupants would never have survived such an explosion. You see, I'd rigged it to explode sky high. There would be no remains, and we'd all be assumed dead." My father looks up at me, his mouth tight, a bitter expression in his eyes. "But then *they* came before we could get away, because of the voicemail I left you, which they'd obviously intercepted. They shot your mother and sister, and I was left for dead like I told you. I managed to escape but once the shower upstairs caught fire, the explosives I'd already rigged sent it rocketing into the sky, just as I had planned... except for your mother and sister, of course. They were never meant to burn."

I watch him carefully. He fiddles with the sleeves on his shirt. He wipes a tear away, then drinks more whiskey. He seems like a man genuinely grieving.

Did Nate lie to me?

"Then I found out that my daughter was living with a hacker, the only other who could have outclassed Horace. It doesn't add up, Beatrice, does it?"

"I don't know, Dad," I muster, because there are two Nates. There's the person he is when he's with me and his kids, and there's the one I never see—the guy he is when he's at work. I've never met him yet.

"He's poison, Beatrice. Poison." He wipes tears from his eyes, but how do I know they aren't fake? How do I know anything?

"What about after Phoebe's birthday?" I contest. "How would we have survived after getting out of the house, unnoticed? Would we have skipped the country? Would we have hidden in a safe house, never to see the light of day again? Tell me. If Horace was dead, and he was meant to be your protection, then how would you have protected us once we got free, huh? How?"

I'm going to believe Nate's theory—that my father escaped with my mother and sister, but not me, because he knew I would never agree to hide. It's the most logical explanation.

When my dad has nothing further, I offer, "After screwing up your freelance work and ending up with a price on your head, you started working for the Collective, and we all got new identities. For a while, with Horace's help, you delayed the inevitable. You didn't have enough money to buy your freedom, as you term it, so you offered to work for it. You offered to do some work for them in exchange for your so-called paradise, but you couldn't afford to take us all away. Just Mum and Phoebe, because I was too famous to just disappear. You'd have had to fork out more for me."

He looks perturbed. He looks guilty. His hand shakes as he picks up the glass and pours yet more whiskey into his mouth.

"You, Phoebe and Mum got out. Meanwhile the house exploded, and the Collective tied up all the loose ends, ensuring your deaths looked real—less hassle for them maybe, if you just disappeared and were never heard of again. You went somewhere, I don't know where. Somewhere remote. But then my actions in the aftermath of the explosion left the Collective bamboozled. Why would I hide? Why would the ignorant daughter resort to all kinds of tactics to stay safe, if she wasn't even meant to know she was in danger? So, they sent Nate in to check it all out, didn't they? To find out what I knew. And when you found out from contacts, or whoever, that Nate and I were cosied up in Montreux and that I was falling in love with him, you couldn't stand it, could you?"

"NO!" he yells, standing up and pointing at me. "You've got it wrong!"

I stand and face him, only the counter between us. "You hated I was with someone from the Collective and that's why, when I flew into Vegas that time, you were already there, waiting for me. You'd been hoping for months I'd make contact, hadn't you?"

"You're so wide off the mark, Bea. I told you... I told you they killed your mother and sister. I watched them die, Bea. I watched them die," he repeats, and he turns his back on me, walking across the room to gather some tissue from the roll, so he can blow his nose and wipe his eyes.

"I've got two versions here. Mine, which makes sense, and yours, which claims my mother and sister are dead, but how am I supposed to believe you let them die? How am I supposed to believe you got *that* sloppy that you let other marksmen swan into your house and take control?"

My father turns on me, railing, his eyes piercing red with rage and tears and exacerbation.

"I told you Bea, didn't I? I told you he's the best. He's buying his freedom too, Bea. He's going to paradise. He'll live forever. He's buying his way there, and now he's working to buy you and the kids their tickets too. But guess what? His freedom has come at a cost. He entered my house and shot me with expert precision... then he went upstairs and shot my entire family. Why do you think I came back, Bea? WHY? For the good of my health? Because I thought I was beyond death? NO! I've come back because you need to know the truth."

"Oh yeah, and what is the truth?"

"HE KILLED YOUR MOTHER AND SISTER!" he yells.

For a few, piercing minutes, I stand perplexed, wondering what to believe.

The jumbled nonsense in my head gradually rearranges itself and my heart tells me something definitive and clear. It tells me that Nate's not a killer. The night I almost got mugged in Montreux—whether it was a set-up or not—Nate showed genuine fear that night. He was genuinely afraid of killing someone. He'd never done it before, I could tell, and he was shocked with himself that he finally realised what I meant to him—that he'd go so far as to kill someone for me. I remember that night and I will never forget it. It was the night we first made love and I felt that fear in his skin and bones as he came inside me and discovered, the same as I did, what people do for one another when they're in love: they let their guard down and open themselves up, exposing every part of their heart. Nate and I were delirious with passion that night, but also exhausted from all the fear. We were starting to care about one another and it was becoming all the more complicated.

"I don't believe it. What motive could he have had?" I demand, because without motive, this makes no sense—and there are a hell of a lot of plot holes in my father's story, too many to count. Why would Nate kill my mother and sister and allow my dad to live?

My father looks me dead in the eye. "You, he wanted you, all along."

"You're insane," I accuse him.

"Look at it this way," he says, coming towards me, "Horace dies and as his successor, Nate's handed our case to manage. He looks through the files and spots you, and he wants you. He decides he's going to have you, but he needs to do it right. Ask yourself Bea! I mean, really, ask yourself! Does a normal feller engineer all kinds of scenarios to get you to trust him, to make sure that you don't ask questions when he works away for months on end? Really? All those years ago, he wanted me out of the picture for sure, because he knew I would forbid you seeing such a man, a man like him. Your mother and sister were collateral damage, but it all worked out great for him. Fearing for your life, you began to trust someone who came along and took that fear away, making you feel safe. It's classic, Bea. We've talked about this so many times before, you and I. It's classic, sweetheart. Stockholm syndrome, through and through."

I stare at him, disgusted. Even if this is true, I hate him right now. Even if Nate is evil and twisted, I hate my father more. I hate him because he brought this down upon me. He was an assassin. He fucked up. He made us leave everything we knew behind. He's the one who did this to me. He did it all. He should have protected me.

"You don't believe me, Bea? You don't trust me."

"You taught me to trust no one," I retaliate.

My mind's going a million miles an hour. What he's saying is all very convincing, but not entirely covering all bases. If Nate is some obsessive douche who did all of this just to get me, why didn't he just come up to me one day and ask me out? I would have said yes. I would have dropped Arthur in a heartbeat for Nate.

Even if the explosion in Edinburgh had never happened, and we'd met on the street or something, then later he'd told me the truth about the Collective and the dangers, and that we'd have to live a quiet life, I still would've stayed with Nate. I would've always loved Nate. No matter the circumstances of meeting, I would've always chosen to love Nate, because of how he is deep down inside. He's my tender, decent guy, caught in a trap he can't escape. Even if he were a killer, he wouldn't have killed my mother and sister and left Dad to live and cause havoc. No way. My dad is trying to twist all of this, so he can use me.

My father and Nate are at loggerheads over something and that's the truth. They're using me to get at one another.

"He grew up with nothing Bea, wanted nothing, only ever knew nothing. He doesn't want things, he's not that kind of person. He wants the chase. He wants what he can't have. He wants the impossible. He doesn't want materials, he wants something beyond... something like you. To him, you are nothing more than a precious trinket, something to attain. Something shinier than anything he'd ever seen before. The cunning ploy he constructed to capture your heart only made the attraction even more appealing to him. The thought that he could pull it off must have been so thrilling to him, Bea. That's how he works. That's how these sociopathic nerds work. I've seen it all. You have to believe me."

"It's just a shame she doesn't believe you, isn't it Bill?" I turn and watch Nate walk into the room, brandishing a pistol in his hand, ready to fire.

My heart almost dies.

Chapter Forty-Five

My dad doesn't have a weapon to draw, or if he does, it's concealed. He stands, stoic, maintaining eye contact with Nate. I move slowly across the room and stand in between them.

"I don't care who's lying, or who's telling the truth here, but nobody must shoot while the children are upstairs. Promise me, Nate."

Nate glances at me, and when he does, I see a different man to the one I thought I knew. I see a rigid soldier, a fighter, someone not to be trifled with. I see hatred for my father, a hatred I don't yet understand, and I see aggression—something he has never demonstrated around me, until now.

Nate lowers his weapon and holsters it. I catch Dad's eye, reminding him I have a gun. It's tucked in the back of my jeans from earlier. Any sudden moves from my dad and Nate would kill him, so he can't draw a weapon, not without risking himself. He seems reassured as I circle the island and show Nate a seat, motioning he sit.

"I'm not even going to ask how you both broke into my house," I begin, "but it makes me wonder if your training goes beyond hacking and assassinating and interrogating. It makes me wonder if it goes oh so much deeper than I could imagine. And that applies for the both of you."

I tidy away my mug, turning my back on them both. In the kitchen window as I swill water around my mug at the sink, I watch in the glass to see if they do anything while my back's turned. My father remains silent and still, while Nate remains furious but not moving, either. They don't attempt to communicate secretly while my back's turned. At least I know I'm not their enemy. Their true enemy is one another, and I am just caught in the crossfire—bait to lure the other.

I turn back around to watch the silent standoff—two men fiercely opposed, unable to draw swords, with two small children upstairs. One is their father, the other their grandfather.

My dad's not always been the warmest man. His default setting is aloof, but maybe his trade has made him like this.

"Sometimes, I used to wonder why you couldn't just be a dentist, you know? I resented the life you'd brought down upon us. I resented that you'd taken me away from everything I knew, that I had to be someone else."

My dad lets his eyes slide sideways, for just a moment, to consider my expression. He quickly turns his focus back to Nate, ready to fight should he have to.

"Dentistry?" He chuckles. "You know the real world is not for me. You know it isn't."

"So, why did you get married? If you'd loved Mum, you would have let her go, right? All my mother ever wanted was a normal life."

"Why don't we ask Nate that same question, hmm?" my father goads.

"I let her go, you fuck," Nate grinds, almost snarling.

"Yeah, and here we are, aren't we?" my father laughs, like he's got the upper hand. "You let her go because it's me you want, not her. You've impressed me, you know? Six months. Six months without her. I read the transcripts, all the sweet nothings you whispered to her at night in Montreux. I know everything."

Nate punches the counter in front of him, and it feels like the whole room shakes in response to his defiance.

I don't know what's happening here, but I guess I can only watch it play out.

"What do you mean, Dad? What are you talking about?"

"Your man here. He's been waiting six months for me to show up like this. He knew I would, right?"

"Right," Nate replies.

"Six months. I thought surely within six weeks he'd need his cock servicing, let alone six months. He's proven himself a worthy opponent, if ever I met one."

Nate grunts and restrains himself from thumping the kitchen island again.

I look between them, seeing my father cool and calm, and Nate as furious as a raging bear, and I still can't tell which of them is the one in the wrong. I'd like to be able to pick a favourite to win right now, but the odds are skew-whiff and don't even make sense. All I know is that I don't like the way my father is talking right now and neither does Nate, so it seems.

"Remember who I am Beatrice," Nate says, grinding his teeth, "remember who I am beyond the job, that's the real me. You know who I am, baby. You know."

He's speaking but not looking at me. He doesn't take his eyes off my father. Pit them against one another, and I reckon they'd both end up dead on the floor. They're equally matched, for sure.

"Dad says you planned all of this, Nate." My husband turns and eyes me for a second, showing me confusion. He quickly turns his gaze back upon his keen opponent. "He says you killed my mother and sister and left him for dead. He says you planned all of this to get me. He says you were handed our case after Horace died and you saw pictures of me and wanted me, but you knew my father would never let you have me, so you bumped them all off—"

Nate appears exasperated, shaking his head. "Why would I touch your sister and mother, Bebe? Why? Ask yourself, deep in your heart, why would I need to kill them? Your father would have been the only one I'd need to have done away with and I wouldn't have done it as shoddily as he faked his own death."

His way of putting it does ring true with me. Why would he have needed to do away with my sister and mother? Why? Phoebe and my mother were blind to my father's truths, because they were too afraid to open their eyes and see what was really going on.

"If I'm the monster he says I am, then why did I give my mother a roof over her head when she turned up on my doorstep, destitute and desperate, with nothing left whatsoever? Why would I forgive a woman who subjected me to her demons and her sick lifestyle if I were a monster? Or is the truth that I could see beyond her mistakes to the woman she once was, the person she should have been. I pitied her. I decided I'd rather conceal her under my roof than let her die in the gutter, even if she did bring her problems back into my life. If I'm the monster he says, slaying a mother and daughter to capture the love and attention of a young woman like you, then why didn't I just lock you in a basement Bebe? Why didn't I use physical violence to break you? Why? I'll tell you why. I'm not the monster he's trying to portray me as. He's the monster, coming up with all this horseshit to make me look bad when he's the one who's bad Bebe, he's the one."

"Don't listen to him Beatrice," my dad growls, "you know what they do to kids in foster homes. You know the truth. You know he's warped. His mother was an addict. He's got all kinds of problems. Don't listen to him, sweetheart."

My focus is sharpened when I hear him call me sweetheart. There's something in the way he says it, patronising maybe. In Yorkshire, sweetheart is used on a daily basis, as a term of endearment after paying the shopkeeper or whatever, but in some places it's a frowned-upon term—not derogatory, but just not welcome. Far too familiar. I think he used it just then to remind me that he's always called me sweetheart because that's all he sees me as—his minion daughter, his lesser. Well, my father and I haven't been familiar in so long—probably never.

I've lain in bed with Nate some nights, just staring into his eyes. I've held him in my hand and watched him come, as he's allowed me full control over his body and his pleasure. He was there when our babies were born. He was there when I was crying because I was in so much pain. He was there when I needed him most, but my father's never been here for me. He was out of the country when I was going through my exams. He missed so many awards ceremonies at school. He even missed me collecting my degree. I went out with my university professor, just to try and get Dad's attention. Dad is the one who has never been here.

I turn and catch Nate's eye. I hope he can see where my loyalty lies. It lies with him.

He's the love of my life, the father of my children. He's the only man I need and want.

I see a tiny flicker of triumph in his eyes before he turns his gaze back onto his opponent.

"I left out some details, Bebe," my husband says. "Before I left six months ago, I left out one big detail."

"Tell me," I implore.

Nate stares my father in the eye as he explains, "The reason I joined the Collective was to find out who he is—this man standing before us right now. Your father runs the show Bebe, but until today I never met him, never saw a picture of him. He has shrouded himself in so much mystery, concealed himself beneath layers of security even I couldn't bypass. It's taken me ten years to get here. Ten years for this chance to look him in the eye. It's taken a series of fuck-ups on his part for us to get here, to where we are right now, but we're here, finally... and now there's no need to lie anymore, because we're all here. I finally got you, Fleming. I got you."

"I don't understand... I can't..." My head is pounding. My father still looks completely indifferent. Vacant, even.

"It was the explosion," Nate explains. "It was splashed all over the news. It had all the tell-tale markers of a Collective plot, designed to transpose an entire family—and yet it had been done completely off the books. It drew my attention and when I realised only three unidentifiable bodies had been found—but that the Williamson family had been a foursome—I tracked you down, Beatrice. I monitored you for a while before I approached you. I'd noticed you were scared, you were hiding. I thought it was strange. I knew I needed you to trust me. I needed you to think that I wasn't someone your father had had dealings with. Then, for you to show up in my neck of the woods in Texas, it was like it was fate telling me to make my move, even though at this point in time, I was only working off a hunch. A hypothesis. Still, I knew from the way you behaved in that store that you weren't just the daughter of some sort of travelling salesman. And as soon as you told me your name was Beatrice and not Annalise, I knew you were his daughter for sure. My father knew your dad and had told me all about Bill and his two girls, you see. And when you told me about having to leave home and take on new identities, that's when it sealed it for me. You were fifteen then. I was sixteen. That's when my father and yours first started up the Collective."

"Oh my god." I put my hands over my face.

"You wanna know why he didn't take you with them, Bebe? You wanna know why?"

"Tell me, Nate."

"He knows you have integrity, that's why. He knows you wouldn't have agreed to it, but your mother and sister? He knew they were weak-minded enough to go along with it all. He knew they wouldn't ask too many questions, not like you. I've waited until now to show you the truth. Look into his eyes, he cannot deny it. He can't deny what and who he is."

I stare at my father and see his cool façade begin to crumble.

"I may have misled on occasion, I may have twisted the truth a smidgen, but my intention has always been this... for us to end up in the same room together, me and him. The real reason I joined the Collective was to get revenge," Nate reveals, "for my father..."

"But Claire-Anne said, she said..."

I realise, looking back, his mother said very little. She said she wasn't the only woman to ever bring up a boy on her own. She misled, but she never lied. She didn't fill me in properly, but...

"When I told you my father used to just show up sometimes, that was true," Nate explains, "and we got close. I was eleven the first time he called round. He'd take me for secret trips to the cinema because we didn't want my foster parents to find out. Then I eventually learnt about his job in the CIA. I knew it was dangerous undercover work, and more importantly, I knew that's why we couldn't have a proper relationship, because he was protecting me. One time, when he was meant to show, he didn't, and I never saw him again. Trouble was, not long before he disappeared, he'd been telling me about a friend called Bill Fleming; that they were building a new initiative together called the Collective, a route out of being owned by the man, as he termed it. It got me thinking... So, I looked up your dad, wanting to know if he knew anything about my dad's disappearance. I was eighteen years old and I travelled to Yorkshire, to the house you grew up in, the place my dad had told me about. A house in the middle of nowhere. At eighteen I was in a foreign country, searching for answers, all on my own, nobody to help me. I shouldn't have wasted my time. When I got there, I found nothing. The house had been vacant for years, I could tell. Furniture you'd left behind had gone mouldy. It was derelict and abandoned, like you'd only been living there in the first place because nobody would visit a house like it. I even talked to people in the nearby village and it was rumoured you'd all died in a helicopter crash on holiday.

"So, I went back home, desolate and alone, unable to let it all die with him. Not knowing the truth burned me up inside, corrupted me. I already knew some stuff about computer hacking. I could do it well and I thought one day, I might use my skills to find out what had really happened to my father. What I didn't anticipate was that one day, the truth would come looking for me."

I turn and watch my father's reaction. His chest is moving more noticeably than before. Does he know he's undone? Or is Nate dredging up bad memories for him?

"My father recruited you?" I ask him.

"I knew nothing about who he really was, and I turned him down at first. I'd had offers from other concerns to work for them. My hacking skills were becoming renowned among circles like your father's. But it was when he mentioned that his business was called the Collective, I thought if nothing else, I could use the job to find out more about my father. Buchanan is my mother's maiden name, so he didn't know who I was."

"Of course, I knew," my dad growls, trying to give off an air of confidence. "The resemblance is uncanny. The only thing I didn't know was that you'd had a relationship with your father."

Nate carries on, not put off... "Your father was SAS, Beatrice. So was mine. My mother was a roadie with a band called the Eclectics and she met my father one night in New York, on tour. Apparently, he told her he was in the British Army, but that he was on holiday. It lasted a week and she found out she was pregnant a few months later, went home to Texas and suffered major withdrawal as she tried to get herself off the drink and drugs."

"Oh, boohoo," my dad hisses.

Nate sharpens his stare and continues, "I was born and she never told my father. She wasn't even sure I was his until I grew up and she knew I was from our striking similarities. Anyway, years later, my father's been promoted and he's working for the CIA in America. He remembers that girl he liked so much and looks up my mother, discovers she's a deadbeat with a kid, and wants nothing to do with her. However, he's good with calculations and realises I could be his kid, and when he looks me up on the databases, he sees his own likeness. So, he finds me, and we start seeing one another in secret, because he's scared for me, because he's doing a job where anyone he loves could get hurt. During our secret meets, he'd tell me about his pal, Bill. Bill was his counterpart across the Pond, he'd say, an old mucker. My dad was British like yours Bebe, but while my dad went across the Pond, yours stayed home. I recently dug deeper, Bebe. I finally got hold of those sealed files I told you about. Bill was never sacked from the Army. It was all a cover. Your father worked for the SAS and was a decorated officer. He was let go and shamed, but secretly, he was transferred to MI5, working in intelligence. He started spying on his former colleagues, you see, those people using their authority to traffic refugees, drugs, weapons... whatever earns them cash. In the military community, everyone knows about the South Pacific island where people go to escape life. It's the worst-kept secret, depending on which company you keep. With the world drowning beneath fear of terror attacks, possible nuclear wars and climate change, well... Your dad spied on his mates who were buying their way there, while secretly joining the ranks of those building their nest eggs from out of criminal activity."

"Oh my god."

"Yeah... He misused his position of power in the MI5 to begin stealing money."

"Dad?" I turn and stare at him.

He shrugs, brushing it off. "I wasn't doing anything different to anyone else. It was just a shame I got caught by the wrong person. It was the MI5, Bea. That's why I needed Horace to get me out."

"Horace? Why do I keep hearing this name, Horace?" I demand.

"My father was called Horace Chichester," Nate boasts, exploding all of my dad's lies. "My dad untangled yours from the mess he was in with MI5, and together, that's when they started concocting this idea for the Collective. My father had wanted out of the CIA for years, but he knew he couldn't just leave and disappear, to start a new life. The work he'd done had got him a bunch of enemies. Anyway, while Horace gathered a team, recruiting people like us—hackers—your dad threw his weight around, scared people into submission. All along, my father was the real brains behind the operation and Bill knew it. Your dad was just a washed-up soldier, whereas mine had the brains to move with the time and recognise it would soon be cyberattacks we'd all be dealing with in future. My father's only fault was that he and your dad had done missions together, there was a bond, and Horace couldn't see Bill Fleming for what he really was: a liability and a fucking evil prick."

"What—" I can't believe what I'm hearing. "W—what is the Collective, really?"

"Money, to put it simply," answers Nate. "The plan was to help relocate people, give them new lives, make them look dead if need be. Charge them big amounts to do so. Then your father and mine were going to take control of this mythical island they all talk about, retreat and escape, prepare for the end of the world—together. Everyone like us knows it's coming, Bebe. We know the signs, you see. Disaster will land on all our heads, eventually, and our fathers were going to make sure all the best people were on this island, a means of survival of the fittest. But then Horace changed his mind about the whole thing when he realised how many people were getting killed for this utopia they were building, and you didn't like it when he questioned you, did you Bill?"

My father's face twitches. "You have such a way with words, Buchanan. Pity you're a liar, huh? Just a dirty rotten liar, who killed my daughter and wife."

"After he bumped off my father, out of rage, stupidity—whatever goes through his thick skull—he recruited me a year later, and the Collective got back up and running. I have the same style as my father, right? Right? I gave new life to your operation, but you didn't know that I knew, that I'd been close to Horace. You didn't know, did you?" Nate turns to glance at me. "The thing is Bebe, your father recruited me through the power of the internet and I never saw his face or heard his real voice. I was sent a new passport and told to fly to Geneva to start a new life, working out of an office there. But eventually, I was breaking down the walls protecting your father, and that's when he knew he had to fake his death a second time. He knew I was coming for him. He knew I was breaking down all the codes my father had written, codes which were protecting your identity. I was untangling those codes the same way he'd written those codes."

"You've got a very active imagination young man, I must say," my father says, maintaining his complete indifference to all the accusations Nate is throwing his way.

"Why stay away from your surviving kid and your grandchildren, huh? Answer me that, *Bill*," he shouts, his voice full of venom. When Nate takes to his feet, my father stands up straighter, too. "He's only here for me, Beatrice. That's all he's here for. To get rid of me. He knows I have more power than he will ever have. He can employ five, ten, twenty hackers in my place, and none of them have the linguistic skills with codes that I do. None of them. Not combined could they outmatch me. For that alone, he wants me dead. My father protected me. He kept me safe. But nobody's safe from you, are they Bill?"

My dad jostles a gun from out of his inside jacket pocket and aims it at Nate.

My husband sighs, as though this was inevitable. He continues to explain, "The Collective is still up and running, Bebe. He will never stop. He's taken control of the island already, he has enough money, and enough people—but none of it will ever be enough. Otherwise, why is he here? Hmm? He's only here for me, because he knows that I know what he is."

"You know nothing," my father spits.

"I don't understand," I say, and they both turn their heads to look at me at the same time. "If you hate my father so much Nate, then what were you doing when you left me? It started..." I have to think back very carefully, as your judgement of time becomes hazy when you're a new mum. "...when I fell pregnant with Seth, and it wasn't long after that, you started working away for longer periods. Why?"

"I'd left my work in Geneva to follow you around the states," Nate confesses. "After that, I knew I was living on borrowed time. You don't leave the Collective. If you do, you die, right Bill?"

My father does nothing but grunt.

"It's because we know too much you see," Nate explains, "that we're not allowed to just up and leave. We're monitored constantly, just like they were monitored constantly when they were paid employees. Anyway, it was after you fell pregnant with Seth that I realised you really did love me. My doubts, by the way, had nothing to do with you or any of this business at all, it was all me.

It was my fault that I doubted you. I doubted you only because of my past... my father... my mother. I never knew love before you, Bebe."

"Ah god, such saccharine vomit..." my father complains.

"I was only away from you because I was following his trail, Bebe," he continues aggressively, glancing very quickly at me. "I was following his murders. I was going to get him, once and for all. I couldn't risk it anymore. I'd bought my mother the ranch under an alias, but I didn't know if Bill knew. I wasn't sure if he knew where we were. After you fell pregnant with Seth, I couldn't stand the thought of something happening. What if he ended me? What if my child didn't grow up with a father? What if my child got hurt? What if you got hurt? I couldn't live anymore while he lived. It's my right to end him. We will never be truly safe until he's dead."

I remember what my dad said about the bullet in Edinburgh, hitting him just to the side of his heart. As he moves, I see the scar I once saw there now gone. Either the scar tissue has miraculously healed, or he was never shot at all. Maybe the last time we saw one another he had used a bit of prosthetic make-up to convince me of his story. Maybe he thought that this time, I'd be so worn down, I would take him at his word on everything. I have to give it to him: he's gone to extreme lengths to try and get me to trust him, and not Nate.

Nate's got his own gun, angled right at my father. If one of them shoots, they'll both die. They both have itchy trigger fingers. The slightest snap will make them both react at the same time, killing one another.

I know what I have to do.

I have to make a choice.

"Where's Mum and Phoebe?" I ask him.

"You'll never know," he says. "It would endanger them to tell you."

"Why?" I ask him. "Why did you do this?"

He doesn't turn to look at me when he speaks, either out of shame, or fear he'll be shot when he takes his attention off Nate, or maybe even sheer indifference to my plight.

"I did it for the long game, Bea," he says, his mouth a furious, hard line. "I did it for eternal life, for the dream. I needed money. I needed power. Nobody lives forever without money or power. I needed both. I needed glory. I don't want to die, I want to live forever. Only money can buy you that."

"And why are you really here? Right here? Right now? Why?"

My father's eye twitches. "It's either me or him, Bea. Me or him. He wants revenge and I can't truly retire to the island until he's dead. If I'm not around, he will destroy everything the Collective has built up. I'm the only thing standing in the way of him crippling the dream. I'm tired of this, so is he. It's either me or him. This has to end, right now."

I take my gun out, and without a second thought, I shoot him in the head.

No thought.

It's my right to end him—nobody else's.

Only someone he wouldn't think capable could end the life of Bill Fleming, an evil wrongdoer, a man of misdemeanour and contempt.

He drops dead instantly, the weapon in his hand rendered useless. Blood and brain tissue drips down the white kitchen cupboards behind him. What made me is now dead, I know, but at the same time I have to console myself that he can't hurt my husband anymore. He can't take away my life from me, not ever again. He can't hurt me. He can't break me.

Arms wrap tight around me. He cuddles me until I can't breathe.

"I love you more than life itself," he murmurs against my hair.

"I love you, too."

Chapter Forty-Six

"I've missed you so much," he murmurs, holding me close. I tip my head backwards and tears leak from the corners of my eyes. "Why didn't you tell me?"

"If I'd told you everything, you wouldn't have believed me. You had to hear it while he was in the room."

"I thought you didn't love me. You left me."

"No, Bebe," he says, wrapping his arms around me and dropping his lips gently onto mine. "I love you very much."

"We're the children of two men who were once friends?"

"Yeah," he agrees, "once."

"And you're sure mine killed yours?"

"Yeah. I checked it out. The day my father failed to meet up with me, all his bank accounts were emptied. Anyway, you saw your father, he didn't try to deny it."

That's true, he didn't.

I have an impulse to look over Nate's shoulder and check my father's really dead. However, Nate holds me tight to his chest and warns, "Don't look, Beatrice. You don't deserve to have his spectre on your conscience."

I nod, going along with him. "Are they alive, do you think?"

"I don't know," Nate says, "I haven't found them yet."

"But you can do anything, right?"

He strokes my cheeks. "I wish I could, but nobody can do anything without reprisals. It's just that some people think they can, but the impossible always comes at a cost."

"Did you know about Vegas?"

"No," he says, frowning. "What happened?"

"I used a number he'd given me a decade ago. He'd told me it would put me in touch with someone who could help, if all else was lost. I was upset you were absent for long periods, and I just, I wanted more information." I start to tremble, afraid he will be upset.

"It's okay, it doesn't matter now. So, what happened?"

"The contact texted back," I admit, "while I was in Vegas, I mean. He told me to meet him on Fremont Street. He crept up on me after a while, took my arm and we went to the back of this Chinese restaurant. I was shocked to learn it was him, my dad. He told me this huge, sweeping story about how he'd made mistakes, blah, blah, blah, and about how he was grieving, that Mum and Phoebe had died after you guys rocked up and shot them, but left him alive. He even said he saw you through the window, watching him trying to crawl to safety. He said you left because the house could have blown up at any second, even though you saw through the window he was alive. Apparently, you'd shot wide of his heart."

Nate's shaking his head. "You have to know, that's total bullshit."

"I know. Tonight, he didn't have the scar on his chest anymore. It'd gone. I'm only telling you all this because I want no more secrets and I only kept this from you because I was protecting you. I didn't know enough, and I was protecting you."

"Listen," he says, "go upstairs, take a bath. I'll deal with this mess. We can't go explaining to the cops that we have the dead body of someone already dead on our hands. Okay? Let me deal with it."

"It'll all be okay?"

"It'll be fine," he says.

"Okay."

I try not to look as I turn and walk out of the room, but I can't help but glance over my shoulder. I can't see his head because the kitchen island is in the way, but I can see Dad's big feet, flopped about.

I take a deep breath and leave Nate to it. He makes a call and all I hear is, "I need an appointment with the undertaker."

I check on the kids and discover they haven't been disturbed. Then I run the taps on full, grateful of the thundering noise of the water hitting the bottom, blocking out all the other noise assaulting my ears:

The gunshot, still ringing in my ears;

All these new revelations, ringing in my ears;

My father's words: *it's me or him.*

Well, I chose Nate, didn't I?

When Nate walks into the bathroom twenty minutes later, I'm buried beneath bubbles, wondering if I ought to let myself sink to the bottom of the tub.

Nate undresses and climbs in behind me, shifting me forwards.

"Is it done?" I ask, shaking.

He wraps his arms around my body, kissing my shoulder. "It's being cleaned up. You won't hear a thing. I promise you, by morning you won't even know he was here."

"Did I do the right thing?"

"Yes," he says, sighing. "Although you really should have let me."

"He'd have seen you coming."

"True."

"You'd have been shot as well."

"Probably."

"What's done is done, right?"

"Right."

There's something on my mind. Something I can't forget...

"When I spoke to my old neighbour that evening at the National Gallery, she gave me your description, told me you'd paid her off not to saying anything. Yet you told me earlier—"

"Beatrice, you're exhausted. We'll clear this up in the morning."

"Do you think you can just waltz back into my life, Nate? You've been gone six months."

"I thought you loved me?"

I turn around and he looks hurt. I move to the other side of the tub, wrapping my arms around myself, trying to steer clear even though his feet are still either side of my legs.

"This is him talking now, Bebe. Him. You know you can trust me."

"Oh, do I? So answer me, why did she say you'd paid her off not to talk to the police or anyone?"

Nate sighs. He's been sighing a lot tonight. Maybe because he's tired of answering me.

Anyway, after another long sigh, he says, "Because I did. I paid her off."

"What? Why? How?"

Nate leans forward, trying to touch me. Maybe he thinks he can distract me, by touching me. As much as I'd like his hands on me right now, my need for clarity outweighs all.

"I was there," Nate admits, and there's something in his guilty demeanour I don't like.

"WHAT? Where? When? What are you talking about?" I demand, tears springing to my eyes.

Oh my god, have I killed the wrong man tonight?

"The morning after, I snuck onto the scene. I flashed a fake badge and snuck in. It was all over the news and it was just a short flight from Geneva to Edinburgh. Plus, there was something about it all. It wasn't just the explosion. It was that Bill had always told my father that he would never return home to Scotland, so it was somewhere I never thought to look... Anyway, I snuck onto the scene and spoke with one of your old neighbours. Apparently the neighbours on the other side were away, playing golf up at St. Andrew's. Anyway, was it Rosie?"

"Yes, Rosie." He remembers! I need him to not say he's a fucked-up prick who has ruined my life. I need him to help me make sense of all this.

"I told Rosie she didn't know what her former neighbours were really like. I told her if she had any sense, to say nothing to the authorities, or she might hinder wider investigations. I said I was from a private firm and that if she told me what she knew, I'd pay off her mortgage."

"Oh my god, so what did she say?"

Nate uses his feet to stroke the outsides of my legs, telling me, "She said she'd seen your father behaving oddly... but she hadn't told the police yet. She hadn't told them because she knew you were still out there, alive, and it could hurt you."

"She'd seen him?"

"Yeah, she'd seen him ride up to the back gate of their house the day before the blast. He'd lugged three big bags up the garden, as she put it, and she could tell they were heavy. She said she knew you were in Florida because you'd told her you were working away when you passed in the street and you had two big bags over your shoulder. She said your mother and sister never left the house, or if they did it was in the dead of night. All she saw after the big bags was your father, sneaking out of the cellar hatch about a half hour before the blast. She'd camped out by the picture window, having turned out all her lights so he wouldn't see her. She said after seeing him lugging three big bags, she knew something was going on."

Yes... Rosie does have a picture window... "So, she just told you all this?"

"Yeah, I told you. I paid off her mortgage."

"So, that's how you knew how to find me? Or where to start looking?"

"Yeah. I waited for weeks until you showed up on a camera in New Orleans. I was tracking you after that. I gotta admit, I liked what I saw as soon as I saw you."

"This is not a time for that," I remind him.

"I'm just saying, I wanted you then, as much as I want you now. In fact, I want you more now."

It hits me like a ton of bricks. "Wait a minute. You knew... all that time? If Rosie told you all that stuff, you knew he'd faked their deaths... you knew everything... so, you knew and you didn't tell me, even when we were lying in bed together, and you were professing to love me, you didn't tell me the truth!"

"You wouldn't have believed me! Besides, I was in an impossible position. I knew if I ever had any chance of grabbing him in the future, I needed you with me. Having you by my side was all that mattered to me, and it wasn't just about the case. It was about needing you, wanting *you*. Okay, so maybe I didn't see you *like that* at first—"

"You were using me," I accuse. "And I was nothing but a fucking case."

"Yeah, but then we fell in love. I fell in love with you."

I put my head in my hands. "You don't love me, you never have. And why on earth would you want me now? I'm a killer. You once told me you'd never had to kill."

"That was before," he says.

"Before what?"

"I had to do something in exchange, Bebe."

"In exchange for what?" My heart's clanging hard against my ribs and all I can think about are my two babies, sleeping next door, both as blonde-haired as their father was when he was a baby. All I can think about is their safety. "What else is a lie? What else haven't you clarified?"

"After you fell pregnant with Seth, something kick-started me, an impulse to protect you and the baby." I gasp out loud and he tries to reach for me again, but I back away, still not convinced. He holds his hands up. "Look, I know what you're thinking, I know. That your father hadn't come for us yet, so why would he then? But you don't know the things he was capable of, I do. I've seen the evidence. I've seen his rap sheet. After we returned from honeymoon, I went to the CIA with what I knew about your father. I said I would do whatever they wanted me to do, as long as it ended with me being able to put a bullet in his brains."

"So, what happened?"

"They gave me the resources I needed and free rein to start looking for him, in exchange for me cracking some viruses. While I've been trying to pin down his location, some people have got in my way and I've had to retire them. That's all. These people aren't anything to anyone, Beatrice. It's nothing. Anyway, they're taking your father away downstairs and now he's gone, it won't be long before we find out where he was hiding. After that, we should be able to find your mother and sister. I hope so, anyway."

I put my head in my hands. "Can it be true?"

"For your sake, I really want it to be, Bebe."

"The thing is, Nate," I say, looking up, "I've got this war going on inside of me now. I've got rid of him from the present, but it's what he did in the past, you see. It's going to haunt me. The thing is—"

"You still don't trust me?" he says, looking pained.

My head feels heavy as I nod. "It's not just that he raised me to be mistrustful. It's also that you lied to me and now you've admitted it, I don't know what to believe."

"I didn't mean to... please, try to understand it from my point of view."

"No," I counter, "you're not seeing it from my point of view. I never lied to you. Maybe once, when I said I was a travel writer, but that's hardly lying in comparison to the lies you've told. I never lied to you about the way you made me feel, about how I felt about you. I never lied to you about the pain my father put me through. You've lied to me about everything. You lied about your father, about what he was to you, you lied—" I stumble, looking for words. "And you never told me about your mother. You never told me! And it hurts that you don't think you can tell me."

"I DON'T WANT TO TELL YOU!" he barks, so loud I'm not sure what was louder—the gunshot earlier or his yelling now.

"Why not?"

"Because it's awful," he says, turning his head so I can't see his eyes, "and I don't want to tell you. Surely you got the gist already? For a young boy to ask to be taken away from his own mother? Surely you already know that what she did was fucking unbearable."

"I hardly know you, Nate. I hardly know you!"

I lift myself out of the bath, wrapping myself in a towel. I don't have to listen to him shouting and yelling, treating me as if I don't care about him—as if I'm only asking out of spite, when it's purely out of love that I want to hear him tell me what it was like.

"Beatrice," he begs, trying to catch me before I leave the room.

"No, don't you dare touch me. Don't you dare."

IT'S STUPID O'CLOCK in the morning when I get fed up of tossing and turning, so I go check on the kids, frightened for them, or something... Maybe it's my guilt. Maybe I think that because I've done something bad, something bad will now happen to me in return. Anyway, the babies are fine. Or maybe they're not babies anymore. They're both walking now, and Seth knows too many words to count. He's very clever, like his dad.

I walk down two flights of stairs, finding Nate asleep on the sofa. He's cradling some of the kids' stuff to his chest—a teddy, a blanket and one of Seth's old baby grows. I see he's had whiskey. The bottle on the table is much depleted. He may have been crying.

I walk to the kitchen and the stink of bleach is high. I inspect every surface and there's not a splash of blood anywhere. In fact, the whole room looks cleaner than ever before. I could almost convince myself he was never here.

I return to the living room and pour myself a whiskey. Nate stirs.

I place the baby monitor on the coffee table in front of me and crawl onto the sofa, curling myself around my husband.

"Beatrice," he murmurs, groggy.

"Hush."

"You don't want rid of me?"

"I'm going to give you one, last chance. A chance to tell me everything. A chance to explain why I should forgive you."

"Okay," he sighs. "Tomorrow."

"Tomorrow."

Now I understand that sigh.

He knew, even before he walked through that door yesterday evening, that I was going to want to know everything as soon as he gave me something.

Chapter Forty-Seven

I don't have to work today and instead of spending the morning running errands and catching up with my agent, I cancel everything so Nate and I can spend time together. The kids are with Tilly the nanny and she's been expressly warned not to allow anyone else in the house until we get back.

Nate and I walk circuits of Central Park as he tells me about the bedwetting, the rough sex his mother would have while he was in the same room, plus the drinking, the drugs, the way she would often lash out at Nate—he tells me it all.

I wonder how he's even sane. I wonder how he survived.

Another part of me feels so unbearably sad for him; I just want to put my arms around him and forget any of this crap ever happened.

A tiny, fragile little voice in the back of my mind wonders if he hasn't been adversely affected by his upbringing. Surely nobody goes through that and escapes untarnished? Or maybe he got rescued by his foster parents just in time?

After he's told me everything I need to know about his mother, we stop by a pretzel stand and take a bench.

"What do we do now?" I ask him.

"What do you want to do?"

"Dream scenario?"

"If you want."

"We go back to Montreux."

"What about your studies?" he asks.

"I can study there, or thereabouts. Letters after my name don't mean as much as they used to anymore."

"I get that."

"Was the cabin your house while you were working in Geneva?"

"My weekend place, yeah," he admits. "We would need somewhere bigger now."

There have been so many lies, so many twists, I don't know what to believe really.

I could keep questioning him until I'm blue in the face and if he doesn't want to tell me something, he won't.

Some of the reasons he's given me for lying and deceiving have been a little far-fetched and out-there, to say the least.

I guess there's only one thing I really need to concern myself worrying about...

Whether I love him enough to stick by him.

"If we move there, you won't be leaving me for months at a time anymore?"

He takes a few big chunks out of his pretzel and tells me assuredly, "No. I promise. I got your father. It's over now."

"What about the Collective?" I ask between bites of pretzel.

"I don't know, Bebe. Maybe someone will try to make a go of it, but your father held a tight noose. Maybe people will just leave it where it is. Forget about it."

"But you'll keep looking for my sister and mother?"

"If you want me to."

"I want you to, as long as your search doesn't take you from me."

"It won't."

We finish our snacks and leave the bench. He puts his arm around me as we walk away.

"Are we good?" he asks.

"We're good."

He kisses my temple and we head for the nearest subway station.

Everything will be fine, just as long as he fulfils his promises today.

Just because my father is now dead, that doesn't mean I can undo what he taught me.

I'll always be me.

I'll be watching and observing.

Nate had better not have lied to me about anything else... let's just say that.

Chapter Forty-Eight

T *wo months later...*
The whole area around the lake is coming to life. Everything is so beautiful. I'm pushing the kids along the promenade and they're laughing and giggling with one another, plucking flowers from the displays as we pass. I'm breathing in the fresh air, doing my gentle morning jog with them. It's fresh but not cold. The spring weather here in Montreux is perfect.

Everything is a lot like it was when we lived here before, except that Nate now spends his free time trying to find my mother and sister for me. So far, he hasn't come up with anything. I don't know if we will ever find them. Perhaps my father was vindictive enough that he never wanted me to see them again.

I'm doing some remote further education courses. I want to become a history teacher and I'm learning French, so I can work at one of the international schools here. Modelling was never really for me. It was always just money but, weirdly, it saved my life too. I don't know what would have become of me if I hadn't been a model—no doubt I'd be facing the same fate my sister and mother are. Perhaps a life of obscurity.

I RETURN HOME WITH the kids after my jog, carrying a bag full of treats for our midmorning snack. The new house we bought in Montreux is white, sits right on the lake on raised ground above the shoreline, but so we can see all that beauty before us—snowy mountains, blue water and green vineyards, as wide as the eye can see.

Nate's ready to welcome us back. He kisses my face even though I'm a bit sweaty. The kids charge into the playroom between the kitchen and living room, heading straight for their toys and blankets. In the kitchen I plate up some donuts while Nate wraps his arms around me, smiling.

"Love you, girl," he says, kissing my cheek.

"Love you, boy," I reply, feeling happier than I've ever felt.

He turns me in his arms and squeezes me tight, sealing his lips over mine and licking into my mouth.

"God, you're gorgeous," I groan.

"Ditto," he replies, grabbing my arse and kissing me some more. No matter how many times we're together, I can't get this fever I have for him out of my veins. It's irreplaceable.

The kids rush in and I hand out donuts, making them sit at the table, or else I know there will be jam all over the playroom.

With donuts and warm milk between us at the kitchen table, I watch Nate watching me. He has that look in his eye, like he wants another baby.

Truly though, I already have everything I want, including some things I never knew I needed—like love, children, a home, a family, a husband who loves me, through and through.

I have life.

Chapter Forty-Nine

N^{ATE}
While Beatrice is in the shower, washing off the sweat from her morning jog, I check on the children in the nursery before venturing to my office at the back of the house. I pull the door almost closed, leaving it an inch open should the kids call out for help.

I stare at my laptop screen, wondering if I should pull the plug on the island.

If I do, then Beatrice will get her mother and sister back, but international security will also be shot to shit.

Slowly but surely, I've been helping the CIA pull in all of Bill Fleming's former colleagues, dropping them in hot water for crimes not associated with the Collective. We have to be careful what these people go down for and what they say while they're in prison. As long as they think they still have some hope of one day reaching the island, everything should be okay.

It's just that I'm constantly wrestling with my conscience and with my love for Beatrice, who desperately wants her family back, I can tell. I've not brought it up with her, but I know she has nightmares about her father. I know there's a cost to our freedom and it's not just me shouldering it, it's her too. She's had to pay dearly for the life we have now. I can't help feeling that if I get her mom and sister back, it'll make up for a lot of shit that's gone down.

The other alternative is that I could take Beatrice to the island myself and we could move there for good. The trouble is, I know she will likely try to go along with it all, but then she'll yearn for real life again. That's who she is.

I can picture her face already... if we were to arrive on the island, she'd see which of the rich and famous never really died. She'd be shocked.

She'd be appalled.

I'm also sick and tired of writing algorithms all day long which are designed to tell us what the people in the programme are currently up to. Whether they be on the island, or hiding in other remote places, I have to make sure they stick by the rules—or else the whole thing could come crashing down all around us.

Bill Fleming was the Collective and now he's gone, it's not like I can just demolish everything. I can't... can I? I don't know... The consequences... I suppose... don't bear thinking about. The truth would come out... military corruption, money laundering, murders gone unpunished, not to mention all those famous people living it up while their fans still mourn them.

On the other hand, I know the brainchild of my father and Beatrice's has merit. I know because I watch the world. I know that supplies are running out, that the gap between the rich and the poor is ever-widening, and I see the world for what it is. As Beatrice once succinctly put it, "There's the world you think you know, then there's the real one." The real one chews people up and spits them out, like my mother, Claire-Anne. She never stood a chance. She was an addict. Nobody cared. Nobody wanted her. It was only crossing paths with another lonely traveller one night that ever brought her any happiness—and it was just unfortunate my father didn't love my mother enough to stay—to save her.

I sit behind my walnut desk, in my expensive house, knowing my dirty money bought all this. But what is it that they say? Every moment is a chance to change, right?

I log into a secure server. I type a message to one of my guys: *It's time.*

Beatrice comes into the room and asks, "What would you like for lunch?"

"We've got some leftover burritos, those will do fine." I minimise all my windows before she comes over.

She sits in my lap and kisses me. My groin tightens and aches in response to her proximity, her scent and her warmth. I love her and because I love her, I know she will never agree to join the people stripping the world of its resources, just to save the 'worthy few'.

"I love you so much, you know that, right?"

"I know." She leaps up from my lap. "Burritos it is. I'll maybe make pasta for dinner. The kids love it."

"Wonderful. Maybe we'll watch a film on TV after the kids are asleep?"

"Nah," she murmurs, "I'd much rather you take me to bed and ravish me."

The burning in my gut reminds me why I love her. She sets my heart and my loins on fire.

"Knew I married the right woman," I growl, watching as she leaves the room.

I log back in and receive an encoded message: *It's done.*

I receive photographic evidence shortly afterwards, proving Bill's eldest child and protégé Arkin Sykes is dead. He's the last of the big chiefs associated with the Collective. Bill had a whole other life before he met Beatrice's mother...

I think Fleming was the type of man who couldn't stand to have people know his true self, and so whenever people discovered the real Bill Fleming, he'd just move on with someone else. Obviously, Beatrice was going to find out about him one day. He wouldn't have liked that.

I suspected he'd faked his death and his wife's and younger daughter's, too and I also knew Beatrice was my only lead to him. It began that she was just a mark to me, but then I fell for her. She's the same as me, after all—my mirror image.

I send my contact a message, while performing another task at the same time: *Disappear for at least six months. I'm sending funds now.*

I receive a reply: *Ok.*

I begin the cleaning process, ripping down the Collective's firewalls and servers, destroying everything we've ever built up. Maybe I'm making a mistake, or maybe I'm listening to reason, and reason dictates my wife would leave me if I didn't do something about all this.

Chaos will ensue, yes, but eventually, order will be restored. Once the truth gets out about the island where the rich and famous go to live, not die—the secrets to long-lasting youth will get out and their price will become so affordable, nobody will care anymore.

All anyone ever wants is what they can't have—a dream to chase—and once they have it, it's not that interesting anymore because there's always a reality nobody ever tells you about. Behind the impossible dream, there's always a dirty undercurrent and a cost. I know about that cost all too well—a childhood that left me cold, unemotional and calculated—at the hands of a heartless mother and her violent boyfriends. It was violence I wanted to escape, so I used my brain instead, and still, I was taken advantage of, only this time it was for my intelligence. Violence and sin shaped me. I was never with a woman until Beatrice. I never thought a woman could act and love as she does. She changed me beyond all recognition. I love Beatrice and because I do, I've changed, for her. She will never know about what I've done today. Never.

People don't control me, I control them, and they know it. I'm a super-hacker... and I'm the best. Nobody ever beats me. My dad taught me everything he knew when he used to come visit me in secret. I just took it all one step further and became even better. I'm the chimera Bill Fleming never imagined might exist—the ultimate weapon, something seemingly unfeasible, something illusory, something existing underground, something there but unseen, keeping everyone safe. People think that life will one day be snuffed out on this planet, but the truth is, we evolve, and I evolved beyond my father, just as Beatrice evolved beyond hers. How we will evolve in the future, I have no idea, but she and I broke the cycle. We evolved. Life... I mean... if we can stand up on two feet after living in the ocean for millions of years... life might find a way, right? It might not be as pretty as we imagine, but life finds a way. We found a way. People will survive, somehow.

So for now, I only have one worry: my own family.

I live to protect my wife and babies, and I will remain the ultimate weapon... until someone comes along to outsmart me, I guess...

About the Author

Sarah pens contemporary and erotic romance as Sarah Michelle Lynch, and other books as S. M. Lynch, her slightly more sinister side . . .

Sarah loves nothing more than to put her feet up with a book and be consumed by a story, so in turn, she endeavours to give you all this and more.

Discover more at: www.sarahmichellelynch.com

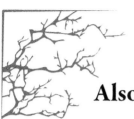

Also by the Author

THE *SUB ROSA* SERIES
Unbind
Unfurl
Unleash
Dom Diaries
Worth It
His Deadly Rose
Epilogue
STANDALONES
Writing on the Wild Side
Fabien: A Vampire Novel
Tainted Lovers
Christmas Lovers
THE *CHAMBERMAID* SERIES
A Fine Profession
A Fine Pursuit
The Chambermaid's Tales
THE *ANGEL AVENUE* SERIES
Angel Avenue
Beyond Angel Avenue
Hetty: An Angel Avenue Spin-off
THE *NIGHTLONG* SERIES
The Contract

The Fix
The Risk
Charity anthologies
Break the Cycle
They Say I'm Doing Well
Poems to My Younger Self
The *UNITY* Series
The Radical
The Informant
The Sentient

Printed in Great Britain
by Amazon

42399411R00199